A TRACE OF SOMETHING STRANGER

ALLISON GIORDANO

SUNGRAZER
PUBLISHING

LOS ANGELES

This novel contains scenes that describe violence and loss, including that of a young person.

My family recently lost someone much too young, who meant the world to us and our community. While I did not change the content of the book following this, my perspective has forever been changed. I hope I treated the subject with sensitivity and empathy.

Rest in peace, Ryan. You are so loved.

I

TEMPEST

Pain explodes against my temple as it smacks into the cool glass of the window. I immediately wrinkle my nose, unimpressed by the bus driver's ability to navigate the bumpy road, and less impressed with myself. If I had been paying attention, I would have noticed that the pavement before us had given way to dirt. But I got lost in my head, and now it hurts nearly as much as my stomach does.

The nausea has little to do with the driver pretending that the long, yellow vehicle we have been trapped in for more than three hours now is a bumper car, though. The obvious answer to my illness is the same as it always is: anxiety. At least that's what my therapist would call it. My parents would have said it was intuition. My mom would have punctuated her thought with a mischievous wink. My dad would have ruffled my unruly hair.

The bus jerks again and my head whips towards the glass from the force of it. I dig my elbow into the vinyl covering below the window and grit my teeth, still bracing for impact.

Thankfully, I've done enough to prevent any further threat of brain damage. For now.

Scowling, I look to my left where my friend Talia sits beside me. She snickers, then shakes her head.

"I still can't believe you decided to come to this thing." She crosses her legs and regards me up and down, as if something in my slouched appearance will reveal the secret reason for my eventual concession.

This thing is the Crescentwood High School's annual field trip to Camp Kenwick. All seniors in good standing are eligible to attend, for two days of connecting with nature. Complete with outdoor activities, campfires, and communal living spaces in rundown wooden cabins. Or, what my classmates are most excited about: no parents, minimal chaperones, and an unlimited supply of marshmallows. It isn't paradise, and it certainly isn't Disney World, like where every neighboring high school goes for their senior trip at the end of the year. It is a step up from a half-day at the Baltimore Aquarium, though. Considering how little fundraising our class did last year, that was a very real possibility.

I'm likely the only member of the student body not looking forward to this excursion. My issue isn't the threat of physical activity or camping. For me, the only problem is spending two full days pretending to be normal.

The prospect is daunting.

I'm not sure if I'll ever feel normal again. Since my parents died, so many emotions have been muted to the point of nonexistence. Even now, I'm only half-listening to my classmates' excited chatter about the latest high school gossip. I'm apparently the only one who doesn't seem to care that Jenny is dating Sam, even though she went out with his best friend, Nick, last year.

There are times when I feel like this is just a funk, and I'm just one day away from being the girl I know I had to have once been. But most of the time, I feel like an alien. Or a half-witted skeleton in a very convincing skin suit.

Dissociation, my therapist called it. Or, depersonalization-derealization disorder. Brought on by acute emotional distress and grief. Check and check. It's characterized by episodes of feeling detached from the world, as if watching a movie on the misadventures of my life, rather than living it myself.

At first, I was thrilled to get any sort of diagnosis. It felt so validating to have a real, scientific explanation for how unreal my life was starting to feel. A legitimate reason for being so estranged from everyone else. But the more I've learned about it over these last few years, the less accurate I feel it is. It's not that I feel unattached, just displaced. I'm still connected to my thoughts, feelings, and experiences. My life doesn't feel unreal by any means, I just don't feel real living it.

"I'm surprised your aunt even let you come on the trip, Tempe," Talia continues, knocking her braided Bantu buns against my head to regain my attention.

My lips twitch into a frown. Between my parents' tragic accident and Aunt Laura spending so much of her time as a nurse in the emergency room, she's absolutely terrified of me getting hurt. I understand, of course, even if I don't always agree.

"I may have implied that this was more of a camp, like camping, than day camp," I admit.

Talia's eyes go wide. "You lied?"

"No!" I say quickly, then add, "I just didn't show her the brochure."

"You're going to be in so much trouble if she finds out."

I sigh. She's probably right.

"I just wanted to give Laura and Brian a night alone for once," I confess. "They've been together for—what? Two years, now? I don't think he's ever spent the night."

"I wouldn't worry about that too much, Tempe," she says with gravity. "They're nurses. That's what on-call rooms are for. Haven't you seen *Grey's Anatomy*?"

I feel my face flush. "That is *not* what I meant."

I again set my attention out the bus's large, smudged windows. There is nothing but miles of dark-green forest ahead of us. I always thought of New Jersey as industrial, but the northeast is surprisingly mountainous. It's so different from Maryland's mostly flat terrain.

My parents and I moved around a lot when I was young, but Maryland is as far north-east as I've ever been before. They were adjunct professors at several universities across the country, hence our nomadic lifestyle for the first decade of my life. I can't help but wonder, and not for the first time, why we ended up planting roots in Crescentwood, of all places.

Despite my parents' interest in academics, I still have no idea what I'm going to do with my life come next year. Talia has it all figured out already; she was just accepted to a university in Boston and is declaring a major in marketing. I can't think about college just yet, not when getting through this year with my sanity intact feels like a behemoth of a task in itself.

When the bus pulls into the parking lot thirty minutes later, there are other students already lugging their bags towards the cabins. Even watching their nondescript backs disappear into the tree line, I can see there are more than a hundred kids—too many to be just from Crescentwood. I don't know why it surprises me that there are other schools here for a field trip as well. We unload from the bus, ordered by

Mrs. Terce to stay together until a camp counselor can give a welcome speech to our late party.

The bus shifts into reverse, kicking up plumes of dirt in its wake. My stomach twists again as it finally pulls away, but this time the feeling is closer to pain than discomfort.

The sun is setting by the time we return from the hike. The obstructed sun casts eerie shadows against the woods, and every time I catch a glimpse in my periphery, I nearly jump out of my skin. Settling into camp did little to lessen my senseless anxiety. I can feel myself starting to spiral in a way I know is indicative of a full-blown dissociative episode. I'm trying my best to keep it at bay until later, when I can work through it in the solitude of the night.

We jog across the soccer field, the ground now patchy and sparse from an early autumn frost, to a wood pavilion where one of the camp counselors waits for us.

"Welcome back, campers! How'd you do?" Remy calls out with a goofy grin.

Talia whoops in response. The two girls from the field hockey team (Jenny of the school scandal among them) and the guys they dragged along join in with hoots and cheers. The "hike" was more of a scavenger hunt than anything, and it put us all in a festive mood.

"We've got a winner here, Remy!" Talia exclaims. She simultaneously shoves me forward and jumps on top of me, squeezing my shoulders.

"Oh yeah? You guys got everything on the list?"

Talia proudly presents her phone to the counselor for comparison. The list contains twenty natural features or creatures that could be found on the trail. Each group was instructed to discover as many as they could, as fast as they could.

"Our girl, Tempest, killed it. She found nearly everything by herself. There wasn't a robin, chipmunk, or aspen that went undetected," she assures him.

I smile, a little embarrassed by the attention, but happy to see my friend so proud. Really, it isn't nearly as impressive as Talia is making it seem. While the rest of the group was too busy chatting amongst themselves or horsing around, I watched. My senses felt sharp out in the woods, the fresh air doing me a lot of good. It even quelled my cramping stomach for a short time. Anyone could have spotted the robin perched on the aspen tree's branch if they had been paying attention.

Remy flips through the images, oohing and aahing under his breath as he makes his examination. He seems truly thrilled with our discoveries even though he must be sick of seeing the same wildlife all the time.

Maybe I should become a camp counselor instead of going to college. I don't know how long I could endure Remy as a coworker, but organizing scavenger hunts and hiking for a living doesn't seem half bad.

"So, we won right?" Jenny asks. Her white sneakers, an ill-advised fashion statement, are somehow caked in mud despite how dry the path had been.

"Oh, it's not a competition," Remy informs us. "Everyone who completes the scavenger hunt is a winner, and this is a mighty fine collection you've brought me! Let me get your prizes."

He leans down to the yellow wheelbarrow beside him and seeks out a couple bags of marshmallows. Talia's face crumples.

"That's such crap!" she argues. "Did we come in first or not?"

Remy frowns and presents her with the goodies as his only reply.

"Second?" she demands, undeterred. A box of graham crackers and a four-pack of Hershey chocolate bars follow.

"Oh, come on! Just tell us," Jenny insists.

With a sigh, Remy finally concedes. "You came in fifth."

"Fifth!" Talia shrieks.

"I did not sweat off fourteen dollars' worth of makeup for fifth place," Jenny's friend agrees.

"How is that possible? We practically had a bloodhound on our team." Talia shoves her thumb in my direction to make her point.

"You were the first from your school," Remy says, seeming relieved to have good news to deliver us. "You even beat out Hartfield High, but the Versi Academy kids flew through the challenge. Don't feel bad about it, though. They're here every year."

I forgot about the other schools since we hadn't seen them after our late arrival. The mandatory safety brief before the hike had been isolated to the Crescentwood kids, and during the welcome speech, we were warned that since the dining hall could only occupy so many people at a time, this evening would be full of activities while the different groups rotated around the campus. Luckily for us, we get first dibs on dinner, so instead of waiting for the rest of our school to finish, we are welcome to head right to the dining hall. Jenny and her friends opt to freshen up in the cabins first, so Talia and I make the trek across the camp by ourselves.

Talia, still fuming from the ego blow of fifth place, tears into the bag of marshmallows as we walk.

"Hey! Save them for tonight," I say. I try to snatch the bag from her hands, but she lunges away from me, taking the bag with her.

"We just spent an hour in the woods getting eaten alive by bugs, I think we deserve a few marshmallows." She finally wrestles one from the bag and regards it appreciatively before popping it into her mouth.

I shake my head. I don't actually care too much about spoiling my appetite for dinner, but we are quite actually in route to the dining hall. That, and I am still so nauseous, thanks to my nerves, that a mound of sugar might actually make me sick.

Thinking about my stomach ache seems to have willed it back with a vengeance. My abdomen cramps painfully, and I have to wonder if maybe it's not anxiety this time. Maybe I'm actually coming down with something.

"I'm starting to think this trip was a bad idea" I mutter, more to myself than to my friend. Despite my words, I don't want her to realize how bad of a mood I'm in. I don't have anyone to blame for signing up but myself. Talia may be my closest friend, but she has plenty of acquaintances she could have hung out with had I decided to stay home.

Thankfully, she's oblivious to my turmoil and beams like she's having the time of her life. It helps to quell the pain—at least a little.

"Trust me," she says. "I have a good feeling about it."

2

JET

High schoolers are idiots. I know because only a few months ago, I was one—though I like to think that I skipped the bumbling-idiocy phase of my life.

For the last thirty minutes, I've been watching a horde of kids head-butt a volleyball over the net, try to spin the ball on their noses, or stick it up their shirts and wail as if they are going into labor with baby Wilson. Brody, at my side, is snickering at their antics, but I'm hardly amused.

Brody notices my expression and nudges me with his shoulder. "Lighten up, Jet."

I don't bother looking back at him. I've been counting the number of Versi Academy students every five minutes to ensure that there are still thirty-six of them. I just finished my count a minute ago, too soon to start again, so now I watch the crowd with rapt focus.

"I'm working," I tell him. He rolls his eyes.

"You realize we're not actually protectors yet. We're basically interns."

"We're cadets," I argue.

The official co-op program starts in college, while pursuing a degree in law & protection at Versi University. There is a high school extracurricular program too, available to seniors who think they may be interested in pursuing the profession. That's how I've gotten so much exposure to protecting already, though I've only been a cadet since college started in August.

"Yeah, exactly. I asked you to come because this is supposed to be fun."

"I am having fun," I say in absolute deadpan. I'm not actually, but I'm not downright miserable either, so it doesn't feel like too egregious of a lie.

Brody is wrong, though. We are here to represent the League of Protectors as chaperones. Sure, this assignment is as low stakes as they come, hence why they allowed a few cadets to take on the responsibility. But it's standard, on an excursion like this, to have some sort of protector presence.

The campus where we all live and go to school is heavily warded to keep anyone unwelcome out, but that means that students are typically kept in, too. Since no one wants to feel trapped, these supervised trips give students a taste of life outside the Versi borders. But anything can go wrong in the human world. Especially now, in the age of social media, when the only thing standing between a teenager and the rest of the world is a photo posted on the internet. It's the League of Protectors' job to ensure that our students are safe and our society stays hidden from curious human eyes. We can't afford to make a single mistake.

Brody is meant to be leading the trip since he's in his second year of the co-op program, though Andre Gonzales was assigned to join us too. I like Andre enough, even though we've never clicked in the way I had with Brody as kids.

It feels close to the five-minute mark now, so I start my scan again, this time mouthing the count under my breath.

Brody shakes his head. "Jet, if this is what it looks like when you're having fun, then you need an intervention even more than I thought. You should really try being a normal college student at some point. Maybe go to a party. Or even," he mocks a gasp, "date."

I frown, but not at Brody's words because I'm not truly listening to them. I start my count again.

"I'm sure Elisa would set you up with one of her friends. Though they're all a little on the wild side, which would probably stress you out. Maybe we could find you someone who is—"

"Thirty-five," I say.

Brody's brow pinches, though his smile never falters. "Okay, I didn't expect that, but if that's what you're into, no judgment here. We should probably just get you on an app, in that case, though."

I roll my eyes. "No, Brody. Thirty-five *students*. We're missing one."

"Missing one?" he echoes. "How could we be missing one?"

I put my hand on his shoulder and give him a sweet smile. "Because their chaperone is an idiot." It takes him a moment too long to understand and look properly affronted, therefore proving my point. "Keep a close eye on the rest of them. I won't be long."

"You know who it is?" he asks. I give a sharp nod.

"Isaac Grant."

It's not a great sign that I know his name so early on in the trip, but it does benefit me in this case. Since I know who it is, and have already committed his trace to memory, it will be easy to track him. Which is good.

If he's unsupervised for too long, he could risk exposing the entire preternatural world.

Isaac couldn't have gotten far considering the intervals of my scans. Even if he was moving at an inhuman speed—which despite his pesterance so far this trip, I truly doubt he's that stupid—I can move just as quickly, away from prying human eyes. I pass into a thick pocket of woods behind a large shack they call the dining hall. There is a buzz of excited chatter from inside that I have to tune out to get focused on the task at hand.

Tracing is not much different than tracking a wild animal. It requires every sense to be on high alert, and a quick processing of every new morsel of information to make fast and accurate decisions. One wrong choice will have you following the wrong path, costing valuable time.

I don't make the wrong choice, though. I never do.

I step onto a path that would look almost indistinguishable to the untrained eye. I was led there by a whiff of a scent that is unique to Isaac. Not a bad scent, and nothing a human would ever be conscious enough to notice, just a hint of something in the wind that has my instincts pulling me this way, instead of that. There is phantom heat clinging to the trees too, as if a warm body just passed through.

Once I'm locked in on Isaac's trace, his scent becomes strong enough to taste. I can see a shimmer of his trace in the air, a perfectly laid out path for me to follow. There is a humming too, faint over the call of birds and scurrying feet of woodland creatures, though the volume of it increases with every step I take in what I know is the right direction.

This skill is a blend of the physical and the metaphysical. It is one that I learned in the Protector Program, though my affinity for it goes far beyond the norm, even for what we are.

My next step brings me into a clearing where the carcasses of three bonfires lie. There are long logs of wood embedded into the ground, as if to be benches, facing each fire. It's nearly abandoned now, still too early in the evening to begin preparations, I presume, but it won't be that way for long.

Isaac is on the far end of the clearing, looking up at a large oak tree. It's the perfect kind for climbing, thick and sturdy, with well-spaced limbs. You could easily secure your foothold on one branch while reaching for another. Guessing from the introspective look on his face as I approach, Isaac's considering that same thing.

Not that it really matters to him. Since Isaac can shapeshift into a monkey, he can successfully climb almost anything in his animal form.

"Don't think about it," I warn, my voice a low growl. The kid stumbles back as if I appeared from thin air and had not made many large, though admittedly silent, strides towards him.

"Woah, where did you—" his question dies out as he realizes who he's talking to. Then he takes a large gulp of air. "Listen, man, I wasn't going to, uh, do anything. Okay?"

"Right," I say, my tone clipped. I've been more irritable than usual today, a fact that unnerves and—yes—irritates me all the more. I can't pin down what has me so on edge, which won't serve Isaac well for this conversation.

Except that I'm certain he has no malicious or criminal intent—he's just dumb and fifteen. He likely resents that he has to remain human for the duration of this trip, but I don't think exposing our secret society is his goal. He just wants to let loose.

I get where he's coming from, I really do, but it's the *one* rule all students must swear by before being allowed on one of these supervised excursions. It's not the only rule, of course, but it's the most important rule in our world.

I decide to let him off with a sigh, though the sound still slips into a rumble of a growl that happens to bare my canines.

"Let's get going or we're going to miss dinner," I tell him. "And *no shifting*. I'm serious, Isaac. If I hear even a whisper about werewolves tonight, you'll have me to answer to."

He swallows hard. "Yes, sir."

I put my hand on his shoulder to push him forward. He takes off in a jog, putting several feet of distance between the two of us as we make the short trek back towards the dining hall. When we break through the woods back into the view of the volleyball courts, Isaac lumbers away from me and back towards his friends with his tail between his legs—figuratively, thank the Universe.

Across the open space, I see Brody talking with one of the camp counselors. A moment later, the counselor leaves and Brody cups his hands in front of his mouth to call the high schoolers to attention.

"Alright, Versi Academy, it's time for dinner. Let's line up to give the Crescentwood kids some breathing room, yeah?"

He is immediately ignored, not that he seems to mind. The hoard of students barrel towards the dining hall at the same moment the kids on the other side throw open the doors and pour out. I shake my head, now a bit amused, though I maintain my watchful perch on the other side of the disarray. I'll do a count the moment I'm inside, though I don't think a single one of the thirty-six students would dare miss dinner.

I'm still overseeing when a shimmer catches my eye. It's not like the trail I saw before when I tuned into Isaac's trace, though it's not dissimilar enough for me to ignore it either. It's like the aura of an ocular migraine, a small floater in my vision's periphery.

I turn to the shimmer, looking for the source, but see nothing unusual. Some are still fighting their way in and out of the dining hall with an equal amount of thoughtless conviction. A new group has entered the mix too. The Hartfield High students are coming to play volleyball while the Crescentwood students are corralled into a corner where they are being given instructions for the third activity in the rotation.

Perhaps the strange shimmer I saw is nothing more than the residual effects of having just tapped into that talent for Isaac a few minutes before. But then I remember the sensation I've been feeling most of the day: on edge, as if standing on the cusp of a cliff and being unsure if the fall is five feet or five hundred.

Again, there's that shift in the atmosphere as the three groups converge, and it's enough for me not to risk ignoring the shimmering warp in my vision. I know I have a job to do inside and that I'm wasting my valuable time by standing here, observing insignificant humans, but something about this situation suddenly feels off-kilter and I find myself rooted in my place. My eyes scan the crowds of kids for whatever the offending thing may be that has me in such a state, but there is still nothing to go off of. No shimmering trail or obvious hum, that's for sure.

I'm not sure how, when, or why I start to trace, only that I find myself doing it. My eyes rake over each person in the clearing while I try to taste a hint of something unfamiliar. There is a confluence by the dining hall door, most of which are fairly unfamiliar given that I don't know all the Versi Academy students personally.

Still, there is one that is stranger than the rest. It is a bit sweet, like the mild nectar of a honeysuckle, nothing more than a wisp of fragrance on the newly autumn wind. I shut out everything except for that scent, that taste, and immediately a shiver shoots down my spine.

There has to be a hum of the trace in this crowd, I just need to hear it over the discord. I close my eyes and try to tune into the sound. At the same time, I let my nose twitch towards the delicate deliciousness.

Even humans have traces, with their own distinctly earthy flavor that marks them as such. Each species has their own identifiers that makes it easy for someone like me to decipher between them. Human traces are so muted that it would take a considerable effort to tune into one and then follow successfully. Yet my senses take several wrong turns in my search, bumping up against the dull hums of one human or another.

I'm about to give up, frustrated by the difficulty since my ability to trace has never failed me before, when I run into a brick wall. Complete and utter silence. Silence like I've never heard from a trace of any living creature. Silence like the work of something unnatural—or preternatural, in our case.

My eyes fly open and are met with the profile of a girl with all the makings of a human, except for a dull barely-there shimmer in the air around her that I ordinarily would have dismissed as a trick of the setting sun. There is nothing particularly disparate about her in the way of most preternatural. No abnormal beauty, unnatural stillness, or a feeling that is inexplicably wild. No, she's kind of pretty—but nothing that would halt you at first glance. She shifts awkwardly on her feet under the attention from her companions, her eyes unfocused as she scans the crowd, though seemingly unseeing.

Then she turns towards me. She looks through me, at some point beyond. Her eyes are as strange as I've ever seen, which is saying something since before now I thought the oddest eyes were the ones that looked back at me in the mirror every morning. Even from this distance, they are a kaleidoscope of deep green and stormy gray, like a storm at sea.

It's a coincidence, it has to be. Plenty of humans have pretty eyes, that doesn't make her preternatural. Maybe there's something wrong with her that dampens her trace. It makes no logical sense, and it may be a mystery, but it's not my problem to solve.

But a human's trace doesn't shimmer, or taste the way hers does. And my first thought, before my analytical brain kicked in, was that her abnormal silence must be due to preternatural manipulation.

My instincts are confirming what should be an impossibility. There is another shapeshifter at Camp Kenwick. And although I can't explain it, I know there is something different about her, something that tells me she isn't part of our world, which could be a very dangerous thing.

I make my way into the dining hall and appear behind Brody, who is just sitting down with a full plate of burgers, hot dogs, and pasta salad. I set a hand on his shoulder and lean in to whisper, "We have a problem."

❦ 3 ❧

TEMPEST

By the time we make it to the bonfire that night, we've eaten more than half the bag of marshmallows. The chocolate isn't faring much better, so we're mostly left with broken bits of graham cracker that Talia is still managing to burn the edges off with two twigs she's holding like chopsticks.

We're arranged around a roaring fire in the center of a large open field on the far side of the campground. There are two additional fires, all with log benches around them for people to sit. I don't think the intention was for the three schools to segregate themselves, but despite the talk of the students today about flirting with the other kids, everyone is now shyly sticking to their usual cliques.

I, for one, am glad for it. The crowd is making me jittery with nerves, and my stomach is still cramping. After picking at my dinner, I finally broke down and popped a couple of Tums to see if that would settle it, but it proved futile. I'm sure all the sugar I've consumed since isn't helping matters.

My classmates are laughing loudly at a story that Heidi

from our European History class is telling, but I tune them out to focus on people watching. It's hard to see with only the orange glow of the fires to light the night. Harsh shadows obscure the profiles of most of the people in my line of sight, so I don't notice what is happening until I'm in it. My vision warps around the edges, giving the scene in front of me a warbled quality. It's not truly my eyesight faltering, it's my cognitive perception that has fallen away.

After staving off a dissociative episode for the better part of the day, it snuck up on me and dragged me under without the normal warning signs I know to take heed of. Unfortunately, recognizing that I'm in a dissociative state is not always enough to bring me back from the edge. Instead, it becomes something akin to an out-of-body experience married with sleep paralysis. I'm still rooted in my body, but half of my mind seems to disconnect from the other. So, while I'm observing myself from a sort of bird's eye view, I am also still acting as me. My lungs inflate and deflate as normal. My eyes still scan the crowd. I hear myself give Talia a generic reply to an equally generic comment, my friend having no idea that I am no longer in control.

My gaze gets locked on the fingers of the flames in front of me, and in my suspended state, I swear they're changing into shapes with the wind.

Thankfully I'm pulled out of it by Talia's touch on my shoulder.

"What do you think, Tempe?" she asks.

The world snaps back into focus with a dizzying clarity. Talia reaches past me to grab the final marshmallow from the crumpled bag and my gaze follows the white glob while I try to orient myself again. "Hmm?"

"Heidi decided the love of her life is that guy from Harfield

High," she tells me, nodding towards a nondescript shadow of a boy at the next fire over getting shoved around by a group of similarly unremarkable guys.

I pretend to need a moment to locate the boy in question, but really I just need an extra second to recover. Then, I snort. "If anyone is having a love affair, they better do it fast. We're leaving tomorrow."

"Oh, why can't you be romantic like the rest of us!" Talia complains. "I, for one, have my eyes on a few guys." Her eyes move to scan the throngs of people around us. Chuckling, I follow her gaze until my eyes meet a pair of startling sapphire blue ones from across the fire.

I take in a sharp breath. They're so unlike anything I've seen before, both in color and intensity. And they're watching me.

I can barely make out his face between the flames and shadows, so I tilt my head to get a better angle. I watch him to see if it will somehow reveal why he's watching me. It doesn't, of course, and after several more seconds of this staring contest, I have to drop my gaze. My cheeks are burning as I look back to the fire.

This time, when I watch the flaming fingers and my mind starts to slip away, I let it. The fire is shifting again. Orange and yellow heat flickers from lions to wolves to beetles. Though I know it isn't real, only a figment of my imagination, I let myself be comforted by the illusion.

I roll myself out of the bottom bunk when the dim red hue of the digital clock on the cabin wall blinks to two a.m. My eyes are heavy with the desire to sleep but it still refuses to come. I head to the bathroom, not because I have to go, but because I need to get out of bed.

My therapist suggested this technique for managing my insomnia—leaving my sleeping area to do something else until I feel tired again. Unfortunately, switching on the fluorescent bathroom lights has me feeling wide awake and I know sleep is still a long way away.

For lack of anything better to do, I read the labels on my cabin-mates toiletries left lying about from the mad rush of twelve teenagers sharing four shower stalls. When that gets boring, I brush my teeth, spit and rinse, and try to brainstorm another way to pass the time.

Only one thing comes to mind. I need a change of scenery.

As quietly as I can manage on the squeaking wood floorboards, I slip out of the bathroom and cross the cabin to where my sneakers lay in a pile by the door. The hinge squeals in protest as I pull it open, but there is only that single sound before I am out in the cool autumn air. Yesterday was the last day of the month, making it now the early hours of October.

I'm not scared as I traverse the quiet campground despite the dark of the night. The chirps of crickets are good company as I head down to the wood dock that overlooks the lake. Rows of dirty kayaks are scattered in front of the boat house, so I keep going to the further of the picnic tables on the sandy shore. I perch myself on the tabletop and stick my feet up on the bench below.

The waxing gibbous moon is just shy of full birth, casting the shore with ghost light. I watch its reflection ripple on the black water of the lake until my eyes begin to fall closed again. The wake gently ebbs and flows against the shore, like nature's lullaby.

"Oh, woah," a guy's deep voice calls out. "I didn't see you there."

My eyes shoot open and I immediately feel alert. I don't think I fell asleep, I swear I only closed my eyes for a moment, but I didn't hear footsteps approaching. I didn't hear anything at all until this guy ten feet away from me cried out.

I'm half a second away from panicking—I've watched enough Dateline to be fearful of meeting anyone in the darkness of night—but the guy chuckles, and the smooth sound of it is disarming.

"That's pretty impressive. People can't usually sneak up on me."

I crack a smile despite my nerves. "I was here the whole time."

"Fair point," he says. He takes a step closer, coming into the moonlight. Once my eyes adjust to the change of shadows, my breath hitches with surprise. It's the guy from the bonfire. The one with the intensely blue eyes.

Without the amber glow of the fire casting shadows against his chin, he seems a little less intimidating, but no less mysterious. Recognizing him, I let my guard down, but only a little.

I'm honestly more afraid of this guy being a camp counselor than a serial killer. The counselors made an entire announcement at dinner time about their zero-tolerance policy for breaking curfew, and the last thing I need is to get in trouble for my late-night excursion.

"Couldn't sleep?" he asks good-naturedly and takes a step closer.

He's in the moon beam now and for the first time, I get a full look at him. I have to hold my breath to catch my gasp from escaping. His skin is tan and clear, and he has thick, black hair that's slightly mussed in the front, like he has been running his hands through it. It gives a rebellious edge to his otherwise rigid appearance.

"Insomnia," I tell him.

"I know the feeling," he says. The smirk that pulls at the corner of his lips has me believing that he truly does. Despite my nerves, I find myself smiling too.

He takes that as an invitation and gestures towards the picnic table. "May I?"

I nod and watch as he climbs up beside me. His posture matches mine, his feet up on the seat below as he leans back on his palms.

"I'm Jet," he offers.

My brow quirks up. That name is almost as unique as mine.

"Tempest," I say. "Some people call me Tempe, like the city."

He hums, like he's considering it carefully. "What school are you from?" he asks after a moment.

"Crescentwood. What about you?"

"Versi. Crescentwood is in Maryland, right?"

I nod. "About thirty minutes from Baltimore."

"Do you get to the city often?"

"Not so much anymore. When my family first moved, we would go back and forth all the time. My parents used to work in the city."

"Used to?"

I nod and turn my gaze away towards the lake to watch the gentle rippling of the water. "I lost them a few years ago."

"I'm sorry," he says, his voice soft.

I rake my teeth over my bottom lip. Even after all this time, nearly four years, it's hard for me to know what to say when someone tells me they're sorry for my loss. I want to agree, but that doesn't seem polite.

I know talking about my dead parents isn't a great anecdote, so I'm grateful that Jet spares me from having to think of a way to change the topic.

"I've never been into city life. I need to be out in nature, like this." He gestures to the glittering lake in front of us.

"You don't get enough of it up in Nowhere, Vermont?" I tease. Earlier tonight, at the bonfire, I heard a few of the kids from Versi Academy talking about their remote boarding school.

"Peru, Vermont," he corrects me kindly. "It is in the middle of nowhere, though. The middle of the Green Mountain National Forest, actually."

My brow pinches as I try to map it in my head. He must have misread my expression because he asks, "Alright, what makes Maryland so special?"

A bitter laugh escapes me. "Absolutely nothing," I say.

I didn't quite realize the extent of my dislike for my current home, but I suppose that living in sixteen cities, between nine states, before my thirteenth birthday could color my opinion without me realizing it.

"It's all perfectly mundane," I continue. "And school is the worst part."

He cocks his head. A silent question.

"It's nothing but repetition and regurgitation," I complain. "They put so much emphasis on setting you up for a successful future but do nothing to propel you towards it. I'm a good student and yet I feel like I have no idea how to apply anything I've learned to the life that I want."

"What kind of life do you want?" he asks, seeming to be genuinely curious.

I falter. It's a fair question, seeing as I was the one to bring up the subject, but no one has ever asked me before. Despite my words, I have no idea how to answer. All I know is that for some reason I'm not ready to commit to the AP-classes-to-college pipeline, and I'm less sure of how I could even afford it.

"Honestly," I start, and it doesn't occur to me until after the word passes my lips that I *want* to be honest with this stranger. Maybe because he's just that. "I haven't thought about it since my parents passed. I've worked through a lot of my grief, but I still don't know how to move forward without them. I feel like I'm stuck in quicksand, drowning in a life that I'm not supposed to be living."

"Sorry," I say quickly, realizing how much I've confessed and how unfair that is to this poor guy who was probably looking for the same escape that I was when he came out here. "This is why I don't sleep," I joke.

"No, that's okay," he says softly.

His eyes shine with compassion as he watches me, and I realize that they aren't sapphire blue at all. They're more vibrant, like Lapis Lazuli—teetering on the edge of looking totally unnatural. There's a glint of curiosity there still, but another emotion too. I can't tell if it's surprise or something else. It's that expression that convinces me more than his words.

We fall into a comfortable quiet. Intimate even.

"I know what it's like to be desperate to reach for something and keep coming up empty-handed," he says, surprising me with his admission.

His brow is furrowed now, and with his deep scowl, he looks as if he is made of nothing but harsh angles. It's his turn to pointedly watch the water, as if afraid to meet my eyes. Before, I wanted to shift away under his severe gaze, but now that it's being withheld from me, I crave it.

Is he always this intense? It works for him, surely. He's alluring without the air of mystery, but with it, even as unromantic as my friend has accused me of being, I can't help but fantasize about the secrets Jet may keep.

I bite my lip, considering my words before speaking again. "This probably sounds dumb—obviously I know that I'm only seventeen—but I just feel like my life has veered completely off-course and I have no idea how to get back on track."

Jet is quiet for a long time. Long enough for me to get self-conscious that I shared too much. That I stretched the vulnerability we've woven too thin and now the thread connecting us is going to snap. But to my surprise, he smiles and—damn. It's a good smile. A great one, actually. Two rows of white teeth that look a little sharp, though it suits him well. It's the kind of smile that makes your heart race, though you don't know if the nerves are from excitement or fear.

"You should transfer to my school. We do things differently than other places." The corners of his lips twitch higher, as if he told a joke, but then he seems to catch himself. He gestures to the camp behind him and explains. "This is a fairly ordinary weekend for us, just without the long bus ride."

"Maybe I should," I tease.

There is still amusement in his eyes, even as his lips fall back into their neutral line, though he's no less beautiful this way.

For a moment, I'm terrified of what comes next. Mostly because I don't know what is meant to come next. I don't usually share secrets with strangers in the middle of the night, and I certainly don't enjoy it as much as I am now. A blush crawls up my neck and onto my cheeks. Thank God for the dark night and cool air.

Jet clears his throat and adjusts himself to sit up a bit straighter. I suck in an anxious breath and look around for something to inspire a subject change. Fortunately, or unfortunately, in this case, I see one. There is a flash of light in the darkness to my right. The white beam of a flashlight moves against the trees across from us and I curse.

"We should go," I say, getting to my feet.

Jet turns his head and must spot the nearby form with the flashlight, but he doesn't seem concerned. "Don't worry about it. I'm actually a chaperone."

I frown. I would have guessed that he was older than me, but he didn't seem that much older.

"I can't really take that chance. If I get in trouble they'll call my aunt and I don't need that." At Jet's frown, I explain. "She worries."

He opens his mouth, probably to argue, but I'm already walking away. I need to get out of here for more reasons than just the threat of getting caught breaking curfew. I don't know what to make of Jet or the connection I've forged with him, however fleeting it may have been.

I wish, for the millionth time since starting high school, that I possessed the ability to act normally in social situations. But no, show me a hot guy by a quiet lake and my instinct is to act like an absolute freak.

"It was nice talking to you," I call back to him, though I keep my voice hushed.

"Goodnight," he says, and his tone is such a rich purr that I feel a shiver spread across my shoulders before shooting down my spine.

I hustle off the sand and set off on the dirt path that leads back to my cabin. I find myself fighting a smile the entire way. I'm across the clearing, only a few strides from the short set of stairs that leads up to the cabin's doorstep when I yawn. My eyes feel heavy too, and I hope it means I can finally get some rest. But as I reach the stairs, a familiar voice calls out for me to stop, though it's not the deep timbre that a small part of me was hoping for. It's Remy, the camp counselor.

"And what exactly do you think you're doing?"

JET

"**I**t would be so great if you could give us a little bit of information," Brody is saying to one of the counselors. He's employing a lethal, megawatt smile that I am reluctant to admit may actually get us further than flashing a badge would.

Brody's sprawled out on the bench seat across from me in the camp's dining hall. We have the entire table to ourselves—or at least we did before he waved over the counselor he is now flirting with. The girl has a head full of kinky curls that she twirls around her finger as she giggles.

Andre is on the other side of the open room, hanging out with Isaac Grant and his friends. It could be easy to mistake Andre's laid-back demeanor as indifference to his role as chaperone, but it's just the opposite. Ever since I told him to keep an eye on Isaac, Andre has dutifully integrated himself into their group, feeling that Isaac needed some extra attention if we wanted to ensure he stayed in line. In a professional sense, it's a smart move, but I appreciate it on a personal level too. Andre just silently assumed the role, leaving me and Brody to spend some quality time together while he's on babysitting duty.

Not that there is much quality time being spent here. We've been obsessively turning over every word Tempest said to me last night, trying to make sense of who she is and what she could be doing here. At least we were, until Brody decided to take a more hands-on approach.

"I'm not really supposed to give info out on any of the campers," the counselor says. She sounds hesitant, but she's also rapidly fluttering her eyelashes at Brody and biting her lip.

I want to roll my eyes, but manage to refrain. After a lifetime of friendship, this is exactly the kind of thing I expect Brody to pull. I was just hoping that a full year of him in the League of Protectors' co-op program would have made him more inclined to rely on real investigative tactics rather than his charm.

"Come on, it's not like we need anything sensitive. My boy Jet is just trash at talking to girls. He has a bit of a crush on someone named Tempest he met last night, but he doesn't know what school she's from. Just let me take a peek at her file so I can be a good wingman."

This time I do roll my eyes. Brody's an idiot, and this is not going to work. Surely this place has to have some procedures to protect the privacy of their campers.

The girl giggles again. "Fine, but we have to be quick about it."

Apparently not.

Brody is on his feet in an instant, sending me a wink and accepting the counselor's hand as she drags him away from his untouched breakfast. I shake my head. Despite how truly annoying my best friend can be, I'm grateful he's on the case, as unprofessionally as he's choosing to go about it.

The truth is that my conversation with Tempest last night left me even more confused. It's clear to me now that Tempest doesn't know what she is, but I can't understand why.

Nagual typically gain the ability to shift sometime around puberty. With raging hormones and all the other embarrassing changes in the human body, our dormant animal form starts to demand attention too. But shifting can't happen without provocation.

The going theory is that by waiting until puberty to shift, it ensures that we are mature enough to use our abilities to carry out the Universe's divine mission: protecting the harmony between humans and the rest of the natural world. By the time a Nagual turns eighteen, the assumption of adulthood in our culture, if they have not triggered their shift, they lose the ability to do so. In the past, the eighteen-year-old deadline was a failsafe, for the off-chance that someone was in a situation in which shifting would jeopardize the Universe's mission, rather than support it. Nowadays, it doesn't serve any real purpose; it's just a good excuse to throw an elaborate birthday party.

There is only one way to trigger a Nagual's first shift: through the Blood Rite. The practice itself sounds a bit barbaric, though anything ancient seems that way through a modern-day lens. It's basically any situation that causes a Nagual to draw blood and simultaneously have blood drawn from them. It's usually part of a fifteenth birthday celebration, since fifteen is typically old enough for our ability to manifest, but not so old that we will suffer from any adverse symptoms. We choose someone close to us, either a friend or family member, and cut their palm. In turn, they cut ours.

There are always a few who opt to go a more traditional route. Instead of cutting palms, they choose to fight. It's always a sparring match, again, between friends or close family. I'm not sure if I would have fought or not, had I been given the choice. But no, my Blood Rite had come about the old-fashioned way: by accident.

When my brother, Kage, was turning fifteen, he decided he wanted to fight for his rite. He chose Brody, who is almost a year younger than him, though they're in the same grade. Brody, of course, was all too eager to learn to shift early and agreed. For a couple of weeks, they sparred in the backyard, practicing for the big day when they were meant to draw blood. I was always there with them, sometimes refereeing and sometimes getting mixed up in the antics.

One time, we were all messing around, and when Kage lunged for Brody, Brody jokingly grabbed me like a human shield. Kage's elbow caught my nose, which, in his defense, had not been there a moment before. In my panic, I grabbed onto Brody.

While I'll tell anyone that I was trying to shove him off of me, I suspect that I may have been trying to cling to him. The blow made me disoriented, and I scratched his forearm just enough to make a couple of beads of blood bubble to the surface of his skin.

The three of us had waited in stillness, wide-eyed with the anticipation of something happening. Kage knew how hard he hit me, and I knew how much pain I was in. Just as Brody knew that while his injury was as superficial as they came, it did draw blood. Then again, I was only thirteen, maybe too young to have triggered the Blood Rite.

The moment I felt the hot trickle of blood on the stretch of flesh between my nose and my upper lip, I shifted into my animal form.

It was as easy as breathing. One second, I was standing, face sore, and the next I was on all fours, my vision almost infrared with the new sensation of becoming a creature other than human. I still remember the first sniff of air, sharp and somehow cold with the scent of freshly cut grass. I remember how soft it felt under my paws. And how, despite my center of gravity being entirely different from what I had ever experienced before, I felt strangely stable on my four powerful feet.

I didn't do anything but stand there and mew in my new, feline voice. It was only my mother, rushing outside in a huff, with a dish towel wrung between her hands, that had me shifting back into my human form. I was afraid that I could hurt her if I didn't yet understand how to operate my new body.

She was furious, saying that we were reckless, and I was much too young to be burdened with my shift. Then it occurred to the four of us, all at the same time, *what* I had shifted into. A panther. It's not an impossibility, of course, but it's rare enough for me to be the only panther shifter on our campus. Kage and Brody still had their Blood Rite a month later, and I came to appreciate the fact that all three of us had each other to learn from as we navigated our new normal.

But that's how easy it is to expose our world. Just one well-timed accident and a first shift can topple everything our community has built to stay hidden, jeopardizing everyone's safety.

For all I know, Tempest could be from a normal Nagual family and has, for whatever reason, chosen not to shift. But if Tempest is actively choosing to forgo her Nagual ability, she would be logged in the LOP's system, and they would have advised her on best practices to avoid triggering her shift— which definitely would have included not attending a camp with a full curriculum of accidents-waiting-to-happen.

No one has to give up their Nagual abilities in order to live amongst humans, of course, but it is something that happens every now and then. Our community at Versi is tight-knit and mostly closed off from the rest of the world, and there is a similar campus called Mayura in Oregon that is the same. There are many families who live throughout the United States that still subscribe to our culture while maintaining the appearance of a human experience, though. That's why the League of Protectors has field offices across the country.

There are also a surprising number of us in the entertainment industry and some who hold political offices. They do their part to uphold the Universe's mission of protecting the natural balance by lobbying for all kinds of environmental and social causes.

My stomach drops when my phone starts buzzing with an incoming call. I should feel relieved, I've been waiting all morning for Lieutenant Delancey to get back to me, but now that the moment has come, I don't feel good about it. I haven't felt good about any decision I've made since arriving at this stupid camp yesterday.

"Hey, Dad," I say as I answer the phone.

"Cadet," he says in a clipped reply. Oof.

I'm used to my dad switching the flip to all-business mode, especially since I've been spending more time around the LOP, but it's not something I've mastered for myself yet. It's hard to reconcile my ranking officer with the man I watched dribble chili down his chin at the dinner table a couple nights ago.

My stomach sinks. I know I made a mistake last night. The second I suspected what Tempest was and that something about her trace was off, I should have called my dad. It was wrong to go to Brody instead. He's usually the one with a hairbrained scheme and I'm the one prepared to get us out of it, so I knew he'd validate my terrible idea to pursue questioning

Tempest on my own. I thought that if I called my dad, he would have told me to stand down, and that wasn't what I wanted to hear.

I'm just not sure why I felt so strongly that it had to be me, and me alone, to do it.

When I called my dad in a panic at nearly three o'clock this morning, he slept through all three of my calls, and I've had no idea what to do with the ticking time bomb I've been sitting on ever since.

"I got your message. Lieutenant Caro and I are driving down from Versi now. The director needs us to handle this matter with discretion."

I frown. The message I left was a rundown of everything pertinent I learned about Tempest, including her hometown and the name of her school. I was thorough in explaining my instinct that she is somehow unaware of what she is, though I glossed over quite a few details about our conversation. Like how I purposely sought her out. And how she surprised me.

I don't know how I expected the LOP to handle this. I may only be in the first semester of law and protection degree, but I've read through the entire League of Protectors manual, twice, and there is definitely no mention of what we should do if we face a shiftless Nagual out in the world. It happens so infrequently that I guess there is no need to outline a specific protocol. But I'm still surprised that two lieutenants would be sent from HQ to deal with the situation directly. Surely one or two officers from a local field office could handle giving her a talking-to and the registration paperwork.

"I contacted the Baltimore field office, but they have no record of a shiftless Nagual in their region," my dad explains. "They cross-referenced the national database and there is no one by the name of Tempest in their system."

"So, Tempest isn't registered as shiftless," I clarify. I suspected as much and I'm still not fully understanding why that would warrant my dad to come to Camp Kenwick himself.

"No, son," he continues, and I'm glad for the reprieve from formality. "There is no one by the name of Tempest in any of our systems. Whoever she is, the LOP has no record of her."

TEMPEST

"**S**top staring. You're so embarrassing," I whine at Talia, who is slack-jawed, gaping at Jet.

We're standing below the rock-climbing wall. The schools have been encouraged to intermingle as we rotate through the four activities planned before lunch and checkout. Our group had been sent to the rock-climbing wall first, which seemed like a horrible idea at eight-thirty in the morning. After this is disc golf, ziplining, and finally, a head-to-head canoe race.

I stand at the base watching as six bodies scale the faux-rock surface. Flailing hands grab at brightly colored holds of all shapes and sizes. Some, mostly the Versi Academy students, don't look half bad. Meanwhile, most of the Crescentwood kids have thoroughly embarrassed themselves, and us, by association. Now, they hang on their harnesses twenty feet above the ground, spinning themselves around like tops as they wait for the counselors to lower them down.

While I'm watching them, Talia is watching Jet. Her eyes are so wide that I'm afraid they might pop out of her skull.

I expected my friend to be excited about my late-night chat with Jet, and boy, did she deliver. When I dropped the bomb this morning, Talia shrieked loud enough to capture the attention of every student in the dining hall and demanded all kinds of juicy details that didn't actually exist. And while I don't really get the excitement for myself, I am secretly reveling in her enthusiasm. *This* is what normalcy feels like; getting excited over boys with your friend.

I know nothing will come of my talk with Jet, and that's okay. It's better even. This way I have a perfect snapshot of the teenage experience without the messy drama of dating, and Talia has something fun to obsess over. We're connected in a way that I've longed for the last three years.

"Well, he clearly likes you," Talia says, pointing right at him. I cringe. "He's looking over here."

Instinctively, I turn, and I'm surprised to see that she's right. I steal a look over my shoulder to where Jet stands amongst a group of Versi students. His rigid posture sets him apart from the rest.

Now seeing him in full daylight, my mouth goes a little dry. The fabric of his dark gray t-shirt stretches against the lean muscles of his biceps. He somehow manages to stand an entire head taller than the high schoolers, and his athletic frame is uniquely lithe. Between that and his keen, bright eyes, he looks like a cat ready to pounce at any moment.

When his eyes meet mine, I expect to see some shift in him, but his expression stays as blank as a fresh sheet of notebook paper. My heart inexplicably sinks. No sign of recognition. None of those smirks I found myself thinking about into the early hours of the morning. For the briefest of moments, I question whether our meeting really happened. There's no way that my dissociations could have devolved into delusions without warning, right?

No, I know our meeting last night was real, and it's frustrating that he'd be so apathetic this morning to let me consider otherwise. Maybe whatever he sees in me in the light of day, he's found lacking. But instead of feeling dejected, I feel like he's issued a challenge. There's a fire that has been lit in my chest; a smoldering ember, waiting to be flamed.

"So, how much trouble did you get in?" Talia asks, turning my attention back to her.

I sigh. I've been purposefully trying not to think about how my evening ended, being scolded by a camp counselor, barely any older than me, about acting irresponsibly. I explained that I have insomnia and I was only putting my therapist's technique into practice, but Remy didn't want to hear it. He took my name down and insisted that if I tried something again there would be severe consequences—which seems excessive in my opinion—and sent me back to my cabin—which I had been in the process of doing anyway when he interrupted me.

"Remy just said he was thinking of calling my aunt," I say. I'm telling myself it's not a big deal either way, but I definitely don't want to stress Laura out over something that was such a nonissue.

Talia rolls her eyes. "He's all talk, I bet. We're leaving in a few hours, anyway. I don't see how it would actually be worth the effort."

I nod, wanting to believe her. I texted my aunt right away to explain the situation myself, but I haven't heard anything back yet. With any luck, she'll sleep late and we'll be packing up to head home by the time she sees the message.

"Alright folks, I hope everyone enjoyed their climb," a

female counselor says, stepping forward. "We're going to do one last round before we send you to the next activity in your rotation. This time, it's a contest!"

The crowd whoops and cheers.

"I need the two strongest contenders from each school to claim a harness," the counselor continues.

There's a slight hesitation as people decide amongst themselves who will compete. In my periphery, I see Jet talking to his companions. I can't tell if he's volunteering, but in that one moment, my heart turns to steel, and without any further consideration, I step forward.

Talia cheers much more than necessary as I claim a harness and begin to climb into it. I meet Jet's gaze, but I still can't read him. His face is a mask of disinterest, and yet there is something wild about his unnaturally blue eyes. Something almost like panic. It's only then that I realize just how out of my depth I am.

My competition is exclusively men, all of whom have so many inches on my perfectly average height of five-five that I'm not sure if they'd be able to see me if we passed on the street or if I would just get trampled by their giant frames.

Down the line, I see Kevin Basie, a soccer player from my school. He talks a big game but never seems to do anything *but* talk. On my left is a guy from Harfield High, and to my right is another student from Versi, though thankfully his lanky frame is a little less intimidating than the others. He looks Latinx with fluffy, brown curls and cinnamon-colored eyes.

"Ready to kick some jock ass?"

It takes me a moment to realize he's talking to me. I send him an apologetic smile. He smiles right back, not missing a beat.

"All these meatheads will be pooped by the second tier," he says reassuringly.

"I hope you're right," I reply, my voice wavering as I look up at the course. I think it's gotten taller in the last few minutes. When I was assigned to climb the first route, they had only let us go up about thirty feet as practice. As the hour progressed, the counselors raised their limit higher and higher until it now sits at fifty feet up. There are bells hung there, one between each pair of pulleys.

I'm not afraid of heights. I'm not even afraid of embarrassing myself—it's hard to be when you're perpetually the new kid, the daughter of the weird hippies, and then the girl with the dead parents. Still, my anxiety is spiking as I step up to challenge a bunch of overconfident guys in a feat of physical prowess. I acted solely on instinct, and now I have to see it through.

"I'm Andre," the guy beside me says as he tightens the strap of his harness against his hip. He's done this before, and not just earlier in this activity. His fingers move confidently over the loops and buckles.

"Tempest," I offer as I try to copy his movements.

"Well, I hope you're fast, Tempest. Because I'm the one to beat." He sends a wink my way and I grin.

The counselors do their safety checks before clipping themselves in to belay.

"Campers at the ready!" one of the counselors' booming voice cuts through the air.

I raise my brow conspiratorially in Andre's direction before turning to face the rock wall. My heart is still hammering with nerves, but the anticipation of the starting bell is turning it into excitement. I mean, what do I have to lose?

"Get set!"

I take in a long, steady breath.

"Go!"

With a whoosh of expelled air, I surge towards the wall. My left foot finds the first protrusion and I launch myself upwards. I immediately regret starting on my left foot, when the right is my dominant, but it doesn't seem to matter when I grab hold of a wide green hold with my right hand, resting my left on a yellow sphere, and heaving myself up again.

The first several feet are easy enough to navigate, but Andre was right about him being the one to beat. He isn't particularly tall, but he's sure about every movement he makes. He finds every hold without hesitation, and he's scaling the second tier before my foot has even left the ridge. It doesn't really matter though. He isn't the one I'm competing against. At a third of the way up, I glance to my left. The Hartfield guy beside me is struggling to find a good spot for his left hand. I keep moving forward, not daring to break my momentum and risk losing my nerve completely.

A small laugh escapes me as I set off again. I have absolutely no idea what I'm doing or why, but it feels good. There is a strange rush to be letting loose in this way, even if it's just a stupid camp contest. For the first time in such a long time, I feel like I'm not holding back. I'm not monitoring my thoughts, my feelings, my behaviors. I'm just existing, living in the moment.

There's clarity in the surrender.

It's not until I'm struggling to find a good grip as I near the forty-foot mark that I look around again. Unsurprisingly, Kevin and the Harfield kid have already tapped out and are being lowered to the ground. The other Hartfield High volunteer is still on the wall but he's struggling to find where next to put his hands. His muscular form doesn't exactly make him nimble, and his own body is starting to weigh him down, just like Andre predicted. The other Versi kid on the far right is suddenly gaining on me, so even though my arms are sore, I force myself to keep moving.

Andre is rounding on the last several feet when he slips. The rope pulls taut as it catches his body with a jerk. He groans, but even that has humor in it. After a moment of orienting himself, he manages to swing his body back towards the colored rocks before the counselors get it in their heads to try to lower him down. It buys me enough time to catch up to him. By the time he is righted, we're neck and neck.

The other Versi student finally gives up. He shouts something to the audience below that has people laughing. I can't hear what he said from my vantage point, but I manage to spare a glance down just in time to see the ghost of Jet's smile as it is schooled back into a scowl.

God, he's beautiful. I don't think I've met a man who is truly beautiful before, but Jet's effortless grace puts him in a league all of his own. When he smirks, like he had so much the night before, warning bells go off far in the back of my mind, predicting danger. But when he smiles, the result is devastating.

I don't let myself get distracted for long, though I do take this moment to recognize that I can take it easy now. I proved my point, having beaten most of the participants in this contest. Now that I accomplished what I set out to do, there would be no shame in letting myself get lowered to the ground, but I am so close to victory.

Andre is just ahead of me, my final opponent in this race. While I'm tired and more than a bit sore, I feel good. I feel better than I have in a long time, in fact. Good enough to continue on, and maybe enough to win.

I suddenly want to win.

I start again with renewed strength. Exhaustion is impacting my speed, so I make up for it by taking longer strides. I stretch myself as I move from rock to rock, but as we near the top, the difficulty seems to be increasing. The holds are spread much further apart than they had been initially. The ones that remain are odd shapes and sizes. My left foot is precariously supporting my weight on an egg-shaped hold. It's much too small for the ball of my foot, but I don't have another option. I just have to hope that my upper body strength can support me when I shift my center of gravity again.

I'm acutely aware of how high up I am, close to the fifty-foot mark now. Even knowing I'm harnessed doesn't assure my brain that I am entirely safe. I know if I look down again, I'll lose my nerve. I'm panting and my arms ache from exertion, but with just a few more hefts, I'll be at the top.

Andre, moving too quickly for his own good, slips again. This time, he remains on the wall, but he slides down at least a foot, knocking his elbow against one protrusion and his chin against another. He groans as he catches himself and looks over to find me just above him. I spare a single second to ensure that he's alright, but he's more disoriented than anything else. He's clearly surprised that I've got an edge on him now. It sparks that competitiveness in me again.

"Time to kick some jock ass," I say with a smirk. I launch myself up as quickly as I can manage without compromising my footing. I wish I could have stayed to see Andre's reaction, but I have to move. As energized as I am by my proximity to the bell, I know against Andre, I can't compromise my lead by sparing another second.

The bell is squarely between the two of us with equal opportunity for either of us to reach it. I have to remedy that.

Andre is already on my tail. This time, when I step up again with my left foot, I decide not to place it on the most convenient hold. Instead, I take a risk, stretching myself. I hold my breath as I reach for a further rock. Then using power in my biceps I've never needed before, I pull myself upright again using a hold the shape of a wedge of lime. I somehow manage it, though I gasp as I right myself, just barely hanging on.

Now, I'm right on Andre's path. He'll have to go all the way around me to reach the bell, and we're only five feet from the top.

"Sneaky!" he yells up, moving at an impressive speed to go around.

I curse as he catches up with me, but I'm only inches from my left hand being close enough to hit the bell. I just have to reach.

Andre tucks his right foot on the rock just on top of my left and lunges upward. I realize what he's doing just in time to launch for the bell too.

I hear it ring. I hear the crowd below us start to cheer, and then I feel the weight of Andre's hand on top of mine. Immediately followed by the weight of his body crashing into me, slamming me into the wall.

"Oof," I groan as my shoulder hits a hold, but I'm already laughing.

I got to the bell first. I won.

Andre lets go of the rock wall and sits back in the harness. He looks just as comfortable swinging around in midair, fifty-five feet up, as he had on the ground. He's beaming at me and throws his own hands up in the air in celebration.

"Way to work Tempest!" he cheers. "That's what I'm talking about!"

I let my body relax, mirroring Andre's seated position. He

swings over and wraps a friendly arm over my shoulders in a gravity-defying hug. He whoops into the open sky, and I laugh, the sound tearing out of me and seeming to crack something open in my chest.

When the counselors lower us down, I even enjoy the ride. For the first time in a long time, I feel entirely present. The world around me is clear and vivid, and I feel very much a part of it. As I hit the floor, I catch Jet's awestruck expression and smirk.

Talia descends on me with the ferocity of a bear, tackling me into a hug. When she starts jumping up and down, I even join in, which seems to excite her even more. I'm laughing so hard that my eyes start to fill with tears. When she finally sets me free, Andre wraps me in a hug as if we've been friends for years. I welcome the affection.

Eventually, when we all settle, I catch another glimpse of Jet's expression and pull up short. He's easy to read now, though that is simply thanks to his scowl. I catch the small shake of his head before he turns on his heels and stalks away from the rock-climbing area with purposeful strides.

6

JET

My heart doesn't retreat from my throat until ten minutes into the disc golf game, once I've decided there would have to be divine intervention in order for Tempest to go through her Blood Rite during what is essentially the world's most boring game of frisbee. I'm glad for it, since it means that I don't have to jump out of my skin as I patiently wait for Tempest to expose our world.

Brody hasn't returned from his escapade with the camp counselor and I'm trying hard not to imagine what they could be doing that is taking so long. Because of it, Andre is now rotating between the other two Versi groups while I'm monitoring both Tempest and Isaac.

If there was any seed of doubt about whether Tempest truly was Nagual, the rock climbing put it to rest. That's the only way someone could have faced off against Andre and *won*. It's not an impossible feat, but it's certainly preternatural.

Preternatural—that's what we call the people of our world. There are more than just the Nagual, the shapeshifters. There are fae, incubi, and magi, just to name a few. We got the name because what we can do is just beyond what is "normal" as far as humans are concerned, since calling anything "supernatural" inspires images of hulking creatures with fangs and wings. Though that descriptor does fit the incubi with alarming accuracy. Still, what we are is *mostly* human. Or close enough to pass as human, at least.

Isaac doesn't seem particularly eager to reveal his animal form this morning and Tempest looks less than enthused about participating in disc golf, so when Brody finally arrives on the outskirts of the course, I'm not too worried about turning my back on them to join him.

I expect Brody to wriggle his brows or give some other sort of indication that he enjoyed playing the role of protector this morning, but his expression is strangely serious.

"I just got off the phone with your dad," he says. "They're about two hours out still but they're sending a team over from the Brooklyn field office in the meantime."

"Okay," I say hesitantly. I can tell there is more to Brody's uncharacteristically sober attitude but I'm almost afraid to ask. Almost. "What is it?"

Brody shakes his head as if he's trying to shake off an odd thought. For a moment, I think he's going to tell me it's nothing and put on a disingenuously bright smile, but he tilts his head, seems to make a decision, and answers.

"Her middle name is Maverick."

I laugh, but it's a panic response. Nothing about this is particularly funny. Not the name itself nor Brody's implication.

"Tempest Maverick Darnell. That's what it says on her permission slip."

"So?" I ask even as anxiety creeps up my spine again. "It could just be a name."

"An orphaned Nagual who doesn't know what she is and just so happens to use *that* name?"

I don't want to see his point, but the fact of the matter is that I do. Maverick is not a name to be used lightly in our culture. There's only one person who uses it. It's the last name of our queen.

The Maverick monarchy has ruled for more than two hundred years and their line has always been women. They've always kept their family name despite their marital status. Melanie Maverick was next in line for the throne, but she abdicated not long before she murdered a member of the League of Protectors and fled Versi with her boyfriend, a magus called Gregor Candor. It has long been suspected that his name was a fake since the LOP could never find any records of his family or where he came from before Versi University. They have been on the run for close to two decades, a feat only made possible thanks to Melanie's training as an agent in the League of Protectors and Gregor's unparalleled talent as a magi with expertise in alchemy.

My instinct is to keep arguing with Brody, to make sense of this situation with facts and figures, but the truth is this seems like too strange of a coincidence to be one at all. I can see the logic in all of this too. By making "Maverick" Tempet's middle name, she'd still have her familial connection to it while legally being able to go through life as Tempest Darnell, flying under the LOP's radar.

There's really only one aspect of this that I can't wrap my head around.

Nagual, given our unique genetic makeup that gives us the ability to shapeshift, can only reproduce with other Nagual. There is an unending debate about whether our abilities are a function of magic or biology. Culturally, we believe that the

Universe gifted the ability to shapeshift on our people, but despite the mythical nature of who and what we are, there is a lot of science that applies too. In recent years, it's been discovered that Nagual and hybrids have different numbers of chromosomes. Magi are still fully human, despite their abilities, and therefore have forty-six chromosomes—twenty-three pairs. Most of the hybrids, though not all, have forty-eight or fifty chromosomes. Nagual have fifty-one.

Others with odd numbers of chromosomes have difficulty reproducing, like mules with sixty-three. For that reason, our experts believe our ability to reproduce with such limitations is brought upon by a similar phenomenon; chromosomes must be an even number because half of each parent's are copied into their child to make pairs. And while Nagual should not be any different, only in the cases of Nagual mating with another Nagual can reproduction occur.

I'm obviously not at all privy to the dynamics of Tempest's parents' relationship, but something isn't quite adding up here. I'm about to tell Brody as much, but he's frowning at something beyond my head.

"She's gone," he says.

I turn around to see for myself. The girl who has been all but plastered to Tempest's side since I first saw them has now joined another group of students and is happily chatting away. Tempest Maverick is nowhere to be seen.

✼ 7 ✼

TEMPEST

My teeth are clenched so hard that my jaw is starting to ache. It turns out that my aunt's Subaru is better suited for the dirt roads than the bus was because it's only ten minutes before we're turning off the isolated road to Camp Kenwick and onto a highway. After another five minutes, I manage to uncurl my fists. There are a series of indentations in the shape of crescent moons that remain from my nails biting into my skin.

"Is it going to be the silent treatment for the entire drive home?" Laura asks me.

I want the answer to be yes. I'm so angry and embarrassed that I'm not even sure I could put words into an intelligible arrangement.

I know Talia thinks my aunt is strict, but I usually disagree with her. Laura is protective, and has been that way since the day she decided to be my legal guardian. I've always tried to be understanding of that. I may have lost my parents that night, but Laura lost her brother. Since then, she worries about me taking unnecessary risks, but it's not like Laura lives in a state of fear. She's a nurse who works primarily in emergency rooms and intensive care units. She charges into danger night after night, faces it down, and tells it to take a hike.

So, when she asked me to hold off on learning how to drive for a few years until she had the time to teach me herself, I understood. It's not like I would have had a car anyway. Her Subaru goes with her to the hospital every day. When the high school went on a day trip to Rehoboth Beach last year for a "Learn to Surf" camp and Laura asked me to stay on the shore, I was disappointed, but I didn't argue with her. And even though I know that shark attacks aren't exactly common in Delaware, I didn't mind not tempting fate.

Only once did Laura go overboard, and it colored Talia's opinion of her. Three years ago, she talked me into trying out for the lacrosse team. Sports were never really my thing since I usually had to spend my free time catching up on the new school's curriculum. Maintaining a good GPA always took precedence. The spring after my parents died, my friend thought joining the team would be a good way to get my mind off my grief, and I was willing to give just about anything a try.

The problem was that I never told my aunt this, not wanting to worry her when there was a chance I wouldn't even make the team. Forty-five minutes into the practice, when I didn't return home, Aunt Laura showed up at school. She panicked at first, not knowing where I was, but once she realized I was on the field, she got really angry. She made me leave right then and there, and spent the ten-minute drive home painting a gruesome picture of every sports injury she had ever seen in the ER.

After imagining cracked skulls, protruding bones, and weeks of itching stitches for the rest of the night, I hadn't been disappointed to formally quit the team the next day. My heart had never really been set on it anyway. Talia decided to sign up for track instead, and Laura enrolled me in SAT prep courses. I think the coach was most disappointed, since she said I had varsity potential.

It had felt end-of-the-world embarrassing at the time, and that was nothing compared to what she subjected me to today.

I feel my phone buzz with another incoming text. I turn it off without even looking at it. I don't need a play-by-play on everything the student body is saying about me right now.

"Tempest, I know you're not happy with me at the moment, but I had to switch shifts and now I'm working a double tomorrow, so I'm not exactly happy with you either."

"You didn't have to come," I grumble, locking my gaze on the businesses that flank the road. "You shouldn't have come," I amend after a minute.

"The counselor called me—"

"I was getting fresh air. I couldn't sleep and I was afraid I'd wake up the whole cabin, so I walked outside for a few minutes."

"That isn't the point, Tempest."

I roll my eyes. I'm never usually like this, so disrespectful. I guess my parents never really gave me a reason to be, but still, I never seemed to develop the attitude that most of my peers did around the age of fourteen. I've definitely never been this way with Laura. She's only twenty-eight and she gave up the last four years of her life, what people say are the best four years, to take care of me. That's why I let her fuss over me. That's why I don't argue even when some of her rules seem unnecessarily strict. But this is just too far.

"After I hung up with the counselor, I looked up this 'camp' and I couldn't believe all the dangerous activities. You signed up without telling me what the trip actually entailed."

"I'm nearly eighteen. It's not like I needed you to sign my permission slip."

"But you're not eighteen yet. I have been expressly clear about what is and is not appropriate, and some of those activities were most certainly not: rock-climbing, ziplining, mountain biking, boating."

"I didn't do half those things," I argue. I don't specify that I didn't do half of them because Laura picked me up before I could.

"I'm more upset that you kept it from me, Tempest!"

"I didn't want you to worry. All we did was go on walks and make s'mores, but I knew if you saw the brochure, you would freak out and not let me go."

"Maybe you shouldn't have gone. Your principal knows you got in trouble. He's going to want to talk to you on Monday."

I roll my eyes again. Of course, my previously squeaky-clean record and 4.0 GPA mean nothing when it's Remy's word against mine.

"We were leaving in a couple of hours anyway. You didn't have to come all this way to lecture me."

"And how could I trust you not to put yourself at risk in that time?"

A frustrated groan finally escapes me, sounding almost like a roar.

"God, Laura! Can't I at least pretend to be normal?" I shout. "I already feel like a freak. Can't I just spend one night with my friends on a totally lame field trip without it disrupting the balance of the Universe, or whatever it is that you're so afraid of?"

My aunt looks stricken. I shake my head and let it rest against the cool glass of the window. I'm suddenly exhausted. I don't know if it's the couple of hours of sleep I managed last night or the emotional outburst, but I'm fighting a losing battle trying to keep my eyes open.

I give up the fight and let the rumble of the road lull me towards sleep. But as I'm about to tumble over the precipice, I hear my aunt murmur, "You've never been normal, Tempest."

I don't wake until Laura is pulling into the driveway of our rancher. The house is not much to look at from the outside, but the frame of the door is painted a conspicuous purple, the last mark of my mother that can be seen on the house. My jaw cracks with a yawn as I push open the passenger door. I retrieve my backpack from the backseat and sling it over my shoulder.

My aunt hasn't tried to talk to me anymore, but once we're both standing in the kitchen, she asks, "What do you want to do for dinner tonight? We can get Chinese and do a *Bachelor in Paradise* watch party. We missed the last two episodes."

I shake my head. I don't even like *The Bachelor*, but my aunt does, so weekly viewings are one of the few rituals we stick to with her crazy work schedule. I'm not ready to forgive her yet, and sitting on the couch with takeout feels like I would be pretending to be okay with what happened today.

"I'm going to shower," I tell her. I plug my phone into the charger by the breadbox and head to my room at the back of the house.

I take a long time washing away the stress of the day and it's nearly three o'clock by the time I resurface. My stomach is reminding me that I haven't eaten since the suspiciously yellow eggs they served at the dining hall this morning.

Laura isn't in the kitchen, so I rummage through the fridge and start to heat up leftover penne alla vodka that she made on

Wednesday. There isn't much parmesan left. In fact, it's such a small amount that it looks like Laura specifically left just enough for me to be able to use for this purpose. My heart softens a bit.

Yes, she crossed a line today. I am only two months from turning eighteen and being fully able to make my own decisions, but I know she's only so worried because she loves me. How can I hold that against her?

While the pasta container oscillates on the microwave plate, I decide to make myself a cup of coffee. It's early enough not to mess with my sleep and I'm still feeling groggy from my late night, long nap, and supremely weird day. Once the coffee starts to drip from the machine into my favorite blue mug, I lean back against the counter and regard the small kitchen.

Like the rest of the house, it's nice, tidy, and quaint. It's exactly the kind of house you'd expect of a hard-working, middle-class family in suburbia with a single, modest income. For that reason alone, it felt too cluttered and cramped when it was me and my parents living here. Especially with all my father's oddments that always seemed to migrate out of his office.

I remember one morning when I was in middle school, I made the mistake of sitting to eat my breakfast at the kitchen island where a farm of Venus fly traps resided. I will go to my grave swearing that one of the toothy plants tried to snap its jaws around the rainbow marshmallow from my bowl of Lucky Charms. When I complained to my dad, he reminded me that Venus fly traps are non-sentient, and their strictly carnivorous diet is simply a by-product of their evolution—but I know what I saw.

Now the house is much more fitting for a family of two who are rarely home, with most of my parents' stuff in storage in the detached garage. This mug, a deep, electric blue, is one from Laura's old apartment, I think. Or maybe she picked it up on sale from Target. There is a small chip on the ceramic brim that darkens as a drip of coffee splashes onto it, catching my attention. The blue is nearly the same startling shade as Jet's eyes—way too peculiar to be real.

For some reason, thinking of him makes me reach for my phone. I'm certain Talia has gotten over Laura's unceremonious arrival by now and has moved on to giving me updates on Jet, which is both ridiculous and appreciated. If my friend is going to creep on him on my behalf, I may as well read the texts, right? But when I reach around the breadbasket for my phone it isn't there. I frown. I was certain I plugged it in, but maybe I only thought about it and left it in my room?

I turn to head to my bedroom, but I catch a glimpse of Laura in the living room through the kitchen's archway. She's standing by the couch with her head bowed over a phone. My phone.

I'm so stunned that I don't say anything for a moment. Laura has never done this before. The invasion of privacy feels like a betrayal, and the shock of it burns hot and bright in the space between my ribs. Before I can say anything though, her gaze jerks up to mine, blazing with anger that I don't think she has any right to feel.

"Who is this?" she demands, waving my phone at me like I should know what's displayed on the screen.

"What?" I move forward and take it from her. "What are you doing with my phone?" I demand in return. I try to make sense of what I'm seeing and why she is so upset about it, but there are a lot of notifications.

"Your phone kept buzzing. I thought your friends were

calling and were worried that they couldn't get a hold of you," my aunt explains.

My text chain with Talia has almost twenty new messages, but that's not what my aunt saw. There is another thread from a number I don't have saved.

It's Jet. We need to talk.

You can't go back to Crescentwood yet.

Answer your phone.

It's important.

I know you have no reason to trust me but I'm going to need you to.

Please.

My heart is racing like a stampede and my breath becomes shallower and more labored with every message I read.

"Who is Jet?" my aunt demands.

I don't know what this is, but it doesn't make sense.

"Some boy from camp," I murmur.

"Why is he texting you those things, Tempest? Who is he?"

I shake my head. "I didn't give him my number. Maybe Talia did. I don't know what he's talking about, though. It sounds important—some kind of emergency. I should give him a call."

I don't even manage to close out of the messages app before my aunt is snatching the phone away.

"*Who* is he?" she asks again and this time I get the sense she's asking me a different question entirely. I don't know that I can give her a satisfactory answer, but I'm starting to get scared and I want to try.

"I don't know," I say calmly. I don't know how I manage it without betraying how sick with nerves I suddenly feel. "He was a chaperone for one of the other schools, but he was my age. Eighteen, I think. We talked last night for a few minutes

A TRACE OF SOMETHING STRANGER

when I went out to get some air. He was nice, but then I saw counselors walking around so I went back to my cabin. That's where Remy found me."

"What school was he from?" she asks, her face a mask of calm that I know must be an eerily similar mirror of my own.

"Some private school in New England," I say, forgetting for a moment the name of the school itself. "In Vermont."

All the color leeches from my aunt's face. "Versi," she says.

My gaze snaps to her. "Yeah. How did you know that?"

She swallows hard. "Pack your things, Tempest. We're leaving."

I shove a handful of long-sleeve shirts into a duffle bag. We've been at this for almost an hour, my lunch and coffee long forgotten on the kitchen counter.

I wasted about twenty minutes following Laura around the house shouting at her, but she finally looked at me with a fierceness I have never seen on her face before and said, "You will be getting in that car tonight, Tempest, whether you are packed or not. You are not eighteen. You do not get a choice in this. You will do as I say."

I was scared before, but after that, I was absolutely terrified. Not of my aunt—of course not. But whatever it is that can scare fearless Laura into having us run from our home in the middle of the night has me absolutely bricking it.

Laura is in her own room, packing her things, but I've heard her making a bunch of calls, her voice a deceptive calm. First, she left a message for Janice in my school's main office telling her that I've had a family emergency, and that I will be taking some time off. Then she talks to her manager at work and her friend Stacy whom she usually trades shifts with. I notice she doesn't call her boyfriend, Brian, probably because she wouldn't get away with the family emergency lie. If it is a lie. I don't have much family left, but there are grandparents I never met in upstate New York. I've gotten a card from them every year since we moved to Crescentwood. It's a birthday-Christmas combo with a twenty-dollar bill stuck inside.

My phone is still in her possession too. I don't know if she doesn't trust me not to contact Jet or if she's fielding more messages and calls from him, but my palms itch to get my hands on it again. I just need to feel like I have some semblance of control in this insanity.

Laura is in my dad's old office now. I hear her banging drawers closed and shuffling through papers. Curiosity has me following the sound.

It doesn't look much like my father's office anymore since we cleared out the jars of dragonfly wings in formaldehyde, mountains of dusty books on Ancient Mesopotamian mythologies, ground quartz that I thought was a jar of Himalayan Sea salt and tried to bake into banana bread when I was thirteen, and other odds and ends that earned my father his eccentric reputation.

I stand in the doorway and watch as Laura hoists herself on top of the cluttered desk. There are papers scattered around the tabletop that look like certificates or some other official documentation. I don't get to take a closer look because Laura is pulling a lumpy black duffle bag from the air vent in the ceiling. She climbs off the desk, but if she notices me standing there, she doesn't let on.

A memory resurfaces of me standing in this very spot watching my dad rummage through his office years ago. He wasn't pulling things out, but hiding them away. I went to ask him for help with my pre-algebra homework and found him messing with the frame of his college degree. I can't for the life of me remember the name of the school printed on the certificate.

I was shorter then and couldn't really see what he was doing, but I got the impression he was hiding something behind it. When he finally looked back at me, he smiled, as if he was pleased that I was sneaking around.

"Just because someone isn't looking for something doesn't mean you should leave it to be found. Knowledge is power, Tempest. It's our job to protect the balance of power."

I don't understand those words any better now than I had back then, though I shudder to remember them.

Aunt Laura unzips the bag and reveals stacks and stacks of hundred-dollar bills. They're bound together by rubber bands like something out of a heist movie. My parents always used to have a lot of cash on hand, but Laura has both a checking and a savings account. I'm not sure where we could possibly be going tonight that can't accept her Visa card. She digs around the bag some more and pulls out a small handgun. I take a sharp breath in, and her eyes find mine.

"What are you doing with that?"

She inspects the firearm, release, and peers into the chamber, and sets it on the table. "Nothing, I hope."

My heart is right back to palpitating again.

Something is wrong here. I knew it from the moment Laura started waving my phone around, but something is very, *very* wrong. And the worst part is, something about this feels familiar too. More long-buried memories are surfacing of my parents packing quickly and throwing our bags haphazardly in the back of a car we didn't own. Stacks of cash being tucked away and phone calls made in harried tones with hurried excuses. I was too young to know what it meant, or at least too young to understand the significance. But I'm starting to understand now.

I take a step forward to read the paper on the desk. It's a birth certificate for the day, month, and year I was born, but I don't know the name written on it. I move the paper away with my pinky, as if it's a sleeping dragon that I'm scared to disturb. Under it is an identical document, still boasting December 3rd, but with yet another name. Oddly enough, on both documents, my middle name is still listed as Maverick. I shiver as if that vent is now blasting me with cool air.

Beneath that is a passport. I recognize the navy cover even though I've never had one for myself. I never needed one since I haven't left the country and have no plans to. Two pages in, I see my smiling image beside another name I don't know. It's a Crescentwood school picture from either the seventh or eighth grade. The expiration date printed on the glossy paper is still four years out.

"What is all this?" I ask my aunt, though I'm starting to get an idea.

"Nothing you need to worry about yet," she says.

I shake my head and stumble back.

"We're not just leaving Crescentwood, are we? And not only for a few days."

"No, honey," she says, kindly. For the first time that night, she stops to look at me. Really look at me. "Your parents were already getting things together for you to go to Toronto when they were killed. They were in Crescentwood too long. They were starting to worry they'd be caught."

"By who?" I ask, though it doesn't feel like the most necessary question.

"By the people you met yesterday. People from Versi. They're killers. They tried to kill your parents when they left.

Your mother did what she must to protect her and your father, but there were deaths. They were running from them for your entire life, Tempest. But when things got quiet, I was old enough to buy a house in my name, so you settled in Crescentwood for a time. Until they came for your parents again."

Laura sends me a sad smile. There are tears in her eyes.

"It wasn't a car crash that killed them, Tempest. It was the shapeshifters."

"Shapeshifters?" I ask, my voice bubbling in a hysterical kind of laugh. "You're not serious."

Laura nods solemnly. "Your mother was one of them. She could turn into a raptor. Your father was different. He had this ability—it's not called magic, though I'm not sure what else to call it since that's exactly what it seemed like. Magic."

I shake my head again and take another step away.

"This— That's not true." It can't be. If magic and monsters are real then what does it make me?

My aunt seems to see the question in my eyes.

"You'd be like her," she says. "But only if you have the Blood Rite before you turn eighteen. You're so close, Tempest. So close to being free from this. All of this."

"I don't understand," I murmur, though that's the understatement of the century. "You're saying that I'm a shapeshifter." Laura nods. Panic grips my throat like a vice. "Wouldn't I know that? Wouldn't I be able to, you know, shapeshift?" I laugh again but the sound is too high-pitched, too breathy.

"Not until you've had the Blood Rite," she clarifies, like that explains it all. "It's why I have kept you away from danger these last few years, Tempest. It could happen so easily. If you were in a car accident, or if you played a sport and got hurt on the field. If you and Talia went through with your hair-brained idea to learn how to skateboard. One slip, one scrape, and you'd be pulled into a world that stole your parents away from us. Away from you."

I'm not sure I believe any of this, and I certainly don't understand it, but one thing is quickly becoming clear.

"I'm supposed to be a shapeshifter," I repeat. "I was supposed to do this blood ritual, but you stopped me?"

Laura blinks as if she can't grasp my meaning. I know the feeling.

"Tempest, if you shift, you become one of them. We're not talking about just a school for shapeshifters. There are villains, there are monsters, there are politics you can't possibly understand. You don't want to be a part of it."

"I don't understand because you've been keeping it from me," I say. "It isn't your decision to make."

Laura's expression shuts down, and becomes hard again.

"This world *killed* your parents, Tempest. These animals tore them apart. They would have done the same to you, but your parents hid you from them. As long as you have the potential to shift, they will come for you. They will try to kill you too. So, I don't care if you feel it's not my decision. A call had to be made and I made it. I lost my brother. He lost the love of his life. I will not lose you too."

I retreat from the room, leaving my bags and everything I just learned behind. Laura is quick on my heels, but she's not quick enough. "Where are you going?"

"I need a minute," I say. I move through the house at a speed I'm sure I never needed to move before. This is all too much. I need some fresh air if I am meant to wrap my head around any of it.

My aunt lied to me. She kept things from me, and still is, from what I can tell. Now she wants me to trust her, and this deranged plan my parents apparently set in motion four years ago. My parents, who aren't the people I thought they were. Who, from the sound of it, weren't really *people* at all.

They may have thought they were keeping these secrets to protect me, but look how it turned out. With me all but walking into the arms of the very people they were trying to hide me from.

"You can't go. We need to leave as soon as we can."

"I'll just be a minute," I shout as I slip through the door and into the cool night air.

I'll have to go back. I know I'll face this, I'll make sense of it, but right now I need a few minutes to step away from it all.

I need my parents.

❧ 8 ❧

TEMPEST

I hate coming here, and yet on my worst days, this is always where I find myself; the place my parents spent their last moments. I'm not a stranger to the onslaught of emotions that hits me when I arrive at the intersection of Park Ave and Crescent Drive. I come here to cry, to plead, to ask the empty air why my parents would be taken from me and what I am meant to do without them.

I'm not usually angry, but tonight I'm filled with the blistering heat of it.

The park that the street is named for has a walking trail that leads to a playground and pavilion about a half mile up. This side of the street is lined by woods—or as much woods as we get in residential Maryland. It's a pocket of trees that spans from this corner to the backside of the high school.

I have to navigate a small incline to get to the tree line, but then I take a seat overlooking the road. Even this early in the night, it's quiet. There isn't a single car on the road.

On Halloween, almost four years ago, my parents were on their way to a costume party on Crescent Drive. They walked, since it's such a short distance from our house. It was later in the night, too late for kids to be trick or treating, and my parents insisted on seeing me off to Hannah Fairfield's backyard party on the other side of town before they headed to the Anderson's. Talia's dad brought me back home around midnight, but my parents hadn't made it back yet. Less than twenty minutes later, the police were at my door. I remember because I hadn't changed yet. I was told that my parents had been struck by what they believed to be a drunk driver, and I was still dressed like a freaking M&M.

Even now, understanding that what I was told was a lie, it doesn't feel any more real. It only brings more questions. Who would have wanted to kill them, and why? How didn't anyone see them get attacked by the road? Could people really have been so distracted by candy and costumes that they didn't notice anything? Though if the night was half as desolate as this one, I'm not entirely surprised. I haven't seen a single living soul since I passed my next-door neighbor parking in his driveway.

I don't have any tears in me today. I'm too confused, too frustrated, and too unsure if I even believe what my aunt said. It's ridiculous, and yet some part of me always felt like I was playing pretend when it came to the mundane. It's bizarre, and yet so much of my childhood was inexplicably strange even without the mention of shapeshifters. It's insane, and yet my aunt has always been hyper-logical, rationalizing everything until there is no room for argument. Surely, if she believes in what she says, there has to be truth to it.

Which brings my spiraling thoughts right back to anger again. It's not an emotion I've had much experience with honestly—my instinct has always been to disconnect and disengage. But now my capacity for anger feels as vast and layered as a canyon.

All my life I felt so different from the people around me. I found every excuse for it. I blamed how often we moved. I blamed my parents' eccentricities. I blamed myself, and eventually, my mental illness. And all that time my family knew the reason why. They knew the truth and yet they still kept it from me.

It's easy to be mad at my aunt when she is the one still here. It's so much harder to be mad at my parents when all I have left of them is memories, ones that I am starting to feel that I cannot trust.

At least I can convince myself that my parents meant to tell me what I am eventually. Even Laura said as much. She's the one who kept the secret selfishly, and she's now the reason I have such little time to make a life-altering decision when I really don't have enough information to do so.

Not that it seems like I have much of a choice. I have to run. I have to go with my aunt. I have to leave my life behind until it's safe to return again. But I won't just let my birthday pass without understanding what I am truly giving up. Even if it seems insane to consider joining a world of monsters that I don't really understand, and that did ultimately take my parents from me, I can't just turn my back on something that could explain why I sometimes feel like I don't belong to myself. I'm halfway to insanity already.

It was just after five when I left, but already the sun was setting. I watch the night darken, minute by minute until the deep blue sky has blanketed enough of the landscape to inhibit the perception of any other color. All the while, I sit and think, letting my hands run over the soft yellowed grass beneath me, but my mind never slips away from me.

Finally, I'm too cold to justify sitting still. I have to walk back, but I'm sure once I'm moving again, I'll feel better. I'm not ready to face all of this, but I'm not sure that I will truly ever be. And my aunt was clear, my time has run out. Heaving a shaky sigh, I rise to my feet.

There is a loud snap from the woods behind me, like a branch breaking under a heavy foot. I whirl towards the sound, but there is nothing I can see. Not that I can see much of anything. With the streetlights as backlight, the woods seem impossibly dark. I pause for only a moment, listening to the chirping of crickets, before deciding I better just get a move on.

Another branch cracks, this time to my right. Instinctively, I spin towards the sound. There is nothing there, not that I really expected there to be. I'm just jumpy after the emotions of the day.

I take another step back towards the road, but as I turn around to go, there is a woman standing ten paces away, between me and the street. A woman that certainly hadn't been there a moment before.

If that isn't scary enough, there is something wrong about the way she looks, like she's more animal than human. She is far too bony, like someone who hasn't seen a proper meal in months. Still, no part of her seems weak for her lack of bulk. She's not tall, but her slender structure gives the illusion of height. Her mousy hair is thrown up in a knot, giving a whole new meaning to the messy bun, and uneven fringes fall into her translucent gray eyes. She roughly pushes them away with long, jagged fingernails. Even from here, I can see where dirt is caked to her skin, and from the scent of her, it's not from a recent romp in the woods.

"Well," she says, flicking her thin, pink tongue over red-stained lips, "isn't this poetic."

❧ 9 ❧
JET

I t's an hour and a half drive between the Philadelphia field office we spent the afternoon holed up in and the Darnell house in Crescentwood, Maryland. It's dark by the time my dad parks out front of a small house on a quiet street. Most of the day has been a blur of frenzied activity. It's hard for me to comprehend that it hasn't even been twenty-four hours since my conversation with Tempest.

I expected us to go after her right away given the urgency of the situation, but suspecting that Tempest may be Melanie Maverick's daughter changed things. Brody called my dad again and we were told to hang tight until he and Lieutenant Caro got to Camp Kenwick. They looped in the director, and after a lengthy discussion, it was decided that Lieutenant Caro would supervise the students returning to Versi with Andre, who is still mostly out of the loop, while my dad went to meet Tempest. Brody and I were allowed to tag along given our investment in the situation. It may be a once-in-a-lifetime shadowing experience.

Despite the stress of the situation, I'm excited to be a part of it. The Protector Program available to high school students sometimes allowed us to shadow real assignments. The last time, everything went wrong, and I haven't been asked to actively participate since, but I've been itching for it. I feel just as strongly now as I did last night that this situation with Tempest, as unclear as it still may be, is meant for me. Her mere existence is breaking all the rules that I've revered, and I have to believe that is the reason why I feel as connected to her as I do.

I always wanted to follow in my father's footsteps, but the primary motivation for me to become a protector is for the sense of control that the creed provides. The League of Protectors serves many purposes, but more than anything, it provides order in a world of chaos.

I've never operated well in shades of gray, and this world, despite some of its stranger elements, has rules. As a protector, I can be the steward of them. It will be my job to safeguard the secret of the preternatural world. I'll protect rogue shapeshifters from their more primal natures. I'll protect humans from those same natures—not that they'll know it. And most importantly, I'll protect humans from the scariest thing of all: the truth.

The agents from the Baltimore office who are meant to be meeting us here haven't made it yet, so my dad goes to knock on the front door alone. He stands on the porch for a long time, but eventually, the door opens and a woman with dyed-blonde hair and a scowl appears. They argue for several minutes—well, she argues, and my dad remains polite and calm. Finally, she allows him inside.

As we wait, I allow myself to try and tune into Tempest's trace. I expect it to be impossible given how difficult it was last time when she had been standing in front of me. This time, it's not difficult at all. It's as easy as it would be to trace Brody in the backseat of the car. Except she isn't nearly so close by. Close enough to register, but not close enough to be in her house. Which is strange.

Without thinking, I step out of the car, letting the door slam. In the nighttime air, I can sense more of her, though something about it feels wrong. Her honeysuckle scent hits me in a rush, making me feel heady and disoriented. Or maybe that's just the overwhelming presence of her. Still, the shimmer of her trail leads out the front door, not into it, and down the street.

Brody is climbing out of the car to stand beside me.

"What is it?"

I shake my head, still not able to make sense of it. "Her trace," I say, "it's too strong."

Brody frowns, clearly not understanding either. I shouldn't sense her so acutely if she isn't nearby, but somehow I can, which is troubling. I'm not sure what it means. I start to follow the trail down the street, leaving Brody hanging back by the car. I walk quickly, too quickly, but something about this is making me nervous. I know now to expect the unexpected where Tempest is concerned, but a trace so potent feels dangerous.

I turn the corner and am hit by the dull hums of three unfamiliar Nagual signatures. They are a little too far off still for me to know anything more than that, so I assume for a moment that they are the protectors from the field office coming to meet us. That is until I realize that the other Nagual aren't coming from the route we came from, off the highway to the north, they came out of nowhere and are now almost exactly where I am sensing Tempest to be.

If Tempest's trace now stands out like a beacon to me, it stands to reason that it would to another Nagual with the ability too.

Cursing the fact I can't shift so early in the night in a residential neighborhood, I take off at a run, faster than any human could. I just hope I'm not too late.

✣ 10 ✣
TEMPEST

My heart has leapt into my throat, but I still manage to ask the stranger, "Can I help you?" All the while, I shift my weight towards the park's trail on my left, a subtle move towards my escape.

"Oh, you can do more than that, girlie," she titters with her strangely childlike pitch.

"It's too bad you didn't take care of her last time," says a new voice, materializing out of the woods to my left.

The last time?

My head jerks towards the smooth baritone. This guy isn't much older than me, and not nearly as emaciated in appearance as his companion. He's well past six feet tall with broad, hunched shoulders and a curly heap of brown hair. His massive frame is blocking the route to civilization I was half a moment from taking.

"Ha!" the woman barks. "Under our noses the whole time, girlie. You made us look like fools. You will pay for that."

"Look, I don't know what this is about," I say, inching away from them both.

My eyes scan the landscape I am much better acquainted with than either of them are. There are houses on the other side of the woods, transverse from where I am now. I know some of the families who live there. Not well, but well enough that they will let me inside if I say I'm being chased by pale-eyed strangers who smell like sour milk.

I know I can be fast when I decide to be. It's probably why the coach wanted me for the field hockey team. I know the woods better than they do. I can cut through to Lees Lane and head to where the Millers live.

"You have no idea how glad we are to see you here," the woman coos at me. "It's a shame you missed it, Savon. You would have liked the way that pesky magi screamed. Then we plucked each of Maverick's feathers clean off."

The man, Savon, shakes his head with a delighted grin. "I was just a pup back then."

My heart stops, then picks up at double time. I suddenly understand what is happening. Or pieces of it, at least. These aren't people, in the same way my parents weren't. That's how they appeared so quickly and silently. These aren't any brutes. They are the same monsters who killed my parents here almost exactly four years ago.

For a moment I feel like I have been turned to stone. My heart stops beating, my blood halts in my veins. There is nothing but oppressive cold and a growing roar in the back of my head as I finally understand who I am looking at.

I don't stand a chance.

Despite this, I make a break for it, knowing this is my only opportunity. I pivot on the ball of my sneakers, sprinting two full strides before a large figure leaps out of the woods. It falls squarely in my path making me stumble back.

A small gray wolf lands on the grass in front of me, blocking the tree line.

A *small* wolf being the size of an overfed Labrador—and not nearly as friendly.

I trip backwards on the sloped ground. A yelp escapes me as I land on my tailbone, but I'm too distracted by the beast in front of me to register the pain. Drool drips from the wolf's maw as it snarls at me. And as if this wasn't enough of a shock, in the blink of an eye the wolf is replaced by a man. A very naked man.

I scramble back, then blink rapidly and rub at my traitorous eyes. I look back at the other two to share in the shock, but if they see anything out of the ordinary, their faces don't show it.

Werewolves then.

I don't know what I expected when my aunt talked about shapeshifters. I think I pictured a hodgepodge of every monster movie I've ever seen. Some human qualities, some animalistic, which was probably why it seemed so impossible to believe. I hadn't expected a full, very real wolf to just become human in a snap. To my relief, the younger man throws a bundle of fabric at the older one. In one fluid motion, he ties a burlap-like sheet around his waist. The relief is short-lived, though.

"She's cute for an abomination," Savon tells the woman. "The Don may want to keep her."

I recoil, though I'm not sure what half of what he said even means. I don't need to, though. From the disgusted curl of his lips, I am absolutely certain that these strangers hate me.

"If the Don wanted her alive, he would have come for her himself," snarls the wolf-man before me. Savon growls in acquiescence, but the woman tsks at the men.

"The Don always appreciates an offering. He may want to keep this one for a pet, pitiful as she is."

"She is a Maverick," Savon agrees. "Could be a use for her."

I use this discourse to climb to my feet again. I know now that running is futile, but I'll be damned if they think they'll take me anywhere alive, especially not to anyone who calls himself a Don and keeps people for pets.

"I won't go with you," I tell them, somehow sounding much calmer than I feel. My heart isn't even beating anymore. It's just fluttering like a wasp's wings.

"Then you'll die here," the older man says, sounding pleased to be getting his way. Maybe he's hungry.

The beastly trio seems to be inching in with every passing moment. They're edging me closer to the tree line, I realize.

"We can do this the easy way or the hard way," the woman sings, like she is excited by the outcome of either scenario.

"The hard way involves Savon tearing your throat out," the older man says.

My eyes flick between them and back to Savon who licks his lips in confirmation.

"Or," the woman offers, "you turn around and walk quietly into the woods with us like a good little girl."

My gaze shifts between all three strangers again. I quickly weigh my options. There aren't very many. Either I go into the woods with them, and they kill me there, or they truly intend to bring me to their leader, which sounds like a fate worse than death. Either way, my life is over.

Or I can let these monsters tear me apart in the same way they did to my parents, in the same place. I wouldn't call this end poetic, like the woman did, but the irony is certainly not lost on me.

With a grounding breath, I make my choice.

I turn to Savon and kick him squarely in the chest with the heel of my sneakers. He howls in surprise, arching his back and instantaneously transforming into a big, black wolf. I gasp, but I don't let myself freeze again. The woman is lunging for me, hands curled like claws. The gray wolf has replaced the older man again, the makeshift skirt tearing at the corner and falling to the ground in a heap.

I dart away as quickly as I can, skirting through the gap between the wolves, hoping that it will surprise them since it is the route that seems least likely for me to take. I make it past and am only a foot from where the woods give way to the park's trail when teeth sink into my left ankle, pulling me to the ground.

I wail from the sudden, agonizing pain as the gray wolf's jaws unlock from my flesh, but I'm coherent enough to roll to my side as Savon's prolonged black maw snaps at my head. I throw up my arms to block my face and kick up with my uninjured leg, like I'm riding a bike with a single pedal. I feel my foot make impact with a furry body, but I keep kicking, unwilling to give up the fight.

I must have landed a better hit than I thought because there is a cry from one of the wolves. Savon has shifted back to human and I can see blood seep out from the corner of his lip. My foot must have caught him right in the mouth. He bares his teeth at me, and I shrink back away from him. But suddenly he's even further away from me.

I went to Disney World when I was a kid—the one aspect of the muggy hellhole that is Orlando, Florida that I actually enjoyed. Hollywood Studios was my favorite park, and the best attraction was the set of *Honey I Shrunk the Kids*. I was obsessed with the giant blades of grass, statues of ants that stood as tall as horses, and overblown tinker toys. This is how the world feels around me now. Everything is much larger than it had been. The yellow grass that I had been letting slide between my fingers earlier in the night is now the entire length of my hand.

No, not hand. *Paw.* A small, brown limb. I cry out in surprise, but the voice that comes out is not my own, though it isn't wholly dissimilar either.

Savon sits back on his heels grinning down at me ferociously. Then the woman shifts back to human again too, but her smile is twice as cruel.

"There she is," her voice says. It's harder for me to understand her words than it should be, though I don't know if that's because of the panic, the pain, or the fact I don't think I'm human at the moment. "Oh, the Don will just *love* this. The last of the Maverick line, reduced to such a pathetic little pest. I could crush her underfoot."

"I'd rather crush her between my teeth," the second man says with a sadistic smile.

Fear has me grasping to feel human again. I was never going to survive this, but at least when I was human, I wasn't a joke to them. Though I'm not sure what exactly I do or how, suddenly I feel myself again—which is a mistake. There is pain, so much pain, as I return to my bleeding body.

The shift leaves me without my clothes too, so that the cold wind brushes against my damaged skin. While the werewolves seem to have no issue with nudity, I take advantage of their distracted laughter to scramble away from them, grabbing for my oversized sweatshirt as I do. It's not quite the length of a dress, but it covers enough of me that I can at least die with some modesty.

I keep scrambling back, closer to the park's trail. I nearly make it to my feet to run, but razor-edged teeth snap at me. I don't even feel where the jaw makes its mark this time. All of me has started to go numb. I don't truly feel the impact of my fall either, I just know I am suddenly on the ground again. My prone arms are the only defense against the prodding snouts that lunge for my throat.

Eventually, my right bicep is caught by the teeth of the gray wolf, and I hear, more than feel, my muscle being ripped away, leaving my sweatshirt shredded. *So much for modesty,* I think, since there is no pain anymore to distract my inner monologue.

My aunt has told me all about adrenaline and the impossible things it can do to a body, so that must be the reason that while I know everything hurts, I don't really feel it anymore. I'm not even sure if I cry out or whimper with each new attack. The only thing I feel is a true cold from the blood that is now seeping into my torn sweatshirt.

My eyes are fastened shut so I can't see the creature that comes to my rescue. I only hear the impact of a fourth body hurdling on top of my own. At the same time, another one of the wolfs' maw chomps down on my thigh, though all I feel is an uncomfortable prickle against my skin.

There is a noise somewhere between a hiss and a snarl that has my eyes going wide to make sense of the sound, but my vision is rapidly tunneling. Shimmering beams of silver begin to dance against the dark, star-lit sky. The cacophony of growls and grunts is deafened by the blood pumping in my ears. Then all my senses seem to fail me at once.

I hear the attack before I see it. There is a chorus of snarls and snapping jaws. I don't wait to understand, and I don't care to ensure my surroundings are secure. It's dark enough and remote enough now that my notice could be blamed on a mountain lion, even if my frame is much too large. I shift, and suddenly the world warps to accommodate my new center of gravity.

My vision is much sharper in the night, as are the rest of my senses. I can hear every crackle of leaves under my paws, taste the metallic threat of snow above us with the rapidly cooling night and the storm clouds overhead. And when the blood-curdling shriek sounds out across the pond, I hear Tempest as if she's standing beside me, screaming into my ear.

I didn't think it was possible for me to move faster, but I do. I'm finally in view of the wolves' scarred and scabbed bodies piling on top of Tempest's limp frame. I don't have to recognize any of them to know exactly who they are. Or what they are, since unlike the rest of the Nagual, these beasts aren't human in any capacity. They are the Full Moon Knights.

I'm close now, a few yards away from being able to launch myself at her attackers, to end this fight right here, right now. But I'm not close enough to do anything when a small mousey-colored wolf chomps down on Tempest's shoulder. She lets out another cry, and the sound breaks something in me.

I'm merciless in a way I don't often get to be. It's hard being a predator like I am when most of the people around me at Versi are so much smaller and more docile. Any sparring, which I do a considerable amount of in preparation for my protector training, requires me to pull back on my instincts tenfold. Wolves are better suited in a match against me, though there is no doubt in my mind that I will win.

Show me a lion shifter and then I'll worry about needing technique to win in a fight.

I pounce on the brown wolf first, simply as retribution for the pain it inflicted on Tempest. My fangs find their mark in its soft flesh, and I snap my jaw hard. The wolf bellows a howl, but I shove it away from me, needing to get to Tempest before they injure her any further.

I'm still too late. The other wolf, a slim gray one with vicious pink scarring, slashes at Tempest's exposed thigh causing fresh blood to seep to the surface. She is too weak to scream out, only a pained noise escaping her parted lips.

My body slams into the gray wolf and we roll down the hill, each snapping and scratching at each other. My claws rake against the flesh of his right cheek. The wolf howls at the full, bright moon and I bare my teeth just before pinning one of his paws under my weight and rolling forward. His bones give a satisfying pop, followed by a crack.

The brown wolf is waiting for me, hungry for a fight, but it's the black wolf that I'm worried about. He's much larger than the rest, but he's no longer attacking. He's just watching me, though I'm not enough of a fool to suspect he's done with her on my account. Unless…

No, I can't go there. Can't think about it. I hiss at the wolves, signaling my eagerness to take them on, but two things happen at once. To my right, the gray wolf limps to his feet, the broken paw tucked into his chest. In front of me, my dad's sleek black car is speeding down the street at four times the limit.

The gray wolf shakes his head and barks at the others. They growl in response, and the black wolf retreats, lumbering into the woods. The brown wolf keeps her eyes trained on me in what I can only describe as a promise of violence. I snarl back, letting her know that I too am waiting for that day.

Finally, she gives the signal to the other wolf and all three of them disappear into the tree line. I want to follow them, but Brody is there at Tempest's side and his tone makes me halt.

"Jet, you need to see this," he says.

I shift in a moment, grateful when my clothing appears on my body again to keep out the evening chill that has now set in. I'm even more grateful to Brody who nicked me one of the charmed belts that come standard-issue with the LOP's uniforms. *Just in case*, he said back at the field office.

I kneel at Tempest's side and press my pointer and middle fingers against her throat. There's blood, so I'm relieved when my touch proves she has no wounds there. Except the blood had to come from somewhere, and there's a hell of a lot of it.

She's alive but her pulse is weak. I do a scan of her other injuries and my heart plummets. So much blood. Torn fabric, thrashed skin, and *more* blood. I press my ear by her lips to hear her breath, but it doesn't come. My heart is hammering against my chest so loud that I'm now afraid I won't be able to hear anything over the sound, so I press my ear to her lips until there is the cool touch of her skin against my own. Only then do I feel the tickle of breath, much too shallow for my comfort.

"We need Fate's Root," I say, and I nearly collapse with the relief that Brody is here with the emergency kit I know will be in the car. Every second could make a difference now. "She won't make it to the hospital."

Brody's eyes are wide as they meet mine. "Are you sure?" he asks.

"It will work," I snap. There's a long beat as we hold eye contact.

Fate's Root is not to be messed around with. It's a powerful medicine, too powerful for most people. If a human were to ingest it, it would burn them up from the inside. Even many of the preternatural couldn't handle the compound. It would only be worth the risk on a Nagual. One who isn't shiftless.

Giving the medicine bundle to Tempest now could very likely kill her, which is obviously Brody's concern. But I'm not convinced she'll live anyway at this point. I'm banking entirely on the fact that if she's lost so much blood in this fight that she must have managed to draw some blood from one of the wolves too. I didn't see her shift myself, but this is a gamble I have no choice but to take.

"I'll get it," Brody says finally. He's already moving towards the car.

I cradle the back of Tempest's head, trying to open her airway, but she's so limp, moving her is like moving a rag doll.

"Stay with me, Tempest." I'm hoping she'll wake from her deathlike slumber from the severity of my tone alone, but she stays unconscious.

"Come on, Tempest. Hang in there for me, okay?" I try

again, this time giving her a little shake. "You need to stay with me, Tempest." I'm pleading now.

She makes a small noise, which sounds like in protest, but then fresh blood sputters from a wound I hadn't seen on her stomach.

"Brody!" I cry out.

"Here," he says, appearing at my side again. I hadn't heard his approach, the sound drowned out by the blood pounding in my ears.

I snatch the glass vial from Brody's hands and uncork the plug with my teeth.

"I'll pry her mouth open," Brody says. "You make sure she swallows it. Are you ready?"

I must nod because a second later Brody has his fingers in Tempest's mouth, prying open her jaw. I take a sharp breath, steeling myself for what may as well be the worst decision I ever make in my life. Then I take the small rod that makes up the medicine bundle from the vial and shove it down Tempest's throat.

It's about the size and shape of a stick of cinnamon, maybe a little shorter, but definitely as thick. From what I understand, it's several herbs and other medicinal compounds, hence its name, cauterized together to be taken like a very, very large pill.

Most try to cough it up, I know from the training we received our first week of the program, but Tempest is listless. She lays perfectly still, like a corpse, seemingly unaffected by the asphyxiation that is surely taking hold. I curse under my breath and shift her weight against me again, trying to use gravity to make the rod go down.

"You need to swallow it, Tempest," I coax, though it's clear she can't hear me. "It's medicine. It's going to save your life, but you have to let it. You can't fight it."

Fate's Root needs to be swallowed to take effect. And if her injuries don't kill her in the next few minutes, the obstruction to her esophagus definitely will.

When nothing happens, I give a rough shake to her shoulders. I cringe as I think about her wounds and the pain it is sure to cause, but there's no choice here. Between pain and death, pain has to win every time.

"Come on, Tempest!" I shout.

Just as I become sure Tempest will choke, her throat bobs once.

There is a long, heavy moment where everything is still. Even the crickets are quiet. Tempest's eyes are open but empty. There is no life detectable in the stormy pools, and I wonder if this will be the second time in as many years that the life of someone I've unexpectedly grown to care about will end here in front of me.

I wonder if it will even be the last.

Then her eyes fly open, and she gasps. Brody and I let out twin sighs of relief.

"Good, Tempest," I murmur and smooth back a lock of hair that's plastered to her forehead. "You did good."

Her eyes fall closed again, but when I check her pulse, it's a bit stronger than it had been. Her breath is coming more easily now too, though it sounds shallow, like she's been buried beneath a pound of gravel. But as long as she's breathing, I'm content.

I sit back on my heels, relief giving way to exhaustion. I see a similar expression on Brody's face, though it's more guarded than I'm used to from him. Brody hasn't done this before— not like I have. He's seen death, but nothing this violent.

In the distance, a siren whirrs. It's not the police or an ambulance, it's the distinctly high pitch of the League of

Protectors' sirens, the sound on a frequency that no human could hear on their own. Even the few magi in our ranks have to use a charmed earpiece to make out the sound.

"I called for them when I was in the car," Brody explains, though I don't really care how they got here, only that they did.

"Thank you," I say.

He shakes his head. "You definitely shouldn't be thanking me. We don't even know if she's alive."

"She's alive," I say. I know she is, it's the only reason why I can be at ease right now. The only reason why I'm not charging into those woods to find the animals that did this to her, besides knowing that they're long gone by now.

I see purple and white flashing lights reflecting against the pavement up the road. Then three sleek black vehicles round the corner, racing towards us.

There are two cars that must have come from the Baltimore office, though my dad is driving the first one. The woman I imagine must be Tempest's aunt jumps out of the passenger seat, running towards us. Her hand is against her mouth, eyes wide with horror, and a choked noise rings out in the quiet.

"We need an ambulance on the corner of Lakeshore Drive," I hear my dad murmuring into his phone. Two other agents join us, but Laura's eyes remain fixed on Tempest's limp form.

"She's going to live," I tell her.

"You—" Laura starts, but falters. "You saved her." She doesn't phrase it like a question, but I see it in her eyes.

"Of course I did," I say gently. "It's my job." Well, it's not yet, but it will be someday. I'm not usually one for breaking the rules, but since doing so saved Tempest's life, I'll happily accept any punishment that comes my way.

Laura shakes her head. "I don't understand," she murmurs, but then she's down on her knees, running her hands over Tempest's brutalized form. She presses her fingers against Tempest's throat and winces as she prods at the rest of the damage. Some of the wounds are starting to heal already. It's a frustratingly slow process, like watching paint dry, but the cell regeneration is so much faster than anything a human could do. I watch Laura's face go slack as she realizes it, too.

My dad is beside me now, frowning down at the scene.

"Who did this?" he asks darkly.

"Wolves," I say. "I'd bet anything it was the Full Moon Knights."

I hear Brody take in a sharp breath. Laura's eyes dart up to my father's.

"I thought it was you who were coming to hurt her. Melanie said the protectors weren't who they pretended to be."

My dad is quiet for a moment, seeming to seriously consider this. "Daria Payne was Melanie's partner at the LOP. It's possible that is who she meant." My father's frown deepens, though it almost seems like a weight is being lifted off of his shoulders too. "She was also a wolf shifter. Daria and her brother are the people Melanie was responsible for having killed, but it's possible that the circumstances around the murders may not be as it seemed."

Any further discussion is cut off by the sudden sound of sirens, the humankind, coming up the street. My father is already digging around his coat pocket for the U.S. government-issued badge that discourages any human law enforcement agencies from asking too many prying questions. It is *way* above their clearance level.

"Jet, Brody, go wait in the car."

Neither of us argue.

I wake to the sound of low, rhythmic beeping. Though it's quiet, it rips me from my slumber like an alarm clock. My sleep was filled with the memories of pain. There's no pain now, only a dull ache that seems to coat my body like a cast. I have to fight through sand-glued eyes and near-blinding sunlight, but eventually, I manage to open them. It feels like it's for the first time.

I'm in a familiar hospital room. Well, the room itself isn't familiar, but the stark white interior and wooden chair are a dead giveaway. I'm at the Aberdeen Regional Hospital, where Laura works. It's comforting to recognize, though as soon as my brain starts to piece together why I would be waking in the hospital, I start to spin out.

I remember everything. I know I was attacked. I know I was hurt, and seeing the wolves lunge for my throat again and again in my mind's eye is nearly as painful as living through the experience. Luckily, I'm well-versed in unpleasant things and banish the memories for the time being, closing myself off from them like shutting off the television.

The small room smells like antiseptic and eucalyptus. The door is directly across from me next to a large window that looks into the hall, half-covered by a thin blue curtain. Beneath it is a chair where my aunt is curled up, sleeping.

Between my bed and the door to the bathroom to my left is a wide window where the glow of the afternoon sun beams through. It radiates pleasant heat on my exposed back. I suppose I slept through most of the day, which must have done me good because I feel surprisingly well-rested. My appendages are stiff and sore, and I can't see the damage beneath my covered wounds, but I feel in much better shape than my memory would have me believe.

There is a nurse in the room with us, studying the vital signs monitor and jotting notes onto a chart. He's a little doughy in the midsection from too many odd-hour shifts and on-the-go meals, but his long face is sweet, and familiar. He's such a welcome sight in all this chaos that I let out an audible sigh. He looks over his clipboard and gives me a warm smile.

"Hey, Tempe. Welcome back to the land of the living."

"Hey Brian," I say. I try to push myself up but he comes to my aid. He rushes to adjust the mechanical bed frame so that I'm seated upright and then offers his arm as I right myself. A sharp pain shoots up my left shoulder making me wince and Brian scowls.

"I can't believe this happened to you," he whispers, shaking his head. He takes a seat on the edge of my bed and rests a supportive hand on my blanket-covered shin. "A wild dog attack like that in the middle of Crescentwood. Who'd have thought?"

I blink, trying to grasp his meaning. I guess telling him that werewolves tried to kill me isn't really on the table. I mean, I'm still having a hard time understanding it even now that I've seen exactly how it works. A dog attack must be the cover story Laura decided on, so I nod, playing along.

"Yeah, it was the last thing I expected to happen either," I say. Boy, isn't that the truth.

"Well, you're healing miraculously, I would say." He nods towards the chart he had been working on. "You should be discharged soon. There are police here, I guess to take your statement about the attack, but you should talk to Laura first. She's been worried sick."

He glances over his shoulder at Laura, still knocked out in the chair. His eyes soften when they look at her, but harden again when they face me.

"I hope they find the animals that did this to you. When dogs are vicious like this, they have to be put down or they'll only attack again, and the next time, the person may not be as lucky as you." Brian pats my shin as he stands. "You've had a tough go of it these past few years, Tempe. Maybe going up to New England and spending some time with your grandparents will be a good thing."

I frown, and murmur an agreement, but that's as much as I'm willing to lie. It's exhausting. I don't know how my aunt managed it for so long.

Laura stirs then, attempting to stretch out in the chair and bumping each of her limbs on the hard, wooden arms. Her eyes flicker open in protest, and at the sight of me, she leaps to her feet.

"Oh, thank God, you're awake," she gasps. She pulls me tight against her chest in a bone-bruising embrace. I don't dare complain though. "I was so worried." Her tears fall on the skin left bare from this flimsy gown.

"I'm okay," I assure her.

"I'll let you two talk," Brian says. "I have to go check in on a few other patients."

Laura moves away from me to wrap Brian in a hug. "Thank you for helping her," she murmurs.

"Tempest, the doctor should be in momentarily," Brian says as he stashes the chart in the hanging plastic basket by the door. "Let me know if there's anything you need. I can steal as many pudding cups as you can handle."

"Chocolate, please," I call after him. He winks, and then leaves us alone in the room.

"Oh Tempest, I can't believe they did this to you." Laura's jaw is trembling as she falls onto the bed with me. "I thought I was going to lose you."

"I shouldn't have run out like that," I say. "I never expected..." I can't finish the sentence, but I don't think I need to. I don't know how to put what happened into words, and I don't know if I should.

The door creaks and the doctor comes in. He exchanges a few words with Laura about my vitals before asking me how I'm feeling. I'm honest about feeling sore, but say I'm not bad, all things considered. Even after the doctor is gone, Laura stays suspiciously silent. She's fussing with my hair and scowling at each bruise on my body that is evidence of what I endured.

"What's going on?" I finally ask.

Laura doesn't answer. Her gaze just traverses my body while she worries her bottom lip.

"Laura," I prompt. I give her a searching look, but any explanation I hoped to pull from her in private is interrupted by the arrival of the "police." I go rigid as Jet walks in with a man who could be his twin except that he looks to be more than twice his age and built like an ox.

I look at my aunt, feeling panic rise in me, but Laura seems relieved to see them. I can't make sense of it. Only hours ago, she insisted these people were out to kill me. She was willing to run to another country to keep me away from them. She was partially right, shapeshifters did come to kill me, but it certainly wasn't Jet or any of the people he's with.

"We're glad to see you're doing well," the older man says. "My name is Lieutenant Delancey of the League of Protectors. You know my son, Jet. If there's anything we can do to make your recovery more comfortable, please don't hesitate to ask."

I let out a nervous breath. "Telling me you arrested those psychos would be a great start."

Lieutenant Delancey gives me a patient smile, but Jet's face is unreadable.

"We can assure you, Ms. Maverick, that a full investigation is in progress."

I frown and pull myself up to sit straighter. There is still a slight twinge of discomfort as I jostle bandages over wounds, but already I feel less pain than I had even minutes before.

"That's not my name," I say.

"It is in their world," Laura replies. I want to argue this or at least get an explanation as to why, but Laura is already moving on, giving me a weighted look that I can't ignore. "Tempest, Jet saved your life."

Her expression seems to say *I was wrong* and *I'm sorry* all in one. It has me softening again, though there is a small, sour piece of my heart that can't help but consider; *if I had known about any of this, then maybe...* But I don't know what that maybe could be. Who knows what would have happened. Things would have played out exactly the same. It doesn't feel fair to hold that against her, but it doesn't feel right to forgive her so easily either.

"You lost a lot of blood and were unresponsive. We almost lost you."

I blink through my shock, trying to piece this together in my head. I was being attacked by the wolf-people, but I fought back. There was pain, so much pain, but I kept fighting until someone came to save me and then—and then darkness like I've never known. But it wasn't sheer nothingness, and it wasn't the empty pit that is my dreamless sleep either. The darkness had mass to it. It felt like swimming, but instead of wetness, there was only warmth. In the unending black, there had been iridescent streaks of silver light, not quite a shape, but it moved deliberately too. It danced around me like it was trying to get my attention. I got the distinct impression it was trying to communicate, but I'm not fluent in light and shadow.

I look up at my aunt, a question in my eyes that I can't voice, but it's Lieutenant Delancey who answers.

"Cadet Delancey took a calculated risk in giving you a medicinal compound known as Fate's Root. It is extremely effective medication, if given within a tight window, that can bring a Nagual back from the brink. However, it can only work if the Nagual has gone through their Blood Rite."

"Nagual?" I ask.

"It is the name we use for shapeshifters. They are just one of the several types of preternatural beings."

That's what I am. A shapeshifter. A Nagual. If I wasn't, I wouldn't be sitting here. I'd be downstairs in the morgue, forever swimming in darkness.

"I think I shifted," I say instead, once I get my ragged breath back under control. "But I don't know what I turned into. The wolves said I was small, pathetic."

"You'll be able to trigger your shift at will now. It may take some time to learn, but it will start to come to you naturally and then we'll know what you are," Jet explains. "But don't believe a word the Full Moon Knights said about you. They're the pathetic ones. They pretend they're fighting for some sort of justice, but they're terrorists. They use violence to push a political agenda that only suits their needs, and I don't think they even know what statement they're trying to make at this point."

"The Full Moon Knights?" I ask.

"They are a group of lycanthrope, a breed of Nagual," Lieutenant Delancey says.

"Werewolves," I murmur. I knew this, of course. I saw them turn from human to wolf, but this situation is still bizarre enough to give me some cognitive dissonance. Werewolves, one of the most famous legends in history, are real, and came to kill me.

"Lycanthrope are the model of the werewolf trope, yes," he continues, "but they are simply Nagual. The same as you, your mother, myself, and my son. The Nagual you encountered last night are members of an extremist group that operates in the preternatural world. They've been on our radar for various crimes and disturbances for more than twenty years, but they hide in the shadows and strike at the moments we least expect. Outside of charging an occasional member with some petty crime or another, we haven't been able to bring them down."

"Why would they come after me?" I ask.

"We have reason to suspect that they are responsible for your parents' death. We're not sure of much else at the moment, but like I said, an investigation has already been launched. I can assure you, Ms. Maverick, we will investigate this to the fullest extent of our creed. The Full Moon Knights have always caused trouble, but an attack of this nature will not go unpunished. I only wish we knew what exactly happened twenty years ago between your mother and Daria Payne. Perhaps all of this could have played out differently."

The heavy weight of finality falls down on my shoulders. That's it, then. I'm a shapeshifter, forced into a world of magic and monsters who are trying to kill me, just like my aunt warned. I feel strangely resigned about it, but being stripped of the opportunity to make the decision feels like an even greater violation than the attack had been.

A voice rings in the back of my head, *was it ever really a choice, though?* I don't know. I didn't exactly want this, and yet, at my core, I know that this is who I am. Maybe this is why I never felt like I was real in my life before. Maybe this was always the answer.

I go to open my mouth, but I haven't decided on what exactly I am going to say. When I do, only a sob escapes. I quickly clamp my lips closed again and train my gaze out the window until I can blink away the pooling tears.

"We want to give you time to rest," the lieutenant says, "but we need to discuss our timeline before any arrangements can be made."

I frown and look to my aunt for an explanation. Her face is pinched as she regards Jet's father.

"I hadn't had the chance to tell her—"

"Tell me what?" I snap. I'm still raw from all the things I learned yesterday. All the things that had been kept from me. Laura swallows hard, but she's resolute when she faces me again.

"You're going to Vermont."

I frown. "Not Canada?"

"No. To Versi. You'll enroll in the academy there and finish out the year."

I bark out a laugh. "No, I won't."

"You will," she insists. I feel my jaw fall open. I blink at her. She can't actually be serious, can she? This is the exact reason I was so upset with her yesterday—why I am still so upset with her. She once again kept information from me and made a crucial choice about my future without even thinking to consult me. I guess I misread her expression earlier, because if she was really sorry, she wouldn't be doing this to me. Again. Not to mention that she sounds like a hypocrite. Yesterday she tore up our house and just about blew up our lives to keep me away from the people at Versi and now she expects me to be okay with being shipped off with them?

I get that there is something else at play here. I get that she didn't know about the Full Moon Knights and she was surprised Jet saved me—I'm surprised too, but this is unforgivable.

"I'm sorry, Tempest, but this changes everything. I—" she shakes her head. "I misunderstood parts of your parents' situation. I knew they were on the run from the law, but I thought the people who wanted to arrest them were the same as the Nagual trying to kill them. Perhaps," her eyes flick up to Lieutenant Delancey, "there's more to it than that."

She settles her gaze back on me and though there is a frown pinched there, her expression is gentle. "But I am not sorry for making the choices I did to keep you safe, including this one."

My eyes burn with another threat of tears and my chest feels hollow, like someone dug inside my rib cage with a spork. And when I speak, that's exactly how my voice sounds too.

"Get out."

Laura's brow twitches then pinches into a furrow. "What?"

"Please," I amend. "Please just go."

Laura is frozen for a moment, but she does eventually get to her feet. Her chin wobbles and I have to look away.

"I'm sorry, Tempest. For so many things," she says weakly before making her way towards the door.

There is a long silence before I face Jet and his father again. Normally, I would be so embarrassed that they witnessed something like this. Normally, I'd feel embarrassed for acting like this, but all I feel is numb right now.

"You have to come with us, Tempest," Jet says finally, though his eyes have softened into something more like what I saw the other night. I can't help but wonder which is the true version of him, or if somehow both versions are equally true.

I shake my head again. Didn't he just hear what I said to my aunt? If I wouldn't blindly trust in her plan, I certainly won't turn around and trust some strange shapeshifter I don't truly know. Even if he did save my life. Jet seems to read this on my face because he starts to explain before I can argue.

"I know all of this is happening quickly, but there is a good reason for that. We all have a signature—we call it a trace. Yours was masked by your father's power for a long time, but after talking with your aunt, we think that my finding you broke the spell, so to speak."

"So, I'm not masked from other shapeshifters anymore," I clarify.

"No," he says seriously. "And your trace is... unique. I'm not sure if it's a result of what your father did to it or something else, but it's more distinct than most."

I swallow as I think this over. Running wouldn't be an option then. I understand now that my parents only managed it with a whole lot of magic and understanding of this world that I definitely don't have.

"The Full Moon Knights can't cross the wards into campus," Lieutenant Delancey says. "And we know that may not be enough, if there is truth to the theory that Daria Payne was a Full Moon Knight in our ranks, but we are committed to ensuring your safety, Tempest. Which we can only do successfully at Versi, at least for now.

"I knew your mother," he continues. "There was even a point where I considered her a close friend." His tone is gentler now than his no-nonsense attitude had been thus far. Jet gives him a surprised look that I don't have the energy to interpret.

"I never wanted to believe she was capable of the cruelty that was displayed by the murder of Daria Payne, but I had to go with what the evidence suggested. I still must. But I can't help but feel like maybe I failed Melanie in all of this. So, if there is something I can do to help her daughter—to help you, I want you to feel confident that I will do it. Which is why I must insist you come with us. The tuition and other details will be worked out with your aunt. We'll arrange getting a dorm for you as well, but in the interim, you're welcome to stay with us."

I frown. Us? As in Lieutenant Delancey and *Jet's* house? With their family?

"That's very generous of you," I say cautiously. He gives me a knowing smile.

"It's the least we can do, given the circumstances. My wife has pull with the administrative offices, too. It won't be a problem getting you enrolled in classes right away."

I massage the sides of my head with three fingers, as if applying pressure will somehow let all this information sink in. This has officially been the strangest twenty-four hours of my life, and the day is still young. There is a part of me, the majority stake, if I'm honest, that feels defeated by all of this. I feel like I've gone ten rounds with destiny, and even though it keeps being called a draw, every inch of my mind, body, and spirit has been bruised.

There is another part of me that is just a bit curious. I can't help but wonder what this secret, warded campus looks like. Or what exactly the curriculum on a magical campus will be. I want to know what I shifted into and why it seemed to surprise the Full Moon Knights. I want to know what an abomination is and why they seem to think I am one. And most of all, I want to know who my parents truly are. Because more than anything else, I wish that this situation made me feel closer to them, rather than feeling like it has illuminated a chasm between us that I never knew existed.

So, while I know I never had a choice in all this, I decide to make it anyway. I take a deep breath and when I release it, I also release the growing weight from my shoulders.

"When do we leave?"

𝕝𝟛 TEMPEST

Throngs of dark green forest blur as they race out of my view from the backseat window. Orange and red leaves are sprinkled in with the brilliant emerald mountainside. Lieutenant Delancey, or Dylan, as he's now asked me to call him, is speeding up an empty road, and Brody Bates is in the front seat.

I don't know what to make of him. He's disruptively attractive, for one thing, and he knows it. It's his fit frame, unnaturally symmetrical bone structure, wavy blonde locks, bright hazel eyes, and disarming grin. But for the entirety of our drive to Vermont, Brody has been singing to himself, humming, or otherwise making some sort of noise. The few times he has quieted down, it's been to turn around and smile at me in a way I think is meant to be charming.

Jet is sitting in the back with me, though I'm not sure why since he's been frustratingly quiet throughout our journey. Most of the ride has been made in silence, though Lieutenant Delancey has asked a few polite questions. He asked about Crescentwood, about my aunt and my friends, about some of the places I visited when I was younger, and my plans for after high school. I answer all of them genuinely, except for the last one. To that, I just reply, "Let's see if I'm not dead by then."

Despite Jet's efforts to appear otherwise preoccupied, I catch the ghost of that smirk I remember from the other night and feel a bit smug about putting it there. He suddenly meets my eye and then peers around me just as there is a break in the forest line.

"We're here," he says.

Light floods the car. Like a veil has been lifted, the green suddenly gives way to reveal an entire city. My eyes take a moment to adjust, but they do in time for me to see a grand, Gothic hall sitting at the head of a large quad. It resembles a cathedral with its gray stone towers and stained-glass windows.

The view is quickly obscured by trees and other buildings as we turn into the campus' main entrance. There is a tall gate with the words *Versi University* inlaid in the iron. At first, I think the gate is ornamental since there isn't any fencing for it to attach to, but Dylan stops at a callbox, and with a few hushed words, the gate opens ahead of us, ushering me into a world made of pure fantasy.

Ahead of me is a main strip of boutique shops. The way they flank each side of the road doesn't look dissimilar from our downtown area of Crescentwood, except these shops look like they're out of a Hallmark movie, just before the towns-people spend a chilly late autumn day putting up wreaths and Christmas lights. It's all candy-colored awnings, pristinely white sidewalks, and overflowing flowerpots. I wonder if that is a function of this magic city or if it's just Vermont.

Dylan doesn't take us down the quaint thoroughfare, but rather, he turns right towards the Gothic building I saw before. It's the largest, sitting in the center of several smaller buildings, all of which wrap around the quad. Most of them are in the same Gothic style, but some are modern: sleek, white, and glass-paned. The road horseshoes around the courtyard but Dylan stops at the first building on the right.

I barely notice Brody exiting the car and exchanging good-byes with the Delancey men because my face is pressed up against the window. The quad is littered with people and animals alike enjoying the modest afternoon weather. Students lay in the grass with open textbooks while dogs, cats, and birds of all species chase each other through the feet of their class-mates. The sight in itself is bizarre, and then I remember that those animals are human. Or not human, obviously, but shapeshifters. Nagual.

That's why they're behaving like this; cohabitating. With a poof of magic, a snap of power, they can shift between human and animal as simply as the Full Moon Knights had.

My heart is pounding again. I'm grateful when Dylan drives around the quad and heads back to the main road where the charming shops that line the street are at least in a realm of normal I can wrap my head around. I actually wilt with relief when we pass sports fields and what looks like a neighborhood pool, already drained and abandoned for the winter.

Beyond what appears to be the main campus is the residen-tial neighborhood. The first few streets are the cookie-cutter homes you'd expect in a housing development, with every lawn covered in bright green grass, clipped short, only marred by a spattering of orange and brown leaves. The further we delve into the residential area, the more unique the houses become. It's like they somehow built this town in reverse. After the modern homes, there are houses with a more Colonial style, and then Victorian.

Dylan takes a left down another road where the style

changes again, some looking like they should be in Beverly Hills rather than Peru, Vermont, and some looking custom-built from an HGTV catalog. That's where Dylan finally pulls into a long, curling driveway at the end of a street that runs parallel to the woods that border the campus' limit. He parks just before an attached garage, adjacent to a large white house with long windows rimmed in iron. The whole house is a stark contrast to the dark greenery that engulfs it.

The woman waiting on the lawn is equally picturesque. She's short, though her build is somehow still willowy. Her hair is cut into a chestnut bob and she has bright blue eyes, though they are several shades lighter than Jet's. She stands on the stone path that leads up to the porch, her hands clasped together by her lips as if in an attempt to hide her smile.

A gray and white tabby cat saunters on the porch's banister, but when it launches off its perch and towards the ground below, it shifts into a woman. Or a girl, I guess, since she appears to be my age. She's clothed, thank god, though I have no idea how that's possible since the first time I faced a shapeshifter he most certainly was not. She wears faded jeans and a stylish leather jacket that contrasts against the purple balayage of her brown hair.

My eyes go wide with surprise—that panicky feeling setting in again. Jet is already leaping from the car, his backpack slung over a single shoulder. He wears a grin as he meets his mom. Dylan follows closely behind, kissing and hugging each member of his family as if their reunion is coming after months of separation and not a couple of days.

I hang back, needing an extra minute in the car before facing them. I close my eyes and take a deep breath. I hope that when I open them, I'll be back in my baby blue bedroom in

Crescentwood where my only worry for the day would be finishing my advanced biology assignment.

Unfortunately, when my eyes flutter open again, drawn from my fantasy by the muffled chatter of the Delancey family, I'm still in this strange place with strange people who aren't entirely people at all.

With a measured sigh, I throw open the door and climb out into my new life.

From the effort that the Delancey family matriarch obviously put into the meal, I'm sure dinner had to have been good, but I honestly couldn't taste it. I'm not hungry. The long drive up here had my stomach doing flips, and given my anxiety, it hasn't been able to recover. I dished myself a polite portion, moved it dutifully around my plate, and tried to keep up with the several conversations the Delanceys were having at once.

Diane, Jet's mother, asked him about the mission while Dylan told the group how proud he is of his son. Jet blushed under the praise, which is hands-down the most endearing expression I've seen on him yet. Meanwhile, Elisa, his sister, filled Jet in on her date from the night before—a classmate who Jet apparently doesn't think is a good influence. Diane then scolded her son and told him to trust his sister's instincts, to which Jet and his dad shared a knowing look. Then, in an effort to change the subject, Diane mentioned someone named Kage who apparently left London for Amsterdam that morning.

My head volleyed between the four of them like I was watching a game of tennis until I gave up on following the thread of the conversation and decided to focus on not eating my meal.

As I clear my plate to the kitchen sink after dinner, Diane

instructs Elisa to show me to my room. The sister, who has been eerily silent so far, appears at my side. Her eyes are blue too, like her mom's light blue, not Jet's electric, but the shrewdness of her gaze is somehow more unnerving than his. She's exceedingly pretty, the kind of girl who should be selling green juice powder on the internet, but the impression is marred by the dangerous edge to her smile.

"Follow me," she says. She leads me out of the kitchen and back into the foyer I saw when I arrived. She turns on her heeled boots and heads up the stairs. "I'm a senior too," she says as if this is the middle of our conversation and not the start of it. "So, we'll be in school together the rest of the year."

"Oh, cool," I say.

She shakes her head as if she's disappointed in my answer.

I want to throw up. Just because I'm used to navigating the politics of high school doesn't mean that I enjoy it. Or that I'm any good at it, even after all my experience.

"This whole operation," she gestures in the air as she reaches the top of the staircase, not pointing at anything in particular, "was supposed to be very hush-hush." For a moment, I think she's trying to reassure me, but as I join her at the landing, her smile turns sharp again. "So naturally everyone is talking about it."

"Great," I mutter. She laughs.

"Don't worry. If you can go up against the Full Moon Knights then you can manage Queen Bee Nixie Cabrera and her pack of purse dogs." She shoves her thumb over her shoulder. "That's my room. The bathroom next to it is mine too but you can use it. Unless you want to smell like bonfire and sea salt, or whatever outdoor activity those 'manly' bath products claim to be scented with."

I almost laugh but Elisa is already barreling down the hall.

"Jet's room is at the end. This is Kage's," she says, pointing at the open door across from us. The bed is neatly made but every surface is littered with books. I wonder if it's being used as storage or if the previous owner robbed a bookstore.

"Kage?" I ask. He's been mentioned a couple of times now and my brain keeps trying to place him.

"Our older brother. He's a college sophomore, studying abroad."

"And this is the guest room. Formerly known as Brody's room, which I'm sure he will tell you a thousand times, as if he didn't choose to move into a dorm."

"Why did Brody live with you?" I ask.

Her smirk twitches into a small frown. "Not my story to tell."

I duck into the room. My bags are already in a corner of the room, so I say I'm going to unpack and try to get to bed early. I never manage the latter, though. My mind is too muddled and my nerves too frayed to even make the attempt at sleep. I'm exhausted, but it's an emotional sort of exhaustion, not the kind that will lend to a few hours of solid shut-eye.

I did decide to unpack my belongings into the guest room, figuring I'll be staying here for a short while. I fill the dresser drawers with my clothes and the nightstands with the other odds and ends my aunt packed: notebooks, chargers, a hairbrush, and my makeup bag. There is a framed photo in the front pocket of my suitcase, a picture of me, my parents, and Aunt Laura at Christmas four years ago. The last Christmas with all of us together. I set it on top of the dresser with a shaky sigh. It looks out of place in its teal blue frame, what used to be my favorite color, now clashing with the white dresser and sage wall paint.

For a while, I consider calling my aunt, but that's another

headache I don't have the energy for tonight. I've been texting her updates on my journey to Versi since I don't want her to worry, but we haven't spoken much more since I told her to leave my hospital room yesterday. Even then it was mostly logistics; what paperwork to give the school administrations, which debit card I should use so she can load my allowance.

I also answered dozens of texts from Talia. Thankfully the rumors of the wild dog attack and my upcoming trip to be close to my grandparents in New England spread through the small town before I had even woken in the hospital, so it didn't take much further encouragement on my part for her to buy the story. I hate lying, so I make a promise to be more forthcoming once I know what is and is not okay to share. I'll just have to be careful not to mention Jet to her. The coincidence of me moving to the same private campus as him just days after our meeting is not something that she would let go of easily, even if she would come to the wrong conclusion.

Finally, I decide I can't stay cooped up any longer. I slip out of the guest room and tiptoe down the stairs. Thankfully this nice, new home doesn't have squeaky floorboards like I'm used to, especially since this house is so eerily quiet. I pass a bathroom and a sunroom where the washer and dryer reside before arriving at the door that leads to the backyard. It's already unlocked, which unnerves me on principle, but considering this house belongs to a family of shapeshifters with a father who works in law enforcement living in a closed community, they probably don't ever have to worry about break-ins.

I walk out into the moonlight, feeling the soft grass beneath my sneakers. A harmony of cicadas, crickets, and hooting owls sing from the edge of the woods like a lullaby. I immediately feel the knot in my chest loosen, so I move towards the concert, entranced by the sound. And I jump out of my skin when a familiar, deep voice calls out, "Can't sleep?"

❧ 14 ❧
JET

My bad nights are plagued by racing thoughts. My worst nights are plagued by silence. Tonight is one of those, hours upon hours of endless nothing until I feel like I'm going crazy. I gave up trying to sleep sometime around one a.m. My first attempt at distraction was to get ahead on some homework, but ten minutes of mindlessly turning pages proved I was way too unfocused. Eventually, I headed outside to my usual perch on the flat rooftop of the first-floor bathroom that overlooks our forested yard.

I need fresh air when I get like this, even if the weather is less than ideal. Tonight is actually pretty mild for October, so I only throw on a sweatshirt before slipping out my door. I'm used to being quiet when I sneak out—my dad's hearing is particularly sensitive, thanks to his Great Dane form—but I don't want to risk waking Tempest either. The light from her room is still seeping out from the crack under the door and, for the briefest moment, I hesitate as I pass, wondering if I should knock. If I should invite her to join me, assuming she is as awake and restless as I am. But in that one moment, I convince myself that it's a supremely bad idea.

Out in the yard, I climb the tree with limbs that twist close enough to the roof for me to sit on the rooftop. We're at the very end of the cul-de-sac, affording us a veil of woods that surrounds our yard, giving us more privacy than the rest of the street. From where I sit, you could pretend that we don't have neighbors and that there is nothing but forest for miles. I don't know why this calms me, only that it does.

I'm not nearly as surprised as I should be when I hear the side door creak open and light footfalls tread out onto the grass a little while later. I know with certainty that it will be Tempest. She steps into my view, but she hasn't noticed me yet. She's watching the woods with the same reverence that I did, and I take a quiet moment to watch her too.

But before long, I hear myself call out, "Can't sleep?"

She whirls towards me, anxiety first flaring in her eyes, and then relief.

"Why are you always sneaking up on me in the dark?" she calls back.

It surprises a small laugh out of me. "Hey, I was here first this time," I tease. "Want to come up?" I gesture to the tree beside me. Tempest moves towards it and begins to climb the branches with ease. I stand, moving towards the edge of the roof and offering her my hand. She hoists herself off the branch and onto the slightly slanted plane. Her hand feels small and warm in mine. I drop it quickly and take my seat again. She joins me, but the space between us feels larger than necessary.

"My dad arranged for someone to give you a campus tour tomorrow," I say after a minute of comfortable silence.

"Really?" she asks, seeming pleased by this. "Not you?"

I shake my head. "I have to catch up on the days I already missed this week."

She nods. "This place is different from what I was expecting. It's different from anything I've experienced before, I think."

"You like it, though?" I don't know why this matters to me, but it does.

"I mean, yeah. It's just that even the greenery and mountains are so foreign to me. Then add the weird magical town at the center of it... It just feels so far removed from the real world."

"This is the real world. For us, at least. And now for you too. It's not really magic either. I know it must seem that way but there's an order to everything."

"How can that be?" she asks, her voice tight with something that sounds almost like desperation. "You're a shapeshifter, which is strange enough in itself, but I know your mom is a cat, and I think she said your dad is a dog? Even that doesn't make any sense."

I have to stifle a laugh because I can understand Tempest's frustration. It does sound absurd. "In most respects, the Nagual gift is hereditary. The Nagual gene, if you want to call it that, is passed down by mating with another Nagual." Tempest frowns at this, but I continue. "My mom is bakeneko, a cat shifter. So is Elisa, and technically, so am I."

"What are you?" she asks.

I feel my smirk spread and my shoulders square without really meaning to. "I'm a panther shifter."

Her eyes go wide. "Let me get this straight. Your sister is a tabby cat, your mom looks like every other shorthair I've seen, and you're a damn panther."

"Yes."

"That's my point! That doesn't make any sense!"

This time I do have to laugh at her distress. "As I was *trying* to explain," I send her a schooling look that she rolls her eyes at, "our Nagual forms are more like a spirit animal than a genotype. There are definitely some metaphysical elements, but most of what we are is ruled by science. Yes, my mom is a cat, and my dad is a dog, but me being a panther is still in the same family of the animal kingdom. A panther is much closer to a Great Dane than a fish or a snake, for example."

Tempest frowns again but considers my words. "So, your form is like a phenotype then. You have a genetic predisposition that you inherited but other factors can influence how it manifests?"

I grin. "Exactly."

"And you have the spirit animal of a panther. That's impressive, I think."

My smirk twitches into a full grin. "I like to think so too."

She smiles too but it only lasts a moment before falling into a contemplative frown.

"If a Nagual can only be born from two Nagual mating, how am I alive then?"

Now I frown. I've been dreading her asking me this question since I still don't really understand it myself. My dad explained it as best as he could after I confronted him about his friendship with Melanie Maverick. I only knew that they were colleagues and that my dad initially headed the case to find her and Gregor Candor after they were named their generation's most prolific killers, but I never knew the extent of their association.

"Well, you know your mom was kind of famous. She was a princess, even if she didn't act like it, and that only made people more interested in her. Then she abdicated her right to the throne to study law and protection at Versi, and was accused of murdering Daria and Shamus Payne, which rocked our world. I mean, I was a newborn when your parents ran and yet I heard whispers about Melanie Maverick for years, almost like it was a ghost story." She frowns down at the roof shingles.

"But your dad was kind of famous too, in a different way. He was young, really young, but he was already known as one of the most brilliant preternatural scholars in recent history. He was an alchemy genius. He developed the LOP's emission elixir and revolutionized the campus wards, including finding a way to let us keep our clothes intact when we shift within the campus boundary."

Tempest wrinkles her nose but there's amusement in her eyes. "So, he was nerd-famous. I bet he loved that."

"I mean, yeah, but he was so much more. Like the preternatural academia's own Isaac Newton. Or DaVinci. Or Socrates. If you ever meet Kage, you'll have to ask him about it. He's kind of obsessed with your dad. He wrote a whole research paper on him last year. Anyway, what I'm saying is that if anyone could have figured out how to use alchemy to bypass biology and reproduce with a Nagual, Gregor Candor was the one."

"Even though it's supposed to be impossible," Tempest clarifies. I nod.

"Your dad did a lot of impossible things. It's what he's known for."

Tempest tucks her knees up against her chest and wraps her arms around herself.

"I wish I knew what I was. The Full Moon Knights seemed surprised, and not in a good way."

"Well, your mom was a harpy," I say. The animal form of every Nagual at Versi isn't common knowledge since there are so many, though a lot of people keep track of the more interesting shifters among us. But people concerned themselves with the details of Melanie Maverick long before she was known as a wanted murderer. "A raptor shifter. And your grandmother, the queen, is a mayura—a peacock."

Tempest snorts loudly. "Sorry," she says. I shake my head to keep from laughing.

"I think I would know if I'm some type of bird shifter though, right? I could have flown away from the Full Moon Knights."

"Maybe, but shifting can be difficult to get a handle on. It's possible that you are one and just didn't know how to take flight on instinct."

"Oh, great. I'm a flightless bird or something equally useless."

"Hey, penguins are far from useless," I say defensively. "They can basically fly underwater. That's awesome."

Tempest waves her hand in a dismissive gesture. My cheeks start to ache and it's only then I realize how long I've been smiling. And yet, instead of clamping my mouth back into a neutral line, I let my cheeks keep cramping.

"The thing is, bakeneko, therianthrope, lycanthrope, and even harpies are all pretty common types of Nagual. I'd be willing to bet that you're something else entirely. Something extraordinary."

My heart races as she turns to look at me. I can only read surprise on her face even though I can tell there is more to her expression than just that. Before I can decipher it, she ducks her head, as if trying to shift away from my steady gaze on her.

Her beauty is not an obvious thing, but it's undeniable. There's something about her that is unassuming, as if she is meant to get lost in a crowd or fade into shadows, and yet I find myself incapable of looking anywhere but at her when she's around. It's alarming how she's managed to worm her way into my consciousness in such a short amount of time. I need to keep focus on my studies and impressing the League of Protectors. I've worked too hard to get distracted now.

But even as I think the words, I do get distracted. There is a stray eyelash that rests on her cheekbone. I shift forward and brush it away with my thumb. Tempest's eyes are wide, her mouth slightly parted in surprise. It has my gaze flickering to her lips and how they part just a bit more as she takes in a sharp breath. Then she is climbing to her feet.

"I probably should try to get some sleep," Tempest says, her voice shaky. She doesn't meet my eye. "Tomorrow is going to be a long day."

I get up too, moving towards the tree so I can help her get down again. She doesn't need any help though. With a couple of confident movements, she's descending the tree's branches with ease.

"Hey Tempest," I call to her. "I know it might feel overwhelming at first, so just remember that you'll get a handle on it eventually. You're one of us now."

She sends a grateful smile back up at me and the wind is nearly knocked from my chest. Her face is flushed, either from the exertion or the embarrassment of a few moments ago, and now she's wearing a full, pleased grin, unlike her usual small smiles. She's not just beautiful in this moment. She's captivating.

"Goodnight, Jet," she says, her lips curving up just a bit more.

"Goodnight," I answer, but not until her feet are hitting the earth again, too far for her to hear.

15

TEMPEST

I'm greeted with a plate piled high with French toast the next morning. It's dusted with powdered sugar and paired with a cup of steaming coffee that I guzzled down before Diane could even finish asking me how I take it.

Elisa is perched on the stool beside me at the kitchen island, swinging her feet and typing on her phone while sucking down chocolate milk. I didn't get the memo that breakfast is a full-glam affair, but she's dressed as if she's about to strut down the streets of SoHo and not like she has calculus first period. Dylan is at the kitchen table reading the Versi Sun publication in the head seat. It seems so novel for a dad to be reading the news-paper at breakfast, but I suppose that social media and cable television is out of the question for sharing news about the preternatural.

Jet was already gone for the day when I arrived, and I'm grateful for it. I don't know what exactly passed between us last night, or if my tired mind was just playing tricks on me and there wasn't really anything that passed between us at all. Maybe he was only just brushing the eyelash away. Maybe that

117

is a totally normal, very casual thing for him to do and I'm just blowing it up in my head because all of this is new and confusing and frustrating, and figuring out the deal with Jet Delancey feels just a little bit easier than figuring out everything else.

I dive into my meal, thanking Diane profusely since it seems like too much work to go through on a typical Wednesday morning. I'm too engrossed in satiating my hunger for the first time in days to realize that only Diane and I are left until she clears my plate away.

"How'd you sleep, Tempest?" she asks.

"Okay," I lie.

She smiles knowingly and I wonder if she's used to Jet telling her the same lie. I gulp down my second cup of black coffee as she disappears into the foyer. She returns a moment later with a pink folder.

"I was able to convince Tracy Mueller to get me your class schedule early. You'll still have to finalize everything with the counselor tomorrow morning, but at least you'll have the course summaries to get acquainted with in the meantime. All your materials should be provided by the teachers on your first day, but let me know right away if you're missing anything."

"Thank you," I say again.

She waves her hand dismissively. "It's nothing. I work for admissions at the University but all it took was a trip down the hall to get you set up with everything you need. I have to head in now but one of Dylan's cadets should be here any minute to show you around campus."

I go make myself look presentable for the day. I don't take long considering that no matter what I do to my hair, its final evolution is always a semi-curly mess. I do minimal makeup since I certainly don't need anything drawing more attention to my strange eyes, and my wardrobe is limited to what I already had packed for my unplanned trip to Toronto with my aunt pre-werewolf attack.

When I do make it back downstairs, Diane is gone, leaving me alone in the Delancey home for the first time. I didn't notice before, I was too distracted by the natural chaos of a big family, but this house is utterly silent. Despite the fact that it's considerably warmer inside than it is outside in the New England autumn, there's not even the hum of a heating unit in the walls.

A knock sounds out against the door, making me jump. When I pull it open, I'm greeted by a familiar head of floppy brown curls and a wide grin. I recognize him right away; Andre, my rock-climbing competition from Camp Kenwick. He pops out earbuds and shoves them into his pocket.

"I hope you're ready to get your steps in for the day," he says in greeting.

I'm smiling like an idiot, but I'm suddenly so glad to have another ally on this campus. I don't know where I stand with Jet, but it feels dangerous to rely exclusively on him. And I honestly have no idea what to make of Elisa, yet. She's kind of scary, but in an endearing way, like a rottweiler.

"Ready as I'll ever be," I say, mustering a bit more cheer than I was feeling before.

Andre leads the way down the sleepy residential street to the corner of Bear Claw Boulevard where there is a stop for the shuttle that will take us to the campus's academic quarter.

"So how did you get stuck on babysitting duty?" I ask him as we wait.

"I volunteered," he says. "Wednesday is my light day and they wanted someone connected to the LOP to help you get situated. People at HQ are pretty freaked out over what happened with you."

"With the Full Moon Knights' attack or the fact that I've existed under their noses for eighteen years?"

He chokes on a laugh. "All of it. They don't like the idea that a Knight could have been in our ranks, even if it was forever ago. And they really don't like not knowing what to do with you."

I want to ask more about the LOP but the shuttle finally arrives. It looks less like the bus I was expecting and more like a trolley car. The doors spring open, but there isn't anyone sitting in the driver's seat. There isn't actually a driver's seat at all. There are only two rows of benches facing each other. Once we're seated, the vehicle pushes forward on its own again.

There's an elderly couple at the front of the trolley who politely ignore us as Andre gives me a driving tour of the crucial landmarks, most of which I clocked on my way in last evening.

"What's your schedule?" Andre asks as the shuttle halts at a crosswalk at the mouth of the academic quarter. A large group of small children, all wearing brightly colored backpacks and adorably petite coats, hats, and scarves, are crossing the street. They wave to the shuttle as if it was put there specifically for their amusement and Andre waves back.

I pull the folded sheet of paper with my class schedule from my pocket. I read the contents off to him: Charms I, Alchemy for Freshman, Freshman Nagual Myth and History, Trigonometry—of course, and Nagual in Literature. The list is accompanied by the names of teachers and various room numbers between several different buildings.

"Oh cool. They got you in a few college-level courses."

"Really?" Andre nods and points to the classes labeled for freshmen.

"A lot of the introductory courses for Versi University are tailored to preternatural new to studying our curriculum. It's smart they're doing it this way rather than sticking you in intro classes with a bunch of fourteen-year-olds. It looks like you can choose an elective too."

He points at the list of four classes at the bottom, not currently assigned to a date and time. "Theoretical Preternatural Principles, Nature as Art, or Zoo. You shouldn't do Zoo yet, though."

"What is it?" I ask.

"It's like a gym class where everyone is in their animal form, and you get to run around crazy obstacle courses."

"It sounds cool."

"It is! But if you can't shift at will yet..."

I nod, burying my hurt feelings. I'm not sure how I should go about learning how to shift properly. I'm not even sure that I want to at this point. My first experience had been more than a little traumatic, so I'm honestly not all that excited to do it again.

"I guess I'll do Theoretical Preternatural Principles then."

Andre nods. "You'll like it. Professor Kilmer is really cool. Ah, look there is the pool house on your right."

I turn to face the glass building. He explains that it is a large complex featuring two Nagual-only pools: saltwater and freshwater. Then there is a sauna, and two general-purpose pools, one indoor and one out, where shifting is prohibited so the magi and hybrids don't have to worry about a shark shifter taking a bite out of them. I can't tell if he's kidding or not.

"Wait, so I know my dad was a magi, but what does that mean? And what is a hybrid?"

"He was a magus—singular," Andre corrects with a smile. "Part of the magi—plural. Basically, it means 'magic-user' but a lot of people, mostly Nagual, have an issue with that definition. They don't like to think of any part of the preternatural experience being 'magic.' They seem to think that it somehow invalidates what we are."

I nod, remembering how Jet implied as much last night. He was careful to talk about Nagual like a genus being defined in a biology textbook, even as he went on to explain that the gift of shapeshifting was bestowed as a blessing by the Universe. I have to agree with Andre. It sounds every bit like magic to me.

"They're usually born into families of magi, though sometimes not—like your dad. Magi are essentially like a witch, warlock, sorcerer, or anything of that grain, except it's not quite like what you see in the movies. They have a keen ability to manipulate natural elements like earth, wind, water, and fire, and this translates to their aptitude for casting spells and creating potions and charms."

"I was going to say, I definitely never saw my dad wearing a pointy hat and painting pentagrams on the wall."

Andre shrugs. "Hybrids are shapeshifters, but they aren't Nagual because their shifted forms aren't animal. The types you are most likely to encounter at Versi are the fae, incubi, and succubi."

Though I'm only conscious of my brow twitching, I realize after a moment that my lips are puckered as if I've been sipping on undiluted cranberry juice. Despite how complicated this world of not-quite-supernatural beings seems to be, the rules, so far, have been pretty clear. There are three main groups of people that make up the preternatural. The Nagual, the magi, and now the hybrids. Except "hybrid" doesn't seem the right thing to call them at all. It seems a little offensive, actually, that there are other types of shapeshifters who exist within the campus wards, and yet they are thrown together under a lesser umbrella.

I want to say as much, but I honestly don't have the words, let alone all the context, to ask the right question. Thankfully, I don't need to. Andre is already nodding as if I've spoken out loud.

"Our ancestors had over-inflated egos when it came to the whole 'divine purpose from the Universe' thing, so they made it clear from the beginning of our time that *we* are different from *them*. There was a war and everything, back in the day. It doesn't help that almost every monster story you've ever heard has originated in some tale of a hybrid or another. Take vampires, for example. You won't find any bloodsuckers here, but creatures of the night who seduce beautiful women to suck out their life force is close enough to the truth of the incubi to cause all kinds of stigmas.

"To be fair, they needed broad categorizations back in the day," Andre continues. "Every culture, religion, myth, legend, and children's bedtime story contains different but eerily similar accounts of magic users, shapeshifters, and other creatures that go bump in the night. A few hundred years ago, the Nagual recognized that all these stories and phenomena were referring to the same things, so they got organized. They took every story from every culture and pooled it into one centralized mythology. They did it as a way for the preternatural to understand themselves and their role in the world. From that, our culture was born. A monarch was established to rule, and a creed of ethics was enacted for preternatural to live by."

"So, everything that I will learn here is a weird combination of every legend of every culture in the world?"

"Wild, right?" Andre says with a wide grin.

I have a hard time comprehending the magnitude of that. Aunt Laura did a decent job of explaining the fundamentals of Christianity to me over the past couple of years. She was raised religious and still participates in some of the traditions, but it all sounded so strange to me. Not nearly as strange as learning about shapeshifters, obviously, but still. I had a hard time wrapping my head around all the names, books, time periods, and stories with their contradicting philosophies. Now, to think that people compiled all of that information, for every single religion and myth, is incomprehensible.

"It's always been different with the magi, though. While Nagual and hybrids have our eternal struggle since we're so similar, the magi kind of operate in their own world. But since they have always been willing to use their abilities to help us out, we've respected them enough to butt out of their business. Even still, it's only been in the last couple hundred years or so that magi have been accepted in our culture as part of the preternatural world. Even less for hybrids. And even more recently, at our campuses."

My frown deepens. "That's messed up."

"I agree," Andre says. "I'm a part of a group called PERA that calls attention to the disparity that magi and hybrids face, and I would honestly say most Nagual are on board nowadays. You'll still find a few families who think back fondly on when the preternatural world 'felt smaller.' And these same people would quickly curse the Full Moon Knights for their small-mindedness and not see the irony of it."

I shudder, the way I seem to whenever something reminds me of the Knights. With everything that has happened these last few days, meeting them seems almost like a nightmare, and I've preferred to think of them that way. So being reminded of their existence as a real threat, and not just a troubling fixture of my imagination, is a shock to my system.

"What is the deal with the Full Moon Knights?" I ask as the shuttle stops again. Andre jumps to his feet and I follow, climbing out into the same area of campus where we dropped off Brody last night. There are several large buildings, all with a dramatically Gothic style, placed around the quad in the shape of a horseshoe. The street arches around through the outskirts of the quad, though it seems to only be used by the shuttles during the day and is empty now that the one we just disembarked from is pulling away.

Andre shrugs at my question. "They're Nagual-supremacists, basically. Lycanthrope have always been the most prominent type of shapeshifter, so there was this group back in the day called the Full Moon Council who tried to overthrow the queen—er, your great-grandma, I guess. They didn't like how inclusive our community was becoming and thought they could do a better job ruling. They failed, obviously, but I think it was one of those guys who created the Full Moon Knights to take down the monarchy, even without having political power behind them."

"And instead, they became a crazy cult," I say.

"Pretty much. Actually, that's exactly what they are. I heard there's some weird blood ritual they do to forever bind themselves to the moon—or something equally unhinged."

"Huh," I murmur, remembering the same milky gray gaze each of the Knights I met the other night possessed. "I wonder if that's why their eyes are like that."

"Their eyes?" Andre asks and I realize he's probably never even seen a Knight for himself. I shudder again and try to shake off the distressing image.

"Nevermind."

Even at this early hour, the green field is littered with students. Most are high school age, but some look to be postgraduates, wrestling with textbooks that weigh more than they do. They look to be studying or conversing with their classmates, but some of the younger kids are playing what looks to be a game of tag in the open space.

One, who I would guess to be a high school freshman, waves to Andre. I've been watching their group in my periphery for a few minutes, but it's only now that I notice that when the person becomes "it" they shift into their animal form. I watch, in awe, as a young boy transforms from a lanky kid with olive skin and oily-dark hair into a snake. He falls about four feet onto the grass and, with a hiss, lunges towards his friends. The girl he slithers up against must be a bakeneko, because she shifts into a Siamese cat. The next kid takes a dog form, and the next, the one who waved to Andre, turns into a monkey. He's small and fluffy, the kind you'd expect to see wearing a top hat in a circus performance—if that sort of thing happens outside of the movies.

I keep watching until I've identified the animal form of nearly everyone in the group, which is how I realize that two of the kids playing don't have animal forms at all. The one girl must be a magus because she doesn't shift and instead manipulates the air around her to reach out and grab the pink-haired boy close enough to her to be tagged. That boy then shifts into a thumb-sized version of himself with delicate, gossamer wings that twinkle in the sunlight.

The game seems to end when another young girl, this one with black hair tied in a tight ponytail, gets tagged. Her friends yell for her to shift with even more enthusiasm than they had for all the others. The girl's cheeks go pink with a furious blush.

"It's not fair!" she complains loudly, but her friends are relentless as they goad her on and laugh. With a defeated sigh, she finally shifts, disappearing completely.

A brown shell falls onto the grass. It lands with a soft *thunk*, and after a long moment, a translucent yellow snail labors out of its hiding place to slink itself forward, millimeter by millimeter.

The students scream in delight and fan out from the sluggish creature. Still, like a good sport, it continues forward, leaving a trail of slime in its torpid wake.

"Sazae-oni," Andre says.

"Bless you?"

He chuckles. "A snail shifter. Snakes are nagas. Dogs are therianthropes. Not all Nagual have their own names. The rest just get 'shifter' tacked onto the end of their animal form."

"What are you?" I ask. I know he's Nagual but not much else. Andre grins, and there is something mischievous about it that has me regretting having asked.

"I'm a boudas," he says, but he doesn't make me wait for an explanation.

When he shifts, my jaw hits the floor.

The creature staring back at me is much smaller than what I would have expected, but it's the familiarity of the form that has me shocked into stillness. Andre is a hyena.

The Lion King prepared me for a mangy creature with mangled fur and wild, clouded eyes, but that image couldn't be further from reality. Andre looks like a cross between a puppy and a cheetah with his dark spots. He has a fox-like tail tucked close to his hind legs and big, soft ears that are slightly pointed at the tips. His tongue hangs as he pants with a smile and his eyes are the same amber brown that I'm growing familiar with.

"No way," I gasp once I can bring myself to speak.

Andre laughs with his mouth wide open. It's a high-pitched chuckle, a uniquely funny sound, and like a contagion, it makes me laugh too. He shifts back in an instant.

"Not what you were expecting?"

"Not at all," I admit.

He winks. "You're at Versi now, chica. You need to get used to the unexpected."

For the next hour, my new friend has me bouncing between the three buildings that will host my classes. There are ten other buildings that encircle the quad, but they only get shoutouts. One serves as a middle school, two make up the high school, and the other eleven are all for Versi University. Behind the Gothic towers are smaller brick buildings in the style of Tudor homes where the schools' administrative offices reside.

"Then there is the preschool and elementary school across the street," Andre tells me, pointing to where we saw all the kids cross earlier that day. I can't actually see the buildings from where we stand between the university's special sciences and literature halls.

"How come the university is so big compared to the other grades? I know not every preternatural family lives on campus, but there can't be that many of us out in the human world, right?"

Andre gives me a pitying look.

"Versi is one of two universities for the preternatural in the entire country," he explains. "Nearly ten thousand Nagual live wherever in the United States and then come to Versi for college. There are less magi and hybrids, but at least a thousand of each here too."

"That many," I say, a bit breathlessly. I honestly wasn't expecting ten thousand across the entire nation, let alone enrolled here with me. I think I had it in my head that Nagual were like the humanoid equivalent of unicorns, but maybe the whole *secret society* thing should have tipped me off.

"More. Versi is kind of small compared to Mayura University in Oregon. And that's not including all the preternatural who don't go to college or go to a human college. Magi and hybrids are harder for us to track in general since a lot of them have their own communities, so we only know how many come to our campuses."

I shake my head. I was planning to do the math, but the equation got away from me with every new nugget of information the Delancey siblings dropped. "Okay, so how many known preternaturals are out there?"

Andre tilts his head thoughtfully. "In the United States or globally?"

"Let's start with the U.S."

"Probably something over three hundred and fifty thousand."

I balk. Three hundred and fifty *thousand* people out there like me. Pretending to be human when they are most definitely not. I can't wrap my head around it. It's a number both scarily huge and uncomfortably small.

Andre points out a few more campus landmarks as we make our way to the library. The Versi Tower sits at the head of the quad and is the tallest of the buildings in the academic quarter. It is of the same architectural design as the rest of them, but this one is somehow grander than the others, making it seem almost like a church rather than a place of learning. There is an oversized clock inlaid in the stone brick. I can feel, more than hear, the loud clicks of every passing minute as I enter what also serves as the university's history hall.

The inside is more casual at least, except for the five stories of a spiraling staircase that leads up towards the clock tower. Andre heads for the stairs, saying that it's the only way to get the full impact of seeing the penthouse library for the first time. I'm out of breath by the time I get to the top though I am glad that we took the stairs. Andre was right, this is the only way I could have truly understood the resplendency of the library.

It's not a penthouse just in the sense that it is the tower's top floor, it's a loft, alcoved in an area that looks like it was meant to be the operational center of the clock tower—if this campus was not powered almost entirely by charms and spells. Though the library itself is quite large, between the massive glass clock faces on the north and south-facing walls and the sheer number of floor-to-ceiling bookshelves in between, it feels cozy.

The walls are painted a color like amber, though it looks different from every angle with the way the light filters in through the glass. Deep burgundy carpets and drapes frame the windows, making the room look like it's radiating warmth. While many of the colossal shelves stand statically, the few where students are browsing shift and rotate in a silent dance.

"Magic," I breathe.

Andre, at my elbow, says, "Nah, just a basic charmed mechanism." I'm about to argue that he's wrong, but then I catch his wink. Not wrong. Just teasing me.

While every part of Versi feels otherworldly to me, this room seems to sparkle with energy. It's a feeling I want to bottle and take tiny sips of every day for the rest of my life. It makes me feel like anything can be possible, and maybe, like it won't be so bad if I do decide to stay.

Like a siren's song, an atrocious painting on a far wall catches my eye. I have to wedge myself between rows of thick wooden tables and chairs to reach it, and yet I find myself surging forward, as if being pulled by a trance. Andre follows dutifully, though he seems only mildly curious about whatever caught my attention.

I'm not an art buff by any means, but my dad had enough interest in history to take me to museums and exhibits when we traveled around. Enough that I recognize this artwork as a William Holbrook Beard.

The one I saw years ago in Indianapolis had a similar uncanny realism despite its surrealistic subject matter. There is a group of men, with the bodies of animals, though they stand upright like humans. They are dressed in old garb: collared shirts with vests and pocket watches. There is a bear, a hare, an otter, a pig, and a fox, standing around an ape wearing a robe and a visor. The ape looks wise and official, like he's leading a lecture. I read now that the placard says *School Rules* and is, in fact, by Beard.

"Are you into art?" Andre asks patiently.

I shake my head. "No, but I've seen his work before. My parents took me to an exhibit, I guess when we were living in Cincinnati." The memories feel disjointed and murky as I try to piece together the timeline, like I was meant to forget them entirely. We were only in Ohio for a couple of months one winter. I remember my parents being on edge the entire time, though they said they didn't like the cold weather. I would guess that it was too close to New England for their comfort, except that we eventually settled in Maryland which was just as far north. I forget why we went at all, only that it had been important to my dad at the time.

"It must have been eight years ago. Or ten? We saw a similar painting there, of a fox," I point to the fox in this painting, "but he was wearing a red robe, like a king, and the other animals seemed to be appealing to him. My parents said the painter was the fox, and I thought they meant figuratively, you know? Like he thought of himself as a king and as clever as a fox. Now, I think they meant it literally."

I reach out my hand as if to touch the brushstrokes and one of those memories flashes in my mind. I had done the same in Indianapolis, but my father grabbed me before I could move an inch, pulling me away from the painting. His roughness startled me. I knew better than to touch, of course, but I hadn't even gotten close. Even to my young mind, it felt like an overreaction from my gentle father. When I looked into his eyes for some sort of understanding, they were full of panic. He surprised me then, and it surprises me now to suddenly remember the scene in perfect clarity.

"Careful where you put your hands, darling. You wouldn't want to lose them." He said it with all the lightness of a joke, but I remember vividly now how startled I had been.

While there's nothing here to prevent me from feeling the embossed paint now, I can't bring myself to try.

I frown at the painting some more. It's strange that it's here. Or, it's strange that I'm remembering seeing a similar painting before when I haven't thought about it once in all this time. But since I've come to Versi—actually since I found out about the Nagual and my parents' role in this world—there has been a clear divide in my mind. My parents, the people I know, do not reconcile with this place and the stories I've heard about them.

Now, for the first time, I can place my parents on this campus, walking these halls, reading from the books in this library. I can see my dad, with his mess of dark curls and wiry glasses, staring at this painting and wondering at Beard's secret meaning for every stroke of paint. I can see my mother, unbothered and ever-vigilant, snaking her arms around his waist, not bothering to see what he sees, knowing she will never understand. I can finally recognize that my parents lived an entire life on this campus that I know nothing about.

My breath is uneven when I turn away. I feel like the bear from the image took a seat on my chest. Even my eyes feel bleary. It's too strong of a reaction to have to an ugly painting, so I try to hide whatever is happening on my face from Andre. I don't need him to see that my heart is breaking in the middle of a public library.

"He was a fox shifter. I think he studied at Versi in the 1840s, or something. I had to take an art history class last semester for a Gen-Ed requirement," Andre says. Then, "Are you hungry? I have a lecture this afternoon but first I need to grab some grub." He pats his very flat stomach with reverence.

"Sure," I say with a smile. I'm determined to shake off whatever it was that gripped me back at the painting. We thankfully take the elevators back down to the ground floor and walk into the bright, late-morning sun.

We're crossing the quad again when I'm suddenly struck with the urge to laugh. I manage to contain it so only an unattractive snort escapes me. To my unending gratitude, Andre sends me a sideways look but doesn't otherwise comment on my odd behavior.

I'm certainly not a stranger to how quickly life can change, but it's almost alarming how fast all of this is starting to feel normal. A strange normal, but normal nonetheless. For a moment there it just felt like I was on my way to grab food with a friend before class, as if everything that I have ever known is not being rewritten.

You're one of us now, Tempest. That's what Jet had said last night. He couldn't have known how much those words would mean to me; how much I have always needed to feel like I was a part of something.

Despite everything, the prospect of being a part of this world, being surrounded by people who were like me and eager to bring me into the fold, has been a silver lining that I never dared to hope for.

16

JET

The fist comes directly at my head with the force of a professional boxer. Still, I dodge the blow with ease and throw back my own hit with the same tenacity.

"It doesn't make any sense," I complain with a strained voice. It's punctuated by the smack of Brody's palm coming up to block my fist, grabbing my hand, and twisting back in a way that could have broken a bone if I wasn't so experienced in hand-to-hand combat. Instead, I shift my weight and jut my elbow forward, right into Brody's stomach. He grunts loudly and releases me. We both reset to go again.

Brody and I like to train outside of the physical curriculum set by our co-op program, though we usually do it in the mornings. On Wednesdays we have an early class, the only one that the two of us share, so training in the evening works better. Most days we spar in our animal forms, or sometimes we take advantage of the unique weaponry that the LOP has on hand for that purpose. Sword fighting had been our favorite activity over the summer even though it is all but useless in a real-life scenario. We haven't touched the blunt swords stocked in the training room at all this week. I know for me, training doesn't feel like a fun exercise anymore. It feels immensely important. So that's why we are brushing up on practical hand-to-hand.

That, and after the news I received this afternoon, I really need to hit something.

"How could the Baltimore field office not manage to find *anything*?" I complain. "The Full Moon Knights are lycanthrope, not ghosts. They can't just disappear."

I make another swing for Brody and this time my fist does land, clipping his left shoulder. I'd bet anything that Brody let me make contact on purpose, knowing I need to let off steam, though I ignore that suspicion and revel in the release.

Brody's been updating me on the hunt for the Full Moon Knights via text since our class ended this morning, but each update has been more unsatisfying than the last. According to the Baltimore field office, who combed Crescentwood for hours after we left with Tempest the night of the attack, there were no tracks or traces of the Knights left to follow. There was no paper trail either. No local hotels, airports, or rental car agencies turned up any record of a connection to the Knights, or anything else out of the ordinary.

There wasn't a shred of evidence on Full Moon Knight activity in the greater Baltimore area either. No recent petty crimes that can be tied to an initiation or any other activity that the LOP can come to expect after a few quiet months. It was like those wolves made the trip to Maryland to see Tempest and nothing else—which may not be so strange in itself, given that they did the same four years ago with Tempest's parents—but the Knights had to know to find Tempest there. The timing of it couldn't have been coincidental, not when I was the one who uncovered Tempest's connection to our world only a few hours before.

So how did the Knights know to materialize in the exactly right place at the exactly right time?

"Isn't this their whole schtick," Brody asks, setting himself up to take yet another hit. Really, I should have suggested we train in the gym today instead of using my best friend as my personal punching bag. "They show up out of the blue, make a mess of things, then disappear into their dens again."

I know the Full Moon Knights are good at covering their tracks, there's a reason why the LOP hasn't been able to apprehend them all these years, but this is something else.

I rub my eyes. It's enough of a distraction that I miss Brody setting himself up on the offensive. He lunges forward in one flawless bound and then his knee is jutting up and into my gut. I grunt loudly, surprised by the force of his blow, though Brody is not apologetic in the least. I wouldn't want him to be. If I can't handle my attention being diverted, then I deserve every bit of pain inflicted by my lack of focus. In a real fight, my opponents would never be so courteous, so it would be a mistake to train that way.

I can't easily accept Brody's explanation, though. Someone should be able to find them, and someone really needs to.

My train of thought is derailed by the appearance of another cadet in the training area. Alejandra Vargas spots Brody and I on one of the training center's sparring mats and races towards us. Her wavy brown hair is pulled back in its usual pony and her face is flushed like she just ran from the fourth floor.

"So?" she demands.

"Hello to you too, Al," Brody says, starting to unwrap his hands. "How was your weekend? Mine was great. Thank you so much for asking."

"Is she here or not?" she asks, crossing her arms and

scowling at him. She goes by Ale, not Al, something that Brody is very aware of and simply chooses to ignore to get a rise out of her.

"Here as in Versi or here as in HQ?"

With an exasperated sigh, she gives up on Brody and looks at me.

"She's staying at my house," I tell her.

"In my room," Brody complains.

"It hasn't been your room in two years," I say, shaking my head. I look back at Ale. "He's just upset because Tempest doesn't like him."

He rolls his eyes. "You don't *know* that."

"Right, well she isn't fawning over him yet and Brody is taking the rejection personally," I say with a smirk.

"Aw, poor Brody's little feelings are hurt," Ale teases, her face lit up with a delighted grin.

"Tempest is welcome to her poor taste," Brody says diplomatically, but then he coughs dramatically and nods his head in my direction. Ale's eyes go wide. I intervene before she can get the wrong idea about Brody's childish retaliation.

"Have you heard anything about the Queen's arrival?" I ask her. Brody heard a rumor this morning that the queen will be making the trip to Versi while she's still stateside to meet Tempest. Since I'm assuming Ale just came from upstairs, I'm hoping she has more insight.

"Saturday," she says. "They're trying to decide if Tempest should meet her at HQ or at the amphitheater."

Brody wrinkles his nose. I can tell he wants to say something, something he probably shouldn't, so I'm glad when the sound of the door interrupts.

"And here is the LOPHQ training center," I hear a familiar voice call out a moment before I see Andre step through the door. Tempest in tow, her eyes going wide as she takes in the expanse of the room.

Alejandra perks up immediately, but Brody pouts—which is dramatic, even for him. I cross my arms over my chest.

"I didn't realize your tour was going to be this thorough," I call out to Andre. He and Tempest turn my way. Andre bounds over on his light footfalls.

"Gotta make sure Tempest knows everything Versi has to offer," he says brightly. He wraps his arm around Ale's shoulder. "Hola, hermosa," he tells her.

"Get off me," she answers with a scowl. Andre raises his hands and takes a half step away, though his grin never falters. Really, Andre and Ale are good friends, it's just that she's about as cuddly as a scorpion.

"What is all this?" Tempest asks as she joins us. She's still looking around the room like she's not sure what to make of it. The large space serves many functions. Navy mats cover half of the floor with five different sections that are taped off for sparring. To the left are rows of exercise equipment and weight racks that look pretty similar to a standard gym. On the far wall is a case of weapons for practice and a rock-climbing wall with five routes rated from 5.8 to 5.12.

I want to laugh. Of course, she takes all the strangeness of shapeshifters in stride but a training facility is what finally gives her pause.

"This is where we hone our badassery," Brody says with a wink. Tempest's eyes widen.

"Ignore him," Ale says, nudging him with her elbow to offer Tempest her hand. "I'm Alejandra and I'm a freshman in the co-op program with these idiots. This is where all protectors train, but us especially since our curriculum has a lot of physical components."

"Train?" she asks. "Like self-defense?"

"Sure. Among other things." Ale nods to the weaponry case.

Tempest looks from me to Andre. "Is that something I can do? Learn self-defense?"

I panic for the length of a single heartbeat, bile churning in my gut as I remember Tempest laying bloody and broken on the side of the road. A protective instinct tells me that I have to keep Tempest away from danger, even if it's simulated.

"That's a great idea," I force out in spite of my more primal nature's impulse. It is a great idea. Sure, Tempest shouldn't ever be put in the position of having to protect herself again, but it will give her some peace of mind if nothing else.

"Yeah, I have all kinds of moves I can teach you," Andre says, ducking low and throwing a couple of punches into the open air. Something white and hot flares in my periphery before I become cognizant of Andre's jovial tone and playful stature. Though it flashes again when Tempest laughs, hiding her lips behind her hand. Andre lunges, but for Alejandra instead, catching her off guard. He flips the short girl over his shoulder. Ale goes beet red as she pounds on Andre's back.

"Let down or I swear to the Universe that I will peck out your eyes and eat your entrails!"

Ale may be full of empty threats, but as a harpy, she is more than capable of doing both of those things with the proper motivation. Also knowing this, Andre drops her again.

"Come on, chica. I'm showing Tempest the rest of the business district and I can't name half the buildings over here, so you're joining us."

"Fine," Ale concedes, fixing her ponytail with a frown. "But I'm doing it for Tempest, not you, pendejo."

They head for the door again. Tempest sends a nervous half-smile in mine and Brody's direction before following.

When they leave, I turn to Brody who is dramatically fluttering his eyelashes at me.

"You're jealous," he accuses.

"Am not," I lie.

"Are too. I bet that was going to be your line. 'I have *all kinds* of moves I can teach you.'"

"You're a *pendejo*," I say, shaking my head as I move out of his range. I keep going towards the door that leads to the outdoor courtyard of the LOPHQ. There is a bin of sports equipment there filled with volleyballs, basketballs, and rackets. I snag one of the tennis balls from the pile and, despite now standing more than sixty feet away, chuck it at the back of Brody's head.

"Ow!" I hear him shout as I push through the doors and out into the fading twilight. It puts me in better spirits.

I'm back in the training center on Saturday, which is when it occurs to me that this has been the longest week of my life. It seems impossible that it was only seven days ago that I met Tempest and everything in our lives flipped on its head. Being back at Versi helped reinstate a sense of normalcy, but somehow that hasn't made me feel better. It's hard to trust in normalcy when there are still so many unknowns and no direction for us to find answers.

It's starting to feel like everyone at the LOP has given up on finding the Full Moon Knights and discovering how they could have known to go after Tempest, which doesn't sit well with me. I'm hoping that I'll learn something new when the director briefs the queen on the investigation today, but if there was anything groundbreaking, I'd already know by now.

While I do train several times a week, I'm rarely by myself. Last night, I couldn't sleep so I got up at dawn to head over to the LOPHQ to work off some of my restless energy in solitude. Nearly two hours later, I'm in the locker room ready to hit the showers when I run into Lieutenant Caro. He has a sweatband pushing back his salt-and-pepper hair, a look that I can say I never expected to see on my superior. There is a pickleball paddle on the bench beside him which tells me that he and I had similar ideas of how to spend our morning.

He's going to be at the meeting with the queen as well, as the LOP's expert on the Full Moon Knights, with him having been lead on several of their cases over the last twenty-some-thing years.

"I can't tell if you've had a good morning or a bad one," he says in greeting, nodding at my shirt that is soaked through with sweat.

"Just getting as much training in as I can, sir," I say.

"Good man." For a moment, he looks content to leave the conversation at that, taking a step towards the individual shower stalls, but then he hangs back. "You know, a lot of the officers are impressed with the work you did to find and safely recover Ms. Maverick."

A balloon of pride swells in my chest from the unexpected praise.

I've always liked Lieutenant Caro. I don't know him well, but he's more laid back than a lot of the other officers. He's done a lot of impressive work over the years that we've studied in some of my lectures. The Full Moon Knight cases notwithstanding, since they seem to be an enigma for the entire organization.

"Thank you, sir," I say, "but it was more of a coincidence than anything."

He shakes his head. "I'm not of the belief that there are coincidences in this world. The Universe has a plan for all of us. All we can do is rise to the occasion." He winks and I give him a polite smile in reply.

His opinion is one that a lot of preternaturals share, but I'm not sure that I do. Thanks to the melting-pot nature of our culture, there is no single theology that we follow, but we do believe in a force that controls all things. The Universe, we call it, for lack of any better term. No one knows if it's a single being, a group of deities, or simply an energetic force that imposes its will on us in the pursuit of maintaining the world's natural balance. Some people take comfort in thinking that everything in life is predetermined, but I have to believe that we are still responsible for the choices we make. Otherwise, what is the point of all of this?

"If you're ever looking to do some extracurricular investigative work, you come to me," Caro continues. "I'm always looking for new talent to take under my wing."

He heads off, leaving me to my own devices. I'm glad about it since I'm smiling as I wonder how soon I can approach him about doing exactly that without seeming too eager.

The LOPHQ is always quiet on the weekends but it's rarely empty. This morning is no exception. In fact, it's busier than usual and I notice quite a few of my classmates hanging around, trying hard to look busy. I'm sure they're all hoping to get a glimpse of the queen. I catch Ale's eye from across the cubicle floor and wave.

"No Brody?" she mouths at me. I shake my head. Brody is

usually unavailable over the weekend, at a party, on a date, or whatever it is he's been up to lately. I'd ask him, but it's hard to keep up with the names of all the girls.

I only get a few minutes at the cubicle cluster that all the co-op program students of my year share before my dad leaves his office on the wall behind me. "Ready, Cadet Delancey?" he asks.

"Yes, sir," I say.

We head up to the sixth floor, the LOPHQ's top floor, where the director's office resides. There is a plush reception area that I must admit is fit for receiving a queen. My father directs me to a conference room on the far side of the space. Lieutenant Caro is already seated at the shiny black conference table behind the glass walls, but the director is nowhere in sight.

"She's escorting the queen up now," he says by way of explanation as I take the seat across from him.

Only a moment later, the elevator dings, and all three of us jump to our feet. Director Sanchez is the first to step out, her red-brown hair clipped up into her usual subdued style. She's fairly young to be a director, a few years younger than my father even, but her air of authority leaves no room to question her fitness for the role. According to my father, the LOP has flourished under her direction over the last several years. She's stern but fair. She is confident and unyielding at times, but empathetic and adaptable. The few times she and I have interacted directly, she made me feel like an equal, not a lowly student. It was that, more than anything else, that garnered my unwavering respect.

"Your Majesty," she says, gesturing for the queen to go ahead of her into the reception area.

But it's not the queen who steps out behind her. First is a

tall, stern-faced man with close-cropped hair wearing an all-black uniform that is not all that dissimilar to ours. Next comes the queen. She's a few inches shorter than the director but she projects an aura of majesty that is unmistakable. She is flanked by an expressionless woman in a too-tight pantsuit and an even tighter bun, clinging to an iPad. The last one out of the elevator is another man, short, broad, and thick with the overhead lights gleaming off of his dark, bald head. These men must be the queen's royal guards.

The guards always start their careers off as protectors, or at least by graduating from the law and protection program at either Versi, Mayura, or one of the European universities. Since there are so few of them, there is no official program or application process. The queen hand picks her guards, and only when one is planning to retire. The whole process is shrouded in mystery, which makes me even more interested in what their training entails. I only know as much as I do because of Brody's father, who for years was part of her guard before his mother got sick and he was reassigned.

Director Sanchez escorts the group to the conference room. My dad and Caro bow when the queen enters, and I hastily follow their lead. Up close, it's clear that she is an older woman, though her fair skin is completely devoid of wrinkles. She uses a cane—or perhaps it's more applicable to call it a staff since she seems to need no help walking—made of a deep cherry wood. The handle is ornately carved into the shape of a peacock with its feathers tucked back. Small gems of blue, purple, and green shine from the eyes of the engraved feathers.

"Allow me to present some of my best officers. This is Lieutenant Caro, Lieutenant Delancey, and Cadet Delancey. He is the one who discovered Tempest Maverick last week and is currently enrolled at Versi University for our law and protection program."

"It's a great pleasure," Queen Madeline says with an ethereal tone. The director has the queen sit at the head of the table, almost opposite to where I sit down at the other end. The woman who came with her takes the seat to her right, and the director, to my surprise, takes the seat to her left rather than the other head like I would have expected. It's a move of clear deference that I find admirable.

"Where is the girl?" the queen asks before the meeting can start. My stomach flips at the sudden hardness of her voice.

"I asked Ms. Maverick to join us at the top of the hour. I figured we'd want some time to debrief with you before she joins us."

My nerves bristle at the mention of Tempest's name. Despite her living in the room almost directly across from mine, I haven't seen her much the rest of this week. My schedule has been just as busy as I usually keep it, and she has been starting classes and adjusting to the new campus. I didn't get the chance to ask her how she's handling all of it. Or how she feels about meeting the queen—her grandmother—for the first time.

"I was told that she has undergone her shift. What manner of Nagual does she claim to be?"

Next to me, my father clears his throat. "It is unknown at this point, Your Grace. Only the Full Moon Knights were present to witness her Blood Rite and Ms. Maverick has not shifted again since."

The queen hums discontentedly.

The director, quick to placate, dives into a carefully prepared presentation of the events that lead to the discovery of Tempest, and her subsequent attack by the Full Moon Knights.

I'm asked to speak about my identification of her, citing how I followed her trace, which my instincts told me had been tampered with. I speak with cool confidence, practiced over the last several days. I'm glad it was decided to host the queen here at the LOPHQ, where I feel like I'm on home turf, rather than in the formal amphitheater. As I speak, the queen's brown eyes watch me acutely. I can't tell what she's thinking, but it's surreal to have her attention at all.

Next, my father takes over the explanation of the case to locate the Knights following their attack. The queen asks several clarifying questions that all the officers take turns addressing. The most sensitive of which is when she asks if we are sure her daughter, Melanie Maverick, is dead. My father is the one to answer, though the queen's expression is carefully neutral as he confirms that both Melanie and Gregor were killed by the Full Moon Knights four years ago.

Lieutenant Caro is just starting to tell her about the road-blocks we're facing in the pursuit of the Knights when the elevator dings. The doors creak open, seeming to suck all the air out of the room. Tempest enters the reception area, being led by Agent Boyd, who works the front desk of the lobby. He gestures for Tempest to head our way, which she does stiffly.

She's nervous. I can tell from the way her eyes scan the room, as if looking for a threat. Her gaze only meets mine for a moment, but then it sharpens as it lands on the queen. Tempest says nothing as she takes the seat at the opposite head of the table, facing the queen. My heart starts to race. I'm suddenly unsure if having her in this meeting is a good idea.

"Granddaughter," the queen greets cooly. "You look so much like your mother." Despite the sentiment, her tone is far from warm.

"I get that a lot," Tempest replies. She's more nervous than I've ever seen her, though she is hiding it under a mask of calm.

The queen's lips pull back in an expression I think is meant to be a smile, though it looks more like a grimace. "I've heard much about you this week."

"Likewise," Tempest replies, her tone unreadable. There is a round of panicked looks between all the protectors at the table.

The director clears her throat. "Thank you for joining us, Ms. Maverick. We were just updating the queen about the progress we've made following the events of last weekend."

Tempest immediately perks up, meeting Director Sanchez's eye. "You've tracked down the Full Moon Knights?"

"Not yet," Sanchez says cautiously. "However, there has been a development in the case that initially warranted the arrest of your parents." Her eyes meet the queen's. "It seems that the circumstances around Melanie's own attack were not what we once believed." Again, she nods to my father to speak.

"Daria Payne, who was Melanie's partner when they started their careers at the LOP, was a lycanthrope. It is still unclear if she was initiated by the Full Moon Knights officially, but we have found evidence to suggest that Shamus Payne, her brother, was in league with them. He was one of the Knights identified at the queen's assassination attempt twenty-four years ago, though he was in our records under an alias. We believe that Daria doctored the paperwork to prevent us from connecting him back to her.

"Motives for the attack are still unclear, but given the Payne's association with the Full Moon Knights, who murdered Melanie and Gregor, and now made an attempt on Tempest's life, we are confident that Melanie Maverick and Gregor Candor should be exonerated of their charges. The evidence suggests that the deaths of the Paynes were in self-defense. We recognize that this does very little now, but it is important their names are cleared of wrongdoing given the new information."

Again, the queen is unemotional as she digests this. I can't decide if it's impressive or unnerving.

"But why would they run in the first place?" Tempest asks, surprising everyone by speaking out.

I find myself scanning her face, looking for any sign of emotion. Strangely, her lack of it is the only commonality I can see between her and her grandmother. They look almost nothing alike, but their steely resolve to seem strong in the face of adversity is like a mirror image.

"I'm sorry?" the queen asks, not seeming sorry at all.

Tempest meets her eyes, unwavering. "My parents were fleeing Versi before the Knights attacked."

"You can't know that," the queen says dismissively.

"Of course I can. I was the one who spent the majority of my life on the run with them."

"They were running from the Full Moon Knights. This is known."

"No," Tempest insists, and there is a crack in her armor. Anger, or frustration at least, is starting to shine through. I find my hand reaching out below the table and catching hers. Her fingers latch onto mine like a vice, gripping tightly. Her skin is unnaturally warm, like the fire of her passion is eating her alive. "If it was only the Knights they were running from, they would have told the LOP the truth of what happened. Daria worked with my mother for years, it doesn't make sense that she would attack her out of the blue. Something had to instigate the attack. It only makes sense that my parents were leaving already."

"That's a really interesting point," my dad agrees, giving Tempest a sideways glance. He seems impressed, and I feel a small jolt of pride at that.

The queen, on the other hand, has cracked her armor too. Her nostrils flare with anger and I can tell by the way the tension in the room has ratcheted up that this break in carefully crafted demeanor is atypical for our monarch. Still, her voice is all cool formality as she says, "I'd recommend that you do not speak on matters of which you cannot understand."

Tempest does not seem keen to argue the point any further. She turns her attention away from the queen, which could be seen as an insult in itself, though the queen is thankfully too distracted to see it that way. She is standing then, the woman with her acting as her shadow. "Elena, be so kind as to see us out. The Prime Minister is expecting me in Yorkshire in the morning and I see no reason to delay."

"Of course," the director says, getting to her feet.

The queen casts one last apathetic look at her granddaughter. Her first guard steps out in front of her as if to protect her from the danger of the empty reception area. "You cannot shift at will yet. I find that most irregular for a Nagual of your age," she says.

It sounds like an accusation. Tempest must hear it too because her fingers are crushing mine again.

"I've had quite an irregular life," Tempest says with a smile that doesn't meet her eyes.

The queen purses her lips and a moment later, she's gone, disappearing into the elevator shaft, and descending to the ground floor with her entourage in tow, leaving only a tense silence behind.

Only Caro seems in good spirits, sending a curious look in

Tempest's direction. "I suppose I shouldn't be surprised that you're so much like your mother."

Tempest doesn't reply. Her eyes are glassy, and she takes a second to blink away the tears.

Caro dismisses himself, leaving only me, my dad, and Tempest behind.

"Your mother's relationship with the queen was always... contentious," my dad offers seemingly in explanation for Queen Madeline's coldness. "Melanie never wanted to be the ruler of the preternatural world, but her mother prized their royal heritage above all else. Melanie resented it. When Melanie abdicated her claim to the throne, whatever fragile peace remained between them was severed. I'm disappointed that the queen would hold your mother's action against you, Tempest, but I suppose I cannot be surprised."

"She doesn't owe me anything," Tempest says hollowly.

"You two are family," my dad says, though I'm not sure if he means for the sentiment to be reassuring to Tempest or reproving of the queen. I'd be surprised. The queen may not be very visible in our day-to-day life at Versi, but she is a very well-respected figurehead. To go against her is to go against everything we stand for. I can't imagine any friendship with Melanie Maverick could have changed my father's opinion on that.

I release Tempest's hand, though I let my knuckles brush her thigh before I stand. She looks up at me, her marbled eyes looking heartbreakingly fragile for the first time since I've known her. She looks back at my dad and climbs to her feet.

"No, we're not. We're strangers."

❧ 17 ❧

TEMPEST

"**D**amn, girl. You can pack a punch," Andre says as his mitts take yet another blow. I slam my fist one more time, for good measure.

We're in the training center nearly an hour after my meeting with my grandmother. Andre and I agreed to start training today, I just didn't anticipate how badly I'd need to let off steam.

I didn't have enough time to develop any sort of expectations around the meeting, and there is obviously an extra layer of weirdness at play with the fact that my grandmother is the ruler of an entire world I am just starting to understand, but the experience was so much more disappointing than I could have imagined. I thought that I would feel some sort of connection to her given that she is the last living member of my mother's side of the family. Instead, I felt like I should be apologizing for my mere existence. That piece of the conversation I am willing to pack away into a neat little box to deal with much further down the road, however, I can't understand her apathy towards learning the truth about what happened to my mom.

I still may not know all the details of how my parents came to be on the run, but my mother was the queen's daughter. She was once her heir to the throne. Queen Madeline could have done *something* to help her. If they did just leave Versi out of fear of the Knights, she could have stopped the LOP's manhunt. And once the truth of Daria Payne's attack was brought to light, she could have had the LOP protect my parents, like they're doing for me now. The fact that she didn't tells me everything I need to know about my grandmother.

I could give the queen the benefit of the doubt and believe that my mom never gave her the opportunity to help. But then, the fact my mom would rather go on the run than go to her own mother speaks volumes.

I don't like her. Worse than that, I don't trust her. If she's the last family I have left, I think I'd rather be alone.

I send Andre a weak smile. "Sorry, I have a lot on my mind."

Andre shrugs before starting to strip off the mitts.

"No worries. You've had a supremely weird week. Anything I can help with, chica?" He grabs for the pair of water bottles we perched on the countertop by the wall. He tosses one to me and I catch it easily.

I snort out a laugh as I put the water bottle to my lips. After taking a sip, I say, "Not unless you can tell me how my grandmother can rule the entirety of the preternatural world but can't find the people who killed her own daughter. Or why the Full Moon Knights seem like these infallible foes." I throw my hands up in frustration.

"I want to know why my parents were fleeing and why Daria Payne and her brother took such drastic measures to stop them. I want to know if that's the reason why they kept us hidden from the rest of the preternatural world for all those years, or if there was some other sort of danger entirely. And I think, most of all, I need to know how my parents managed to have me."

Andre frowns. "What do you mean?"

I let out a sigh, but it comes out more like a huff.

"It's just that people keep saying that it's impossible for my parents to have conceived me, and yet no one but the Full Moon Knights seem all that concerned that they did. And I get it, I guess. This is a magical campus, and my dad was particularly skilled with magic, there's bound to be some gray area. I think I just need some sort of clarity before I can start to accept how truly weird all of this is."

I run my free hand against my forehead, feeling suddenly exhausted by my outburst. I didn't mean to give so much of my frustration away. I anxiously meet Andre's eye, expecting him to be uncomfortable, or at least uninterested in my rant, but he's watching with a sympathetic smile. It's somehow different from the pitying looks I'm so used to receiving from the people around me. The ones who want to be "nice" but also don't want to get too close in case tragedy turns out to be a contagious affliction.

"Okay, I definitely can't give you the answers to any of that, but I do know where you can find some."

"Where?" I ask with a frown. I really hope that if there was some sort of magical database that could tell me everything about preternatural history, as well as my own, that someone would have hooked me up on my first day.

"The library," Andre says, like it's obvious. Which to be fair, it should have been. Libraries may not be quite as magical as Google, but once upon a time, they were *the place* to go for research.

"You think the answers to my questions will be there?"

"Sure. The library has all kinds of books on charms, spells, and potions. Our newspaper gets archived there too. You can probably find out more about your parents and the Full Moon Knights from those than a textbook. Even if we don't, you'll probably learn a lot from us looking. Besides, it would be fun."

I narrow my eyes on my new friend. "I'm supposed to believe that you would find after-school study sessions fun?"

Andre stammers back with a gasp, dramatically clutching at his heart. "You doubt my scholastic prowess!" he accuses, his tone dripping with melodrama.

I laugh. "I just think you have better things to do with your free time."

"Just the opposite. Befriending the mysterious—and potentially dangerous—" he waggles his eyebrows, "new girl has only made me more intriguing to my lady admirers."

I play-punch his shoulder. His serious facade falls away into one of his signature wide-mouth grins.

"Are there lady admirers?" I ask with narrowed eyes.

To my shock, Andre blushes. "Maybe one."

"Tell me everything," I insist. His blush deepens, making me laugh. I know Andre to be nothing but a jokester so seeing him so flustered has joy bubbling in my chest.

"There's not much to tell," he says mildly, suddenly busying himself with putting the gear away and packing up his bag. I follow suit, allowing him his few moments of shyness. "Her name is Lacey, but I don't know her that well yet. We're supposed to be going out this weekend."

With everything packed away, we head towards the door and walk up the single flight of steps up to the LOPHQ's lobby.

"Fine, I'll withhold my interrogation for now."

"Thank you. Want to hit the library after class on Monday?"

"Absolutely," I say, smiling at him. He slings his arm over my shoulder, giving it a friendly squeeze as we enter the lobby. It seems to be a subtle sign that he's got my back, and I gratefully lean into his embrace.

❧ 18 ❧
JET

Tempest is alone in the kitchen when I finally get home. I hesitate in the doorway for a moment too long, debating if I should sneak up to my room or give in to my growling stomach.

After the meeting with the queen, I went to my dad's office to listen in on the debrief between him, Caro, and the director. None of them were happy about the lack of answers they were able to provide, but none of them could decide on a clear path forward, either. With all of the LOP's resources and our natural capabilities, it's rare for investigations to drag out like this, though that has always been the case where the Full Moon Knights are concerned. As a general rule, protectors follow the evidence. In this case, where there really isn't any, we're not just at an impasse, we're at a cliff's edge.

I spent the rest of my day shadowing agents at HQ, trying to get a sense of their investigative process and secretly hoping that I'd come up with an idea for a new path we could pursue. In the end, the only thing I can be sure of is that going twelve hours without eating makes me extraordinarily grumpy.

Tempest is also having a late dinner, some sort of pasta dish she is eating out of the glass left-over container. She's more sullen than I've seen her to date. Quiet seems to be her default, but there's usually an obvious ember of fire in her. Tonight, it's like that fire's been winked out, which makes my chest tighten uncomfortably.

I don't like the feeling. I don't like that I care so much. It's not that I want to be impartial to her, it's that I can't seem to stop myself from getting sucked into her orbit, and that lack of control is unnerving.

As much as I want to see the Full Moon Knights apprehended for all their various crimes, I'd be lying to say that the urge to protect her, to keep her safe, hasn't been my strongest instinct this week.

Brody is right that I'm jealous, but I'm also grateful that Andre took up the mantle of being the one to train her in self-defense. She's already been a dangerous distraction. I don't think I could trust myself to be even closer to her. And yet, I find myself heading into the kitchen to face her before I make the conscious decision to do it.

"Hey," she says, sounding a little surprised by my arrival.

I let my gaze glance over her, as if I hadn't just been studying her in the shadows. "Long day?" I ask as I open the fridge door across from where she sits at the kitchen island. There is another container of pasta waiting, a perfect portion that my mom likely left for me.

She lets out a hollow laugh. "You could say that. You?"

I nod. "And they keep getting longer."

Tempest laughs again and my chest contracts further. I don't even bother heating up my meal. I just pop off the lid and stand on the opposite side of the counter from Tempest. It's stupid that I'm refusing to get comfortable by eating beside her, as if that will somehow counteract how comfortable I instinctively feel in her presence.

"How have your classes been so far?" I ask, immediately glad that I did when the corner of her lips kick up into a small smile.

"It's actually been kind of amazing. Your mom pulled some strings so I'm taking a couple of college-level courses. I'll need some time to catch up in alchemy but I'm really liking Theoretical Preternatural Principals. Did you know that Hercules was a Nagual?" she asks. I shake my head. "A lot of the heroes and monsters from Greek mythology are. Satyrs—those are the half-goat half-human things—are Nagual too. They were often depicted anthropomorphically, but it was really an artistic representation of their Nagual ability, sometimes human, sometimes animal, that got misinterpreted in history."

"I know about satyrs. We have them on campus."

Tempest's eyes widen, the trajectory of her fork stopping just shy of her gaping mouth. "You're kidding."

I chuckle. "I'm not, but I don't understand how that means Hercules was Nagual too."

"Well, if Greek mythology was full of Nagual: satyrs, harpies, centaurs, and maybe even the minotaur, then it stands to reason that Hercules could have been one as well. The story goes that he slayed a lion and then wore its pelt, making him nearly invincible in battle, but if you can believe that Hercules was a lion shifter then it would actually explain his depictions with the pelt and his superhuman abilities that made people believe he was a demigod, like his speed and strength."

"Great Universe," I say, shaking my head. I'm watching Tempest with fresh eyes. "I can't believe I didn't see it before."

"See what?" she demands. That fire that I've grown accustomed to is kindling again.

"You're a nerd."

Her cheeks flush pink. "I am not! It's just that I like those stories. I like to read, and researching all this is fun."

"You're as bad as Kage," I accuse, making her blush deepen.

"Do you miss him?" she asks, her voice soft.

I nod, and it's only then that I realize how much. "He's my best friend, I mean, besides Brody. The three of us have been inseparable since we were kids, or we had been until Kage started traveling all the time. Like I said, he's a huge nerd, always had his head in books, but then he woke up one day and it was like he wanted to experience as much life as possible, all at once. He did an exchange program with Mayura during his senior year of high school and has studied abroad nearly every semester since."

Tempest is quiet for a long moment. Her focus is pinned on the fork she's twirling in linguini strands. "Is it stupid that I'm even jealous of you missing your brother? I know it must be hard for you, but at least you know he'll come home eventually."

I guessed that her somber mood had a lot to do with her meeting her grandmother this morning, but I didn't realize exactly how it was affecting her. I appreciate that she's confiding in me now.

I duck my head so that I meet her eyes. Reluctantly they flitter up to mine.

"It's not stupid. But you still have family."

She presses her eyes closed for a second longer than she needs to blink.

"I know. And I have been talking to my aunt, not quite like normal but as close as I think we can get to it right now. I think that's part of the reason why I'm still so mad at her though. She's all I have left and yet she sent me away."

"I get it," I say. "Or I can understand where you're coming from, at least. But I can understand her perspective too. You're all *she* has left, and sending you away was the only way to ensure you would be safe." I don't say that I relate more to her Aunt Laura than I do to Tempest. Even knowing how Tempest feels about it, and how it violated her trust. I would have made the same decision had I been in the same position, even knowing it wasn't mine to make.

Tempest is quiet again until she finally gets to her feet. She comes around the corner to rinse her container and stick it in the dishwasher. I finish my last few bites and then do the same. We maneuver around each other easily, and it feels strangely domestic in the quiet kitchen with only the dim lighting from under the cabinets illuminating the space.

A part of me hopes that Tempest will just head to bed without saying anything more, and for a second, I think she will as she steps towards the doorway, but she turns back to me with only a couple of feet between us.

"Thank you," she says, meeting my eyes. I give a curt nod in reply, though I don't move my gaze. She swallows hard before turning to leave again.

I don't expel my breath until I hear the creak of the stair third from the top, the only one that ever makes a noise. I'm once again glad that she's the one to walk away. I don't know that I would be strong enough to do it.

❧ 19 ❧
TEMPEST

The Grove stands alone, covered by a spattering of
trees. It's a squat log cabin that seems out of place on
the Versi campus. With colorful stained glass
window hangings and tinkling wind chimes, the bustling cafe
looks almost as if it was erected in a fairy forest and not twenty
yards from the academic quarter.

On Monday afternoon, every table, both inside and out on
the wrap-around porch, is overcrowded with students
pretending to do homework while they snack on pastries and
sip confectionery beverages.

I'm exhausted after the long day of classes, and being in
such an over-stimulating environment is the last thing I want
to do, but I promised Andre I would meet him here, so I
battled my way into a corner booth. Now I'm managing my
exhaustion with a hazelnut latte and a serving of pain au
chocolat that looks suspiciously like the face of a panda bear.

I jump in surprise when Andre slides onto the bench across
from me. Even though I've been waiting for him to come over
from the LOPHQ, I'm on edge. Most of my day I've been

gawked at, but I feel on full display here. It's always like this when I change schools, so I knew to expect the curious gazes, but this time there is an edge to it. Curiosity is still here, but there's also an unsettling feeling of being known. These students, and even some of my new teachers and the school staff, look at me like they know I'm a ticking time bomb, and they're morbidly fascinated to witness when I'll go off.

"Hola, chica," Andre says. He leans over and tears the face right off of my panda pain au chocolat. "How was class today?"

"Long," I say. "Is it weird that I get alchemy so much better than chemistry, even though I still don't really get it at all?"

"Of course not," he says while chewing. He swallows his bite. "You're hard-wired for the preternatural. But you should probably check out a book on alchemy basics at the library today to get you up to speed. Ready to head over?"

I nod and start packing up the homework I had been blankly staring at while nursing my coffee. The table jostles as someone bumps into it with a force that has to be deliberate.

"Dirty abomination," a stranger snarls under their breath. I wince, and not just from the hateful tone. That word, *abomination*, is one that I've heard snarled at me before. The Full Moon Knights had said it, and while I don't understand the context any better now, it's alarming all the same. It makes the hair on the back of my neck stand on end.

I whip my head around, looking for the culprit, but they're lost in the crowd of people. At a table across the way, there is a girl openly frowning at me with such obvious disdain that I'm almost certain she knows what just happened, and whose side she's on. Andre must have heard too because he's staring down a lanky kid that I recognize from one of my classes this morning with murder in his eyes.

"Let's go," he says, more serious than I've seen him before.

I hurriedly shove the textbook into my bag and scurry behind him out the door.

"Why abomination?" I ask as we approach the busy quad.

"It's just a nasty insult," he says, still more brusquely than I'm used to.

"Yeah, but why do they think I'm one?" I press. I understand the definition of the word, it means to be vile or abhorred, but I honestly can't understand why someone would say it to me. And the way it was said, both by the guy in the cafe and the Full Moon Knights back in Maryland, makes it sound like it's more than just a creative adjective.

Andre sighs. "You know how you were saying the other day that it doesn't seem like people care that your parents were not meant to conceive you?" I nod. "Well, some people care. A lot. That guy is Kent, he's part of Nixie Cabrera's clique. She thinks she's hot shit because she's in one of Versi's founding families, and she's one of those who makes it clear she preferred how the school was when her ancestors founded it."

"You mean when it was exclusively for Nagual."

"Yup," Andre says with a frown. "People used to call hybrids 'abominations' and said that they were a perversion of nature—which is so wrong, for so many reasons. Thankfully, not many people use it anymore, but clearly Ken and Nixie are the exception."

My feelings clearly aren't hurt over some stranger's ignorant comment, but it's interesting that anyone would lump me in with hybrids. "But I'm Nagual."

"Of course you are," Andre agrees. The door to Versi Hall is already open wide so we pass right through. "But your dad's a magi, which is... unique."

"Huh," I say as I consider it. As much as people have told me that I'm unusual, I hadn't thought about my situation like that before. It certainly doesn't excuse the Full Moon Knights' hateful behavior, but for all my speculation on why they would come after me and my family, it never occurred to me that it could be personal.

The library is surprisingly quiet at four o'clock on a Monday, but I suppose it makes sense since it seemed like the entirety of the student body was either soaking up one of the last nice days of the year out in the quad or at the Grove. There is a single librarian perched at the front desk between the spiraling staircase and elevator bank, engrossed in a thick book. Although I felt such a strong connection to the Versi Tower's library on my first day, I've been too overwhelmed with everything else this week to even think about going back.

"Hey, how was your date?" I ask Andre as we claim a table on the far side of the library.

I'm glad to see him smile again. "It was good," he says shyly.

"Are you going out again?" I ask, but I don't press for more details.

His ears turn pink. "She said she'd like to, but who knows. She could blow me off."

"No way," I say. "You're a catch. She'd be crazy to let you slip through her fingers." I'm laying it on thick, but Andre immediately perks up, sending me a cheeky wink and a grin.

"I know right?" he teases. "Muchas gracias, mi amiga."

"Da nada," I reply, employing my very limited knowledge of public-school-level Spanish.

Andre opens the lid of his laptop.

"I have to send a message to one of my professors, but you should get started," he says, typing on his computer and nodding at the library shelves, which are unusually stagnant. The first time I was here, the towering bookcases seemed to be in constant motion, shuffling themselves around students. Now, they look grand, but very much like the racks of every other library I've ever patronized.

But as I approach, one of the shelves creaks to life. It moves as if on a track out from its place beside the others to present itself to me. My lips quirk up into a delighted grin. I wonder if it's just the most eager shelf of the bunch or if there is some kind of enchantment in this place that decides what section of literature I may find most interesting.

I search for a label or some kind of iconography that will tell me what genre I'm looking at, but the bookcase itself is bare. While some of the texts have the titles and authors printed on the spine, some are nothing more than binding. I reach out at eye level for the first book I see, just to read what is printed on the cover to give me a clue. To my surprise, it reads *The Abridged History of Madeline Maverick's Ascension to Queendom*. Curious, I peer at the titles of the two books beside it to see if they also are lessons in the Maverick royal line, but neither are anything relevant to the subject. One is a spell book for magi children and the other is some sort of theoretical bestiary with hand-drawn images. The page I flip to shows two different renderings of a creature with the body of a lion, head of a goat, and the tail of a snake, labeled a chimera.

I tuck the book about my grandmother under my arm, and as I do, the bookshelf retreats, quickly replaced by another. This time, the shelf directly in my line of sight is full of newspapers stacked in protective laminate. Trusting in the magic of the library, I grab for the one on top and again I'm treated to it showing me exactly what I had been looking for. It's an article dated from thirty years ago with sepia-colored ink. The image shows a grand amphitheater full of partygoers dressed in vintage finery, covering their mouths in horror. *Ethereal Ball ends in terror— Who are the Full Moon Knights?*

"Finding everything okay?" Andre asks as he comes to my side. I look up at him, and despite the frightening subject matter, I can't fight the grin that overtakes my face. "Oh no," he murmurs. "This is going to be a long night."

"You've got to be kidding me," I complain, throwing my hands out in frustration. It knocks the manila folder off the corner of my dad's desk, sending a small stack of papers to the ground.

Brody kneels to pick it up, leaving me to my staring contest with my dad.

"There's nothing more we can do, Jet," Lieutenant Delancey says cooly, his gaze drifting between me and Brody. "We cannot continue to tread on Maryland's jurisdiction and HQ can no longer spare the resources. The Maryland field office will continue to comb the area, and in the meantime, we'll pursue a new direction with the investigation. We have some old leads that may help us identify the whereabouts of the Full Moon Knights, so it's time that we turn our attention to a new avenue that may actually give us a chance of closing this case."

"It just feels like no one at the LOP is actually taking this seriously," I continue, my frustration only mounting. "We're talking about Tempest's life, dad. She isn't safe until all the Full

Moon Knights are behind bars. We shouldn't be pursuing *new* avenues, we should be pursuing all of them."

I pushed too far, I can see it the moment the words leave my lips. My dad's eyes narrow and his lips press into a firm line. "The severity of this situation is not lost on anyone at the LOP, son. The director, Lieutenant Caro, and I have all invested an exorbitant amount of time into facilitating a thorough investigation in the area around Crescentwood. We will continue to put our best efforts, and best agents, on this case, but there are procedures in place for a reason, Jet. Our resources are not unlimited, but I can assure you that we are not giving up."

I shove my hair off my forehead to disguise how my shoulders are shaking with anger. I've always understood the importance of rules. They have been my guiding light for as long as I can remember, yet now they feel like a joke.

Surely this case is important enough to come at it from all angles. What if there is still evidence to be found near Crescentwood? How can the right answer be to walk away?

"There has to be something we can do," Brody says. His lips are pursed with frustration, though he seems to have a much better handle on his emotions than I do at the moment. "Send Jet and I down there. We can examine the area with fresh eyes. There may be lingering traces that Jet can follow."

My dad opens his mouth, starting to argue, but I press on. "We wouldn't need any resources. Just let us take a car down for the weekend. Maybe something was overlooked."

"Absolutely not. You're only cadets. You don't have authorization to take on an assignment without supervision, especially not with a situation this volatile" I want to argue more but my dad holds up his hand in a silencing gesture. "Enough. The director would simply not allow any cadet to involve themselves in this capacity. I appreciate your dedication to the

LOP, and to Tempest, but continuing the investigation in Maryland is out of the question."

I'm about to argue more but the moment I take to inhale a calming breath allows me to actually digest his words. He didn't say that we couldn't help, only that we couldn't go to Maryland ourselves. Maybe there is a way for Brody and I to get involved in the case. An idea sparks that turns my anger into excitement, though I try to temper it and project cool professionalism.

"Let us take a look at the old case files, at least," I say. My dad's eyes narrow on me and I expect him to refuse outright again, so I continue before he can. "You know we're asked to do grunt work all the time. This would be no different."

"Just last week Caro asked me to type up all of his notes from the property line dispute with the fae families on Wolf Den Way," Brody offers.

"See," I say, holding out my arm to him. "Just let us read through the files and we can call it an independent study or something. If you feel like we're falling behind in classes, we can end it." I hate to give him any sort of out when I feel this is so imperative, but I know my father won't just let us dive into this without due consideration. "Just let us try, dad. Please."

I think this is a great idea and if my dad can't see that, I'll take Lieutenant Caro up on his offer and go to him with my proposal. Sure, my dad won't like me going over his head, or around it in this case, but this is worth the backlash.

Thankfully, it doesn't seem like my subterfuge will be necessary. He's quiet for a few moments as he thinks it over, but when he lets out a long sigh, I know we've won.

"Fine," he says. He hands over his entry key to the archive room. I take the charmed talisman in my hands, a silver emblem of the LOP on a keyring. "But I don't want either of you hanging around the archives. Get everything you need out of there tonight. Those files aren't to leave the headquarters. You do your research here, during business hours. I don't want you working overtime on this. You get six hours a week for the 'independent study' or I'll end it right away."

"Ten," I barter.

His eyes narrow again. "Eight."

"Deal," I say.

The archive room is massive, but diligently organized. Very few things in the LOPHQ are enchanted given the finicky nature of charms, which means there's no chance of the file boxes we're looking for appearing in front of us. We have to search through the wire racks, all cataloged by year, and then sort through them alphabetically. My dad gave us access to the digital database that lists all the available casefiles on the Full Moon Knights, so we know what we're looking for, but finding them in this room may take some time.

I don't hesitate to start, perusing a row of shelves under the bright overhead lights. Even with a full rack of file boxes between us, I feel Brody's gaze on me.

"Don't try to tell me I'm wrong," I say. A gap in the boxes in the 1989 section lets me see him shake his head.

"You're not wrong. If Tempest ever steps foot off this campus, her life is in danger. Closing this case as quickly as possible needs to be everyone's priority."

"Then what is that look for?" I insist.

Brody sighs deeply. The frown he wears when he comes around to my row is so unlike his usual carefree smile that I have no choice but to consider it. He crosses his arms over his broad chest.

"You're taking this case personally. You have been since you met Tempest."

I frown. I don't see the problem in making it personal, especially if that's what it takes for us to find answers. I don't think it's a problem to want Tempest to be safe either.

"I want to put away the Full Moon Knights. I want to make sure they can never hurt her, or anyone else, again."

"So do I, but this is about more than just work. It's about more than Tempest even." I open my mouth to argue but Brody cuts me off with a sharp look. "This is about Kiara."

I flinch away from his words. Suddenly my nails are digging into the flesh of my palms, like my panther's claws are trying to make an unceremonious appearance.

"Nothing about what happened to Kiara is the same."

"No, but the last girl you were involved with died. Now, as much as you want to deny it, you like Tempest and she is in real danger. I know how you are. I know that you're trying to take control of this situation. I respect it, but I think it's time you realize that you're just making things worse."

I want to argue, but his assessment has cracked open my chest, leaving me feeling exposed. At the same time, I don't know how he can think it would be better for me to take a step back from this.

"I'm trying to keep her from getting hurt," I insist.

Brody shakes his head. "It's not Tempest that I'm worried about. I know that you're not going to let anything happen to her. But *someone* is going to get hurt if you keep obsessing over the Full Moon Knights like this."

"Who?" I ask in a small voice, but I know the answer even before Brody says it. He reaches out his arm and squeezes my shoulder.

"You, dude."

21

TEMPEST

"Leave me here to die," Andre pronounces. He's laying sprawled out on the mat like a starfish basking in the summer sun. He darts his tongue out for effect and closes his eyes. I chuckle, picking myself up off the ground.

Andre knocked me to the floor with a particularly skillful takedown. I tried to dodge, but he expected this, flipping my arm around so that it was pinned against my back. He swept his leg and knocked me off my feet. I hit the ground with a solid thud, but not before I tightened my grip on the arm that had me pinned. It was likely more a product of surprise than anything, but I managed to shift our weight and send Andre flipping over me, landing smack on his back.

I offer him my hand so he can climb to his feet.

"Let's go again," I say eagerly. Andre shakes his head.

"I think that's enough for the day. Maybe for the week." He rubs at his back, but I think he's just being dramatic.

We've met a few times to train in between our library study sessions this week. Andre has been a great teacher and we've already covered most of the basics; how to escape a hold from three different angles, how to break the hand or foot of a potential attacker, and several different take-down moves in case I ever need to be on the offensive. It felt like an entire semester's worth of classes packed into our four sessions so far. I was a little worried that we moved too quickly through the instruction and that Andre would be happy to get me out of his hair, but he's been eager to schedule our next session.

He even mentioned that we could start covering some of the physical curriculum that the protectors use as part of their onboarding program. The idea is more exciting than I thought it would be.

"Let's try having you shift again," Andre offers instead. I groan.

So far all of my attempts have gone nowhere. I just feel stupid standing around waiting for something magical or divine to happen. Andre, of course, is a thorough and diligent coach. And considering the ease in which he's taught me how to defend myself in just a week, and his tutoring in all matters of the preternatural, I think it's safe to say that the fault lies with me.

"You'll feel better," he goads, nudging me towards the center of the mat again. "Shifting won't heal an injury, but the injury won't manifest in your animal form since it was acquired in your human form."

I widen my eyes with surprise. "Really?" He nods. "So, when I was attacked by the Full Moon Knights, I could have saved myself from almost dying if I shifted?"

He tilts his head as he considers this. "Technically. But you'd have to have enough energy to make the shift in the first place and honestly, the exertion of it, with your injuries being so severe, could have killed you faster. It's a helpful trick if you have a sprained ankle or a broken nose and want to get from the far side of campus to the hospital, but it's never going to save you from a fatal wound." He claps his hands together. "Enough gabbing. Clear your mind."

I groan again. I'm almost as bad at this as I am shifting. Still, I try to quiet the cacophony of thoughts in my head.

"Try to tap into the primal part of yourself. Remember you have an animal inside you, lurking below the surface. It's always there, but seek it out now. Invite it to come out to play."

I do as he says but it feels entirely wrong. I don't feel like I have an animal inside me, like Andre said I should. I feel exactly as I always have, long before my Blood Rite when I somehow unlocked this other piece of myself. It seems so distant, in fact, that I've been starting to wonder if I had been wrong that day. I know *something* happened, and I obviously completed the Blood Right, but if I was capable of shifting, wouldn't it have happened by now? Everyone talks about it like it's a totally natural thing, and yet nothing about it feels natural to me.

"Maybe we need to try a new tactic," Andre says, breaking me free of my ruminations.

"Like what?"

He gives me a sly smile. "Well, the first time you shifted it was triggered by the adrenaline of a life-threatening situation, right?"

I nod. He knows this, so I'm not sure why he's asking me. And I don't trust the mischievous glint in his eyes.

"So, maybe that's how we'll trigger it again."

With a gnash of his teeth, Andre lunges for me, shifting seamlessly into a hyena. I yelp as I dodge him, shock spiking my blood pressure. Andre's warm brown fur brushes my fingers as his body hurtles past me. I've seen Andre in his shifted form before, but again I am floored by just how cute he is. Despite his threat to scare me into shifting, I'm smiling.

I dart away from him on instinct, but I know Andre could never hurt me. Even as he charges me again, he's bouncing lightly on his paws and tittering with pitchy laughter. Like a contagion, it has me laughing too, even though I squeal when he lunges again. He chases me around the mat for a full minute, until my abdomen aches with laughter, and someone interrupts us.

"The two of you are having way too much fun to be training," says a deep male voice.

I look up to see Dylan Delancey. Andre immediately shifts back at my side. "Sir," he says in greeting.

Dylan waves his hand dismissively. "No need for formality, I'm clocked out for the day." He turns his attention back to me. "I just heard from Diane that a dorm has opened up and you can move in as soon as Sunday. I figured I'd come deliver the news myself and check up on your progress."

"Girl's got some moves," Andre says cheerily.

Dylan nods towards the mats. "Show me."

My nerves spike immediately but Andre sends me a wink.

With the added pressure of Dylan's watchful gaze, I suddenly forget everything that I've learned about both defensive and offensive maneuvers. I try to recall what we covered in our instruction today: groin kicks, elbow strikes, and how to break free of four different grips. But Andre is letting me make the first move, which hasn't come easily to me. Thankfully, he registers my hesitation and changes tactics, lunging for me. I dodge easily.

We move around each other for a couple of minutes, looking for weaknesses in our posture and trying to get in a hit or kick when we can. We seem pretty evenly matched, which tells me that Andre is holding back in an effort to make me look good. Even though I know that going head-to-head with Andre, he would certainly come out on top, I do want to prove myself and all I have been able to learn this week.

Muscle memory has me employing the cross-hook-uppercut combo sequence that Andre and I practiced earlier. He bobs out of the way for the cross and hook, but it's the uppercut that surprises him. He reels back, nearly stumbling off the mat as his chin tips up to the ceiling from the force of my fist.

I don't have any fear that he actually got hurt thanks to the headgear, but he takes a second to steady himself and rolls his neck as he recovers from the impact. All the while, I keep my defensive pose. My gloved hands are up by my face, ready for anything.

"I think we could be looking at a future cadet. What do you think, Gonzales?"

Andre relaxes and looks back at me, his lips spread wide into a grin.

I drop my fists and look at Dylan in surprise. "You think I should join the Protector Program?" I ask.

"I think you could. You have a lot to learn but I would say you have a natural inclination for it." He gestures to my gloved hands. "And your mother would have been one of the best of us. I don't think I'm the only one who wonders if you'd be an asset to the LOP."

I can't say that I've thought about getting involved with the protectors before now. I'm still so new to campus and just starting to find my footing with my classes. But I do know that sparring with Andre has been the most fun I've had in a very long time. It's enough to make me wonder if I might find protecting as fulfilling as Jet and Andre seem to.

"I'll think about it," I say with a genuine smile.

Dylan nods, seeming pleased. "The Protector Program, our afterschool program for high school students, is already halfway through this semester. We could have you shadow a few lectures this fall if you're interested, and you'd be eligible to formally join for the spring."

We chat about the details for the next several minutes, Andre giving me encouraging smiles and excited nudges with his elbow all the while. Finally, with a promise that I can shadow my first class next week, Dylan bids us a good night, leaving me and Andre alone in the training center again.

"This is amazing, Tempest. I think you're going to love it."

I return his smile. "I kind of think so too," I admit.

22

JET

The stack of the Full Moon Knights' case files is suspiciously short. There are dozens of files for all the trouble that they've caused over the years, but each accounting is sparse. If this happened once or twice, I'd chalk it up to oversight and the intention to follow up that just became deprioritized over time. But the lack of essential details on the number of violent demonstrations in the last twenty years is seeming more and more intentional as I dig into them.

The most thorough documentation that we have on file is the transcript from the interrogation of Dannon Carter after the assassination attempt on the queen twenty-four years ago. My father was one of the agents who conducted it, but most of Dannon's responses were insignificant rhetoric on the Knights needing to take the state of the preternatural world into their hands.

The rest was incoherent ramblings about the illegitimacy of the Maverick line, the "poison" infesting the preternatural— which I eventually understood to mean magi, hybrids, and any advancements they have made to our world—and how he wouldn't actually go to jail because his brother would let him go freely. I did a little digging into his brother but wasn't able to find anyone who shared his surname through the Versi database. I make a note to ask my father to look into it as I let out a long sigh.

Brody, who has been sitting in the cubicle next to me, looks up from his own stack of files and rubs at his eyes. "I think my brain is melting," he says.

"Want to grab dinner?" I ask.

He shakes his head. "I've got plans."

I managed to forget it was a Friday night. The days keep flying by.

"You know who's probably free for dinner?" Brody asks leadingly. I groan, already knowing where he's going with this. "Your dad said he was going to go talk to Tempest downstairs. You should go ask her."

"We have dinner together all the time," I say. I'm being purposefully obtuse, and Brody knows it. He rolls his eyes.

"And she's moving out this weekend. All the more reason to ask her out already."

"It's not a good idea. I have to focus on finding the Full Moon Knights. I can't afford any distractions."

He shakes his head. "That makes no sense. You're desperate to protect her, but you're too afraid to actually spend any time with her."

"I'm not afraid," I argue.

"Fine." He gets to his feet, grabbing his jacket off the back of his chair. "Well, I'm going to go say hi to my friend Andre on my way out. You're welcome to join me or you can stay and brood by yourself."

Grumbling, I stand, though I leave my stuff at my desk. I've barely scratched the surface of all these case files this week, so I have a long night ahead of me.

Andre and Tempest aren't doing much training when we arrive at the basement floor. Tempest is sitting on the mats while Andre bounces around her. I can't tell if he's telling a story, doing a demo, or auditioning to be the next Energizer Bunny. She laughs at something he says, and my lips quirk up into a smile. She seems more at ease than I've seen her since that first night at Camp Kenwick. Maybe more. Even then she had been muted, uncertain. Now she seems kind of happy.

"Hey!" Andre calls out as he sees us approaching. "Guess who's going to be joining the Protector Program?"

I frown, unsure if he actually expects me to guess. Tempest rolls her eyes.

"I'm not joining yet. I'm just shadowing."

My frown deepens. "You can't join the Protector Program." Three sets of eyes turn on me.

Tempest crosses her arms. "Excuse me?"

"It's too dangerous," I say.

Tempest's brows jump up her forehead. "It's too dangerous for me, but it wasn't for you."

I huff out a breath of frustration.

"Okay," Brody says. "I actually need to get going. I just wanted to say hi. So, hi, and, uh, bye." He takes a step away and then another.

"That's not what I mean," I argue. "The Protector Program lets students shadow assignments outside of Versi, which can't even be a consideration for you until the Full Moon Knights are apprehended."

"I know that," Tempest replies. She gets to her feet and takes a step closer to face me. "I'm not an idiot, Jet. I'm not planning to run out into danger. But I'm not just going to put my life on hold until they're arrested either."

"Why can't you?" I ask her. It's not a genuine question, it's just a plea of desperation that I'm frustrated enough to actually voice. But it's the wrong thing to say. Tempest's frown turns into a full-blown scowl.

"Maybe because the LOP has been trying and failing to apprehend them for more than twenty years. And since they still don't have any real leads, I can't exactly trust that they're any closer now."

"Can't you just trust me?"

"You know what?" Andre calls out from behind Tempest. "I actually need to head out too." Tempest and I both turn to shoot sharp glares in his direction. He's standing by the countertop with his bag slung over his shoulder. Slowly, he lowers it back down to the floor. "Nevermind. I can hang a little longer."

"Look, I appreciate the concern," Tempest starts, not sounding very appreciative, "and I know I can't leave campus until I get the all-clear, but I'm not going to sit around and wait until then. I do trust that you're doing everything you can, Jet. In the meantime, you need to trust that I know what I'm doing. Because I do know what I am doing. I could be good at this, even your dad thinks so. And maybe becoming a protector isn't what I want, but that will be my decision. Not yours or anyone else's."

"Prove it," I say. Tempest's brows arch up again.

It is a challenge, but it's not that I don't think she's capable. Tempest has proven to me time and time again that she can handle so much more than most people could, but I need to see it for myself. I need to feel it, or I'll go out of my mind.

"You think you have what it takes to train with protectors? Prove it."

23

TEMPEST

Jet nods towards the mats. I'm clenching my jaw hard enough that it's starting to ache. I stride towards where I left my boxing gloves and start to tug them on. Andre lets out a nervous laugh. His eyes dart between us, wide with alarm.

"Now is probably a good time for me to remind you that Tempest has had exactly one week of self-defense training and probably shouldn't be sparring for real."

We ignore him.

I take a minute to shake off my jitters. Jet does his own, tempered version of a warmup, rolling his neck and flexing his forearms in a way that makes the one prominent vein jump.

Finally, without saying a word, I know it's time. Neither of us are wearing additional protective gear, but I don't even want it. I don't expect this session to be anything like it's been with Andre. As much as I believe that Andre can easily beat me in a real fight, I'm willing to bet that Jet could do it in half the time.

This is a test. It's not about me being better, it's about proving that I can learn. That someday, once the Full Moon

Knights are out of the picture, that I will be able to protect myself.

I square my shoulders as Jet stares me down. His eyes seem almost aggressively blue now. It's razor-sharp and solid, like an icicle that could glide through skin and between ribs to pierce a heart.

I fully expect him to be on the offensive, but I want to surprise him, so I don't hesitate. I move towards him, tucking my elbow and then throwing it right towards his obnoxiously pretty face. He blocks the blow easily and then spins on his heels. He grabs for me, but I'm already lunging to the other side of the matted ring, never having turned my back to him. In one smooth stride, he surges forward. He's faster and more decisive than I had been, but I still manage to step out of his reach. He bares his teeth, a snarl slipping out in his frustration, so that's when I strike.

I swing at him, the force of my determination drawing out a grunt as my fist connects with his jaw. He takes the hit, which is a small win in itself, but then dodges me. I reset my stance rather than push on the offensive again. This time, he throws out his arm to hit me, but I block it. He does it again on the other side, and I realize too late that his goal isn't to make contact with me like I initially assumed. He just wants to get close.

I duck with only a second to spare, feeling his arms graze my shoulder as he reaches for where my waist had just been. I don't waste any more time playing now. While he's still off his center of gravity, I knee him in the gut. He hisses in surprise. This time when I surge towards him, I raise my leg to kick. But I feint low so that when he moves to block his shin from impact, or prevent me from sweeping out his legs, I actually go high.

The heel of my foot connects with the center of his chest, making him stumble back. I allow myself a self-satisfied smile, but just that moment of losing focus allows him to make his counterattack. He surges forward, capturing both of my wrists in his hands and tugging me close to him. Then, in a move that feels more like a dance, he spins me so that the back of my body is flush with the front of him, and my arms are crossed against my chest. I slam my foot down on his instep, which surprises him enough to loosen his grip on my wrists, but not enough to get me free.

I buck against the backwards embrace. Jet's grip is strong, constricting my shoulders as he pins them against his chest.

"Not bad," he purrs. Actually purrs, because he's a damn panther. I keep forgetting that.

Frustration flares as I try to remember the focus of all of Andre's lessons. Yes, I've learned how to fight too, but it's always been about self-defense. I have to fight back with strategy. It's about outsmarting my opponent since I'll never be able to outmuscle them.

I squat down, rooting my feet to the matted floor. Despite my racing heart and spiking adrenaline, I feel good. I feel each passing second of the frenzied fight like it's twice as long. I grab for Jet's arms, still wrapped around my chest and shoulders, and pull down hard. At the same time, I pick up my left foot and plant it behind his right. My body is pressed against his without a millimeter of space between us. His grasp on me is still strong, but that's exactly what I need in order to make this move successful.

With a burst of speed, I lunge forward and down, wrapping my forearms around the backs of his knees. Then I thrust upwards, using his body weight and rigidity against him, and sending him crashing to the ground. A noise between a roar and a groan rips out of me from the sheer force of it. Jet's back smacks into the mat and a grunt escapes him.

I have exactly one second to admire my handiwork before a large form pounces on me, tackling me to the ground with almost no effort. The force of landing on the mat startles me, though not nearly as much as the sight of a black panther holding me down. Both of his front paws pin my wrists and the weight of him prevents me from even considering escape. His face is so close to mine that I feel the tickle of his whiskers on my cheeks. His eyes are the same luminous blue that they've always been and focusing on them quells some of my body's primal panic as the caveman part of my brain tries to convince the rest of me that I'm about to die.

Jet opens his mouth and roars. I flinch and turn my head away as hot, minty breath blows onto me. Then, in a blink, he's shifted again, his human form still keeping me pinned in the same way I had been under his animal form.

"That's not fair," I manage to get out between panted breaths. Though those eyes are exactly the same as they had been a moment before, it's much harder to meet them now.

"The Full Moon Knights won't play fair either. If they ever get near you again, they will use everything in their arsenal."

"I know," I murmur, meeting his gaze now, but shifting uncomfortably under their hardness. Jet's expression softens a bit, and his posture does too, though he doesn't immediately climb off of me, and I'm not exactly encouraging him to.

A throat clears. "I really do have to go," Andre says. "I'm going out with Lacey tonight."

"Have fun," I say weakly as Andre scurries for the door, giving an awkward wave above his head.

When the door shuts behind him, I finally shove Jet off of me. He rolls easily and is standing again in one swift movement. Meanwhile, I stumble to my feet and have to shake out my stiff limbs.

"You did really well," he says, offering me my water bottle. I accept it gratefully and take several long gulps before capping it again.

"Thank you. But even if I hadn't, whether or not I join the Protector Program isn't your decision. I just found out that I've spent my entire life getting jerked around by the choices that other people have made for me. Everyone who has ever meant to love me has lied to me and made decisions without consulting me that have altered the direction of my life. I know you're coming from a good place, Jet, but you absolutely do not have the right to do the same."

"You're right. I'm sorry."

My mouth gapes like a fish trying to take a gulp of water but only getting air instead.

"You—what?"

"I'm sorry," he says again. He shoves his hair back, an anxious tick that I'm surprised I can now recognize. "I know that I can't make choices for you, and I'm sorry that I made it seem like I did. I just panicked. You're already in such an unsafe situation with the Knights as it is, and I feel responsible for that."

"Jet," I say, reaching out to brush the bare stretch of skin above his elbow. "You're not the reason the Full Moon Knights attacked me."

"I could have been. We don't know how they got to you so soon after I realized who you were. Maybe it was me uncovering your trace or maybe it was something else, but either way, it was because of me." I shake my head, but Jet continues on. "It was, Tempest, and I'm going to make it up to you. But that's not the only reason why I panicked." He swallows hard.

"This happened to me before. That's why I need you to understand how dangerous protecting can be, even without the threat of the Full Moon Knights."

Jet doesn't meet my eye, as if gathering up the courage to say something more.

"There was a girl named Kiara in the Protector Program with me. She was—we were dating, I guess. It was complicated. But she died on an assignment, and it was all my fault."

❦ 24 ❦
JET

I don't mean to tell Tempest about Kiara, but I need her to understand why I've been constantly teetering on the edge of panic since I met her. I didn't fully understand it myself until Brody called me out on it, but I'm glad he did. I need Tempest to know. I need her to understand, not just why I acted like a jerk, but to understand me. And so, the words start spilling out.

"Sometimes the Protector Program lets students shadow actual assignments. It's meant to be low stakes. Kiara and I were invited to go with a couple of agents to make a house call in New York State. There was a selkie family, seal shifters, who were having trouble with their human neighbor. At first, he was just saying that he thought there were mermaids in the lake they lived on, but then he started to become suspicious of this Nagual family who lived down the street.

"The agents were going to pose as local law enforcement and talk to him. They got confoundment charms to place around the family's property and inside the man's house. It's a pretty basic enchantment that would make him overlook anything preternatural he may see. So, when the agents went to the man's house, Kiara and I were meant to place the charms around the Selkie family's property. But as soon as we showed up, we knew something was wrong. Everything was too quiet."

I take a deep breath and shake my head, trying to free the images from my mind. It's amazing that my brain has managed to lose so many of the details from all those months ago, and yet some of the memories are seared into my brain, clear as day. I can remember the exact pattern of the crickets chirping that evening and how the setting sun's reflection gleamed off the eerie stillness of the lake.

"Things had been weird with Kiara and me for a little while by then. I thought we were moving towards a relationship, but she got busy and distant. This was one of the first times I had the opportunity to talk to her in weeks, so I let that distract me. The agents sent us a message saying the man wasn't home like they expected and that we needed to regroup, but we ignored it. Only for a minute, but that was long enough.

"When we entered the house, the dad was in the living room, unconscious, bleeding, and barely breathing. We realized then what we were dealing with, but we couldn't wait for the agents to tell us what to do. The mother and the two little girls were missing, and we had every reason to believe they were already hurt, or about to be. Kiara saw through the open back-door that the family had a boat and it looked like people were on it. So, we ran out there."

Pressure curls around my hand, followed by comforting warmth. I glance down to where Tempest is now holding it, before moving my eyes up to meet her own. They are wide and sad, and impossibly earnest. I feel emotion getting caught in my throat, so I try to clear it, but it becomes a choke instead.

"We messed up. We know we did, but with the rest of the

family in danger, there was no real choice to make. Besides, the agents were already on their way. We couldn't just sit around waiting. So, we boarded the fishing boat. We didn't see the man right away, but we found the mother and daughters tied up below deck. We helped them back up, but once we did the man was there, wielding some sort of harpoon. I wasn't supposed to shift since he was human, and in that second, I delayed, he swung the blunt side of the weapon and hit Kiara with enough force that she was flung overboard. Then he turned on the mother.

"The agents had arrived then. One went inside to give the father Fate's Root—I was later told. The other came to help, but thankfully the daughters had made it off the boat, so he had to take a moment to make sure that the girls were alright before coming to my aid.

"I intercepted the harpoon and got clipped in the side. Thankfully the blade was dull. I was at more risk of infection than anything serious, but the blow still managed to hit the mom. She wasn't hurt, but the shock of it made her shift, which shut the man right up. It also bought the agent enough time to incapacitate him.

"I tried to get to Kiara to help her as soon as I could, but everything had happened so fast. Both the agents were preoccupied, and they never even saw Kiara fall off the boat. I was bleeding, but I waded into the water to find her. I looked until the human emergency services arrived to take the man and the agents could help me, but she was just gone. We got search and rescue involved and everything, but she was never found. Kiara may have been Nagual, but she was a naga, a snake shifter, not a selkie, and the kelp was so dense in that area that it was off-limits to swimmers."

That horrible feeling in my throat is finally lessening, but when I go to speak, it makes my voice break. "She was gone."

Tempest is silent for a long moment, but I can feel the heat of her gaze on me. I don't dare meet her eyes again though. My vision has gone glassy and I'm afraid if I face her and see the sympathy I know will be in her intense, marbled eyes, I'll start crying in earnest, and I've already cried enough for Kiara since March.

"I am so sorry, Jet. But you have to know that none of that is your fault. I don't think it was anyone's fault, besides that horrible man."

I shake my head. "It wasn't really his fault either. I mean, I could never justify what he did, but there's a reason the protectors exist. It's to protect our own kind, but humans too. They can become obsessed with the preternatural if they are too exposed to our world. No one knew how far his preoccupation had gone, but I wish that we had. If we hadn't been so blindsided, Kiara might still be alive."

I finally meet Tempest's eyes. "After everything that happened, I'm a little overprotective of the people I care about." Then, feeling self-conscious about my admission, I glance down again to where our hands are joined. Hers are smaller than mine and paler, but they don't look weak. In fact, her knuckles are scraped and scabbed from the training she's been doing, and I can feel the roughness of her calluses, so much like my own. I clear my throat again.

"But that's not an excuse. If you want to become a protector, then that's what I want for you too. I just want you to know what you're signing up for."

"I understand. Thank you, Jet."

I'm not sure what she's thanking me for, but I nod anyway. She finally drops my hand.

"Hey, are you hungry?" I blurt out. She blinks back at me in surprise. "I was going to head to the Grove for food, but Brody is busy. And I know Andre is busy. Unless you have plans with your other friends."

"Friends?" she repeats. I can't decipher her tone, so I continue.

"Yeah. I thought we could grab dinner together instead. Since we're friends."

Part of me wants to snatch it back, to confess that where she's concerned friendship has always been the furthest thing from my mind. But I meant what I said to Brody, and what I said about Kiara. I can't afford to be distracted right now, not when Tempest's safety is still at risk. I just need a little more time.

I'm nervous to look at her, anxiety making my body hum, but when I do, I'm surprised to find her lips twitching up into a smile.

"Yeah, I'd like that," she says. "Let's go."

25

TEMPEST

My hand is pressed against my mouth, physically holding in my laughter as Jet finishes telling his story. Once he, Brody, and Kage went camping and Brody was convinced that the black bear that broke into their s'mores stash while they were on a hike was a bear-shifter and tried reasoning with the animal for a full five minutes. Apparently, Kage was uselessly calling out bear facts in an attempt to convince his friend not to get so friendly, and finally Jet had to shift and drag Brody away by the hood of his sweatshirt before he got himself hurt.

Thankfully, the sudden appearance of a panther was enough to scare the poor bear into running off, leaving enough of their food untouched for them to still manage to make dinner.

"I think we all learned an important lesson that night."

"Don't befriend stray bears?" I offer.

Jet shakes his head. "Don't let Brody be in charge of packing."

I laugh again and watch as the corner of Jet's smirk

twitches higher. We're at the Grove, of course, but our meals have long since been discarded, leaving a pile of trays and wrappers between us on the table. It's actually quiet for once with most of the student body already getting their weekend festivities underway.

Darkness has set it, exhaustion coming with it. I know I should say goodnight and head back to the house to make an effort at catching up on the sleep I have been sorely lacking lately, but I'm not ready to end my night with Jet just yet. We've never done something so normal, and it feels really nice. I've considered him an ally since we met, and I've appreciated the way that we have confided in each other these last couple of weeks, but we've never got to the place where I've felt like I can call him a friend.

Now, I think we're on our way and the prospect makes my chest feel tingly, as if there is an anthill where my heart should be. The sensation is peculiarly pleasant.

My gaze must have strayed out the window for longer than I thought because when I turn back to face Jet, he is watching me with open curiosity. He looks like there is a question he wants to ask, but he gives a small shake of his head as if he's decided against it.

I wonder if he's thinking about my dissociations and how I haven't had a single one since my going through my Blood Rite. It was explained to me that my first shift coming so close to my eighteenth birthday could have resulted in all kinds of strange manifestations as my animal form tried to reject its dormancy. From their limited knowledge of the subject, shifting could have cured my affliction just as easily. Despite not having felt my mind creep away from me these last couple of weeks, I'm not sure if I believe that theory. It sounds too good to be true.

"Come with me," Jet says instead.

He gets to his feet, not giving me the opportunity to ask too many questions, though I still manage to croak out, "Where?" as I trail behind him towards the door.

"To the roof," he says. "Obviously."

"Obviously," I mutter, but I'm trying to school a smile off my face.

The roof in question is not actually at the Grove, which I should have expected given that it's a one-story cabin. However, that building does seem to have some sort of magical property that makes the inside twice as large as it appears from the outside, so I couldn't be sure.

Jet leads me back across the street to the LOPHQ. We walk side-by-side, our shoulders brushing on more than one occasion, though neither of us apologize for it or acknowledge our closeness. The tingly feeling that has been building all night only continues to grow. We take the elevator to the fifth floor, though I don't get to explore this level at all. Jet makes a hard left turn to the staircase. We go up two flights to a door marked *roof access.*

Though I was just outside a minute before, stepping out into the night again feels much cooler than it had when I was seven floors below. I cross to the edge of the building, resting my elbows on the rail that overlooks Versi. Jet comes to my side, matching my stance. I shudder, but not from the cold. I don't think I will ever get used to the feeling of his presence beside me.

The roof is atop one of the tallest buildings at Versi and provides a unique view of the campus. While I still think of Versi as small, especially compared to some of the cities I've lived in, from this perspective, it looks huge. The academic quarter is across from us, Versi Tower standing just a hair taller than HQ with the bell tower's spire, but the Grove is nothing more than a speck tucked in between the trees. Main Street is lit by two neat rows of street lamps—which I now know are not powered by electricity or gas, but fire that never dies out.

Beyond the buildings are thousands of twinkling lights from the residential neighborhood. Yet, despite its vastness, the tree line creates a clear border around the campus where all light and life disappear into what feels like endless darkness.

"It's beautiful," I say, my gaze trained out on the blue-black night. Maybe it's just a product of his panther's instinct to perch, but I can see why Jet likes hanging out on rooftops so much. The world is different here. You feel insignificant being so far from it, something that shouldn't come as such a comfort to me. But there is beauty in letting go. It's more than freedom. It's peace.

I can understand how Jet would find peace in it too. The fact that he wanted me to share this with him makes me feel oddly warm.

"It is," he murmurs. I must have turned my body away from the rail to subtly face him some time in the last minute. It's only then I realize he isn't watching the skyline at all, he's watching me. His posture has mirrored mine, but if that's intentional or subconscious, I can't guess.

I feel my face flush. This isn't the first time that I've felt this between us. A little zip of an electric current that sparks hope and curiosity. I've been afraid to explore it. I haven't wanted to even think about and give life to a fantasy that I simply do not have the bandwidth to indulge in at the moment. But with the way he's looking at me, and the confidence that the darkness of night affords me, I suddenly want to play out the fantasy.

"Jet, I—" The words die on my tongue since my brain hasn't actually thought of anything to say. There are words, I suddenly feel full of them, the weight compressing my chest, but I can't seem to arrange them in my head let alone give them voice.

The intensity of his gaze on me tells me he has words too, or thoughts at least, but he doesn't speak them either.

There is a moment that stretches eons. There's only the darkness, the quiet, and Jet just *looking* at me. I'm not sure what to do with that. I feel overheated and I'm afraid my palms are going to sweat.

"I know," he says finally. But I'm not sure what he thinks he knows because then he's standing upright and rolling back his shoulders. He nods his head towards the door we exited from. "Ready?"

I nod, though I take a moment to gather myself, taking a deep inhale before tearing my gaze away from the glittering horizon.

We make the long trek back to the Delancey house in companionable quiet. Elisa is out but his parents are in the living room when we get back. I say a brief hello but then make for the stairs to turn in for the night.

Jet catches my hand from the bottom step, briefly interlacing our fingers and giving a gentle squeeze. Before I can turn back to face him, he's letting go. I continue up the stairs to my room, but I swear I can feel his eyes on me until I turn the corner that obscures me from his view. It's only then that I take my first full breath since the rooftop.

Since my knowledge of anything preternatural is essentially nonexistent, as Andre and I continue to hit the library over the next week, most of the actual research comes down to him. My role has been regulated to standing in the center of the ever-shifting shelves and waiting for them to present me with any materials they deem important. Then I return to our desk in the corner of the library to add the textbooks, articles, magazines, memos, and memoirs to our already impressive stacks.

In the last several days, I've managed to answer many of my questions, but a lot of what I've learned has just allowed me to understand the mechanics of the preternatural world better.

Potions and charms sounded like voodoo to me when I first came to Versi and it was hard to comprehend what elements of the campus were magic and what was not, especially when everything seems so extraordinary. Now I know that the practice of alchemy, which is responsible for things from the medicine bundles and potions used by the preternatural doctors, like Fate's root, is a rather simple science. It's the mixing of organic and inorganic compounds to create a particular reaction, much like chemistry, but the magi's unique bioavailability that allows them to manipulate elements like fire, earth, air, and water can acutely influence the reactions. Magi aren't the only ones who can do alchemy, of course, but the materials I use in class must first be transmuted by a magus, or I'm useless in the lab.

Enchantment is a bit trickier. Spells and charms are less tangible mediums, though a lot of the concepts are the same. It is more of a manipulation of the available energy around any particular thing. Charming the library shelves to move is actually a pretty simple feat, but enchanting them to understand a person's desires and rearrange themselves to tailor to that individual is powerful magic.

My grandmother's history turns out to be fairly boring. My ancestors apparently ascended to power in the late eighteen hundreds, following the reign of the Tennouji line. Queen Madeline was raised by the last queen with the intention of taking over the throne once she turned twenty-five, as all the Maverick women in their line had done before her.

Other than the aftermath of the unrest between the previous queen and the Full Moon Council, my grandmother's reign was not very notable until an article speculating on my mom sparked intrigue around the line of succession. Seemingly out of the blue, my mom decided to come to Versi University to study law and protection, out of everything. Since neither Queen Madeline nor Melanie spoke to sources, there wasn't anything beyond speculation around the unprecedented decision, but my mom quickly made a name for herself beyond her birthright. Even just after she graduated, one article wondered if Melanie was being groomed to take the position of the director in a few years, and what that would mean for her throne.

Then, seemingly all at once, Melanie announced that she abdicated, the queen named a new heir from one of the noble families in Europe, and Melanie and Gregor fled from Versi, accused of a double homicide. All coverage from then on was on the failing manhunt for my parents.

Information on the Full Moon Knights turns out to be the easiest to come by, though most of what I learn leaves me with more questions. Their group officially formed twenty-four years ago when the band of lycanthrope attempted an assassination of Queen Madeline at the annual Ethereal Ball. They failed, of course, thanks to the royal guard. One Knight was incarcerated, a man named Dannon Carter. He told everyone their manifesto: they wanted to return to the age of Nagual-supremacy, where Nagual were the ideal beings with their divine blessing and inhumane abilities. They said the Maverick monarchy was allowing the Nagual to be weakened by their association with magi and hybrids. The man later died in prison due to self-inflicted wounds and the other Knights disappeared, wanting to create their own society without the influence of other preternatural.

It is partly reassuring to know that the Full Moon Knights are nothing more than a band of discontented outcasts who are willing to go to extreme measures to assert their agenda, but it is mostly disconcerting. It doesn't seem possible that a rogue group has been able to evade arrest for all these years. To me, they don't exactly seem to be thriving in their ostracized community. Yes, they may have physical prowess and are still capable of terrible acts of violence, but they seemed disorganized, erratic, and almost sickly.

It's stranger still that they could make an attempt on the queen's life and stage public demonstrations, and yet putting an end to their terror has never seemed to be enough of a priority. In fact, as much as the newspapers, and the queen, according to the articles' sources, were quick to condemn their actions, they always seemed to be painted as more of a nuisance than a threat to public safety—which is beyond frustrating for me, since those nuisances cost me my parent's lives, and nearly mine too.

Despite all my research, almost every afternoon of this week with Andre's help, the only thing I haven't found any sort of answer to is the question of how my parents were able to conceive me. The magic bookshelves haven't provided any text or tome, and nothing I've come across even hinted at an answer. Andre and I have poured over books, documents, files, and diaries. We've studied topics ranging from fertility and the history of magi, to divine blessings and miracles, hoping for even a crumb of information that could lead us to a starting point for where to look. No matter what we've tried, each time we've come away empty-handed. Yet, I can't shake the feeling that the answer is right in front of me.

"Andre, is it possible for a charm to somehow hide information?" I ask on Wednesday night.

He squints up at me from the thick book he has been reading named *Japanese Mid-Century Folklore Volume IV.* "Sure. Several ways."

I find myself fighting off a laugh. The past few days we've had our little study group, Andre has taken to wearing grandpa-style reading glasses. It feels wrong to tease him when he's clearly so invested in helping me out, but it's hard to keep a straight face when I look at the small wire rims and his beady little eyes.

"That's not very helpful, abuelo," I say, not able to help myself. Andre only grins and pushes the spectacles up the bridge of his nose.

"There are both spells and hexes that can suppress memories—which is a manner of hiding information, right? There are also a few charms that can cast different sorts of masking glamours. They could make something invisible or hide something in plain sight but curse anyone who looks at it to find it too unimportant to look at."

"What about making a specific passage of text disappear or disguising an entire book to look like another one?" I look at the pile in front of us and again wonder why a library enchanted to give me exactly what I want seems to be incapable of pointing me to the one thing I really need.

"It's possible," Andre admits with a shrug. "It could be a trickery hex, an illusion spell, or a confoundment charm. It could be that only a gifted magus is able to uncover it, or that it's tuned to a specific group of people or person."

"Or no one," I say with a sigh. I close my own book, *Medieval Witchcraft and Sorcery: A Comprehensive Guide*, and while I don't mean to slam it, the book is so thick that it makes a loud thump that startles me into jumping.

"Unfortunately," Andre agrees with a sigh. "You think it's possible someone is trying to keep the information from you?"

I shake my head. "No, nothing like that. Though... I don't know. I get that my dad was really good at alchemy but it's just so weird that there aren't any other children of magi and Nagual running around. I'm not saying that I agree with the people who call me an abomination, but if it requires some really complex spell in order for me to have been born, then maybe the information is dangerous. Maybe my dad was the one who hid the truth of what he did so that other people couldn't replicate it."

And maybe I shouldn't be so obsessed with finding out anything more either. It's not like it matters at this point. I was just hoping for some sort of clarity, because the more normal my strange reality becomes, the more alone I feel in it.

With what is meant to be another sigh, but comes out more like a groan, I let my head fall forward in defeat. It lands against the heavy book with a soft thump.

"Cheer up, chica. We'll figure something else out. Didn't you say you still have a lot of your parents' stuff in storage? Maybe we're just looking in the wrong place." I'm not sure why but my mind immediately flashes to my father messing with his degree hanging on the wall back in his office in Crescentwood and how it's now sitting under a tarp in our garage.

I turn my head over so that I can face Andre, my cheek still pressed into the soft cover of the book. "It doesn't really matter anyway. Midterms are coming up so we should probably start using our study group to actually study for our classes."

"If that's what you want," Andre says magnanimously, but he fixes me with a watchful gaze. After a long moment, I finally pick my head back up. When I do, Andre continues, "I know you know that figuring out how your parents managed to have you isn't going to bring them back, but there's no harm in wanting to understand them better. Or wanting to understand yourself better."

I give him a small smile. "Thanks for saying that. You're my hero." I let my tone slip into teasing again, otherwise I may start crying.

"I get that a lot." Andre puffs out his chest, seamlessly falling back into our typical easy banter as if he didn't just see into my broken heart and offer a way for me to put the pieces back together again.

"I'm just trying to make a difference in this world," he continues. "Whether it's as a protector out on assignment, talking about magi and hybrid advocacy, or helping you with your alchemy homework."

I narrow my eyes at him. "You've never once helped me with my alchemy homework."

He pouts. "Maybe that's because I'm never compensated for my heroism. Buy me a slice of apple pie at the Grove and I'll read over your lab report. I'm starving."

I roll my eyes even as I laugh. "Fine. I do think I owe you the whole pie after all your help the last couple of weeks."

26

TEMPEST

The bell rings out through the quiet classroom on Friday afternoon, signaling the end of my week. I look up from my Theoretical Preternatural Principles textbook as my classmates funnel out through the door. I jump to my feet, scooping up my books and not bothering to shove them into my bag as I rush into the dramatically arched corridor of Therianthrope Hall.

"Dee!" I call after a short girl with a silky sheet of hair that falls to her sacrum.

While most of my peers have already dispersed, Dee hangs back at the sound of me calling for her. She tucks a lock of dark hair behind her ear.

"Oh, hi, Tempest," she says. While she meets my eyes for a moment, she quickly ducks her head and seems to concentrate on counting the floor tiles.

"Hey," I say with a smile. "I wanted to thank you. Professor Kilmer has been letting me use your notes the past couple of weeks. I'm still catching up, but it's honestly been such a huge help."

While the professor told me that the notes belonged to his best student, Deepti Somat, it took me a long time to place her in the class. She goes by Dee, for one thing, and from what I can tell she's incredibly shy. She sits in the farthest corner of the room and never raises her hand. It took Professor Kilmer calling her out last class to answer his question for me to learn her name. She then proceeded to give an analysis of the connection between Pagan and Japanese supernatural allusions that lasted more than ten minutes and was hands-down the most fascinating topic we've covered in the course so far.

She's also gorgeous, with a golden-brown complexion that is utterly flawless, like there's a filter permanently fixed on her heart-shaped face.

"It's no trouble. The exercise of taking notes has been proven to open new pathways in our brains to encode information, which allows for us to better retain said information." Her ears flush pink, as if she's embarrassed by what she said. "So, uh, I don't really need them."

I give her an encouraging smile. "I didn't know that. Once I make it through this midterm, I'll have to give it a try."

"I could help you study," she says brightly, but after a moment her excitement seems to dim again. "Er, I'm sure you have plenty of friends to study with. It's just that I'm a tutor, so if you, you know, needed a tutor, I could do that. Tutor you, that is." She goes to tuck her hair behind her again despite it remaining perfectly in place.

"I mean, I could definitely use some help," I say. "Actually, would you want to grab coffee now? We can talk about the midterm, or we could just hang out."

"Yeah?" Dee brightens again. "Coffee sounds great."

"Great," I echo with a smile.

Dee lets out an awkward titter as we step out into the afternoon sun dipping over the academic quarter.

"Sorry, I'm so nervous. I'm new to campus this year and I haven't made very many friends yet."

"Believe me, I get it," I say.

Life has been so busy lately that I haven't felt too lonely, but I still almost laughed out loud when Dee said she thought I had a bunch of friends willing to help me study. It's true for Andre, of course, and his friendship is something I am so grateful for, but I already feel like I monopolize enough of his time. I think I'm getting close to being able to call Brody and Alejandra friends too. I'm supposed to train with them, Andre, and Jet tomorrow morning, and I'm really looking forward to it.

With Jet, I'm not sure what to call the connection between us, but "friends" doesn't seem to cut it. Our dinner last week was really nice, and our moment on the rooftop felt important somehow, despite the lack of anything having actually passed between us. I haven't seen much of him over the week, but he did help me with my move on Sunday. By which I mean he drove me to the other side of campus and offered to carry my two pieces of luggage up to my second-floor dorm, which I declined.

The dorm is actually much nicer than I thought it would be. I even get my own bathroom.

I will miss the Delancey family chaos though. I didn't like feeling as if I was an imposition, but I liked how noisy their home always was with the family's comings and goings. Their dinners were loud and the conversations hard to follow, but it was filled with life and love. It's so different from anything I've known before. Even when my parents were alive, our family of three felt small.

Dee and I walk in amiable silence on our short trek to the Grove. It's as busy as ever when we arrive, which seems to freak Dee out. She curls into herself, seeming smaller in all aspects.

"You're a college freshman, right?" I ask, hoping to distract her from her nerves. "Are you majoring in Theoretical Mythology or another subject?"

The course is offered as a gen-ed elective, but it's a course requirement for anyone getting a degree in Theoretical Mythology, so our class is a mix of students. She perks up immediately.

"I'm in the alchemy program actually," she answers as we slide into an available booth.

I have to stop myself from getting back to my feet and cheering. Universe knows that if I need tutoring in any subject, that's the one. Considering how I made a point to ensure that Dee knew I wanted to befriend her, not hire her to tutor me, I keep a lid on my excitement for the time being. I will definitely ask for her help before my midterm, though.

"Are you a magus?" I ask.

"A succubus," she says. "But I've always been better with inorganic compounds than organic life forms." She giggles nervously again, but I'm too hung up on her words to put her at ease.

I was told that there are succubi on campus, and incubi as well, but I haven't met one yet. It's shocking because Dee looks nothing like how I have previously imagined the creatures. I pictured something like a vampire with inky black wings. Dee is stunningly pretty, but her sweet demeanor and socially awkward energy are the last things I would expect of a being who is said to live for seduction. After these last several weeks, I should know better than to expect anything but the unexpected.

"Professor Kilmer's class is just an easy way to pad my eighteen-credit semester," Dee says. My eyes widen slightly. While it's my favorite class by far, I certainly wouldn't call Theoretical Preternatural Principles easy. I change my mind; I'm hiring Dee to tutor me immediately.

"This is a potentially dumb question, but how does theoretical mythology differ from regular mythology?" I ask her.

She laughs, which makes me grin. "For us preternatural, mythology is usually referring to the known theology of the Nagual and magi. Theoretical mythology tackles a much broader scope, like fairytales or unconfirmed legends about lesser-known beings, like the fae, for example."

"That makes sense," I say. I'm not very far along in my Nagual Myth and History class yet, but I can see how the two subjects differ in their instruction.

"I can give you an example, if you'd like," Dee offers, seeming at ease now that we're on an academic subject. Maybe Jet is right that I am a nerd because I definitely feel more comfortable too. Either that says something critical about the kind of person I am, or I really need to dedicate some time to familiarizing myself with Versi's course offerings.

"What do you know about the abditory aether?" Dee must see from my expression that the answer is absolutely nothing. "Or the Lost Book?" I shake my head and she sighs. "I guess I shouldn't be surprised. It's not a Nagual legend, but it is interesting. It actually explains the connection between our world and the spirit world. For the sake of this story, we have to consider that there is a third dimension; the demon realm."

I frown. "The whole preternatural thing is complicated enough without bringing science fiction into it. Please tell me we can't time travel because then I'm really done."

She giggles again. "No time traveling, and the multiple

dimensions theory isn't as complicated as it sounds. We have our world and then the spirit world: where people go when they pass, and restless souls are said to linger. There have always been theories about the existence of more realms, but it's been unproven. The demon realm in particular is nothing more than a horror story that preternatural tell naughty children, but a long time ago there was a vicious rumor that incubi and succubi came from the demon realm. No one is supposed to be able to cross these dimensions, but of course, there are stories of people who have managed it, so some Nagual tried to imply that we did."

"That's horrible," I say. Dee nods. "Why would anyone think something like that?"

Dee shrugs, but the way her eyes dart away from mine tells me that she knows the answer, she's just not comfortable having to share it.

"We, succubi and incubi, can do more than just shift into wings. We consume life force, or energy, from other people. It's not a lot, not enough to incapacitate or kill, but you can probably imagine how that would get us a bad reputation. We have ways of doing it safely now, mostly with volunteer programs, but hundreds of years ago, our kind had no choice but to take it from others. That earned us our reputation as seducers and villains. It's not entirely true, though. Many of our communities found ways to take life force consensually. There is a church in Romania said to be touched by the heavens. There were claims that if people stayed in the church overnight, an angel would come and give them a kiss. People traveled across Europe for the angel kisses, saying they had magical powers or healing properties. This church has stained-glass windows depicting this scene to this day.

"But it wasn't true. There were no angels, and the kisses were not magic. Winged creatures did kiss the humans who visited, but it was incubi. Their wings are identical to the angel motif, just with black or gray feathers instead of white. Succubi are different, our wings are featherless and leathery, more like bats. As for the kisses, they are said to give a heady, almost euphoric sensation. I wouldn't know." She blushes furiously.

"I, uh, haven't even been kissed, for one thing. Not properly, at least. The transfer of life force doesn't feel quite like that for me, though." She doesn't linger on the subject, instead transitioning back to my lesson. "This arrangement let the incubi feed with ease, and then pass the energy onto the succubi in their community with the humans as eager volunteers."

I frown. "But it was still a trick. They didn't know what they were signing up for."

"That's true," Dee says with a nod. "But exposing themselves in the name of honesty was not an option. We always had that in common with the Nagual. This may have been deceitful, but it was the lesser evil. The humans in this community were protected by the fact that the incubi never needed to go too far with their feed out of desperation."

I can understand this, but I still don't like it. Dee gives me a sympathetic smile.

"Like I said, things are different now. That same church actually plays into the story of the Lost Book, if you would still like to hear about it."

"Of course," I say, my eagerness eliciting another delighted giggle from Dee. "Well, I said that this rumor about our kind was started, but it was more than just that. Before, things between the Nagual and other preternatural beings were contentious, but never violent. After, Nagual started to seek us out in our communities. They claimed it was part of their divine mission to protect humans from monsters like the incubi, and that was actually what sparked the Preternatural War in the 1800s. Years went by with our people at war until a man named Hektor Verostoia, an incubi from the same group in Romania who fed at the church, sought to cross into another realm. He wanted to prove, or, disprove, I suppose, that our people came from elsewhere.

"He enlisted magi to help him since everyone agreed that this would be a nonviolent way to put an end to the war. It took many years, but he managed it. He didn't go to a demon realm, of course, but a limbo state where he was not alive or dead, thought to be the spirit world. He was not here nor there. He existed in a suspended state, able to watch the world as if through a looking glass."

A shudder racks through me. Though I know this is just a story, one of a theoretical nature, I feel a strange kinship to Hektor. Sometimes when my dissociations got bad, it made me feel as if I was in a suspended state. Nothing truly exists, and I don't feel real, I just watch the world around me as if through an insurmountable distance. I don't think what I experience is any legitimate sort of purgatory, but the parallel is unnerving.

"He learned something when he was in that state, not about the origin of our kind, which he no longer thought would actually put an end to the war. The Nagual were already trying to discredit him and his experiments with the magi. Nothing he could say about his kind would change their minds, but the information he learned was leverage they did not have before. He wrote down what he learned in what eventually became the Lost Book and went to the monarch, now the Mavericks, with it. Whatever was in there was enough to get them to agree to a ceasefire. The war ended right then. The queen wanted to destroy the book, so Hektor ran off with it, swearing to put the book somewhere no one could ever find it unless it was needed again."

"He brought it to the church," I guess.

Dee nods, but there is a mischievous glint in her dark eyes. "Yes, but he put it inside the abditory aether. He had never been able to cross worlds again after the first time, it is said that the Universe would not allow for it now that his quest for knowledge had been accomplished, but the magi helped him to open a small pocket that would be able to hold the book and it could only be opened again by someone of his blood. Or so the story goes."

Her words have something fractured clicking together in my brain.

Magi experiments, the Universe allowing something impossible, a hiding place in a pocket of purgatory only to be opened by someone of their bloodline—though the circumstances are completely different, it strikes a chord with my own quest to discover what my parents did in order to conceive me. Maybe it's crazy to be connecting these pieces when I still don't understand what exactly I am meant to be putting together, but something about it feels right too. There's a sensation crawling up my neck that is telling me not to ignore this.

As much as I've struggled to reconcile the parents I knew with the people who lived and studied here, this feels inexplicably right. My father loved obscure stories and mythologies. He loved finding meaning in what others would consider the mundane. He loved nothing more than to prove an impossibility to be possible, and that was just with science as a tool. Here he had an entire world of magic to inspire him. I can certainly believe that if my dad were to hear this story, he would try to make his own abditory aether, and if he was successful, it would be the perfect place to hide something he didn't want to be readily found.

And if he managed to do all this—and it is a big if, I know —I think I have a good idea of where to start looking.

Dee and I chat for a bit longer, but when we finally part ways, I head back towards the academic quarter. It's quiet at this time of night and when I arrive at the library, it's empty save for the librarian, Hugh, who I've come to know after the last few weeks. He's sitting at the front desk between the grand staircase and the elevator thumbing through the same thick book he's been reading all month. The vinyl player behind his desk fills the space with pleasant jazz and he hums along in time with the tune.

He smiles as I approach from the elevator bay. "Why Miss Maverick, what brings you in this evening?" He has the remnants of a southern drawl, the only evidence that he is a transplant like me and was not, in fact, born and raised within the walls of this library.

"I'm just looking for some answers," I explain.

"You came to the right place then! I was going to put on a pot of decaf in the back office, can I offer you a cup?"

"That would be lovely, thank you."

I listen to his footsteps growing distant as he passes the stagnant bookshelves. There is an employee office back by the elevator bank with a kitchenette and a coffee machine that whirrs much louder than I think should be allowed in a library.

Grateful for the privacy, I don't hesitate. I rush over to the William Holbrook Beard painting and examine it with fresh eyes.

When I heard Dee's story, the first thing I thought of was my dad's office again and the degree he had hanging above his desk. I was young in that memory, but something about how he had been handling it struck me as odd, even then. I think that's why it keeps replaying in my mind. I'm no longer sure that my dad had been hiding something behind it. I think I may have caught him hiding something *inside* of it. Or beyond it—I don't have the mechanics of this theoretical magic worked out just yet.

I almost called my aunt when I left the coffee shop to ask her to find the degree in the garage, but decided against it. Even if she did drag it out, I'm not sure there would be anything to see. I think I have to be there and interact with the magic myself. Which I won't be able to do for a while since I'm restricted to Versi.

That brought me to my second theory. Because my dad would have likely been at Versi when he discovered what he did. If he decided then that he didn't want the information to be found out, he would have hidden it right away. He would have hidden it here.

And the only other time I remember him acting strangely around a wall fixing was in Indianapolis, while looking at a painting by William Holbrook Beard.

I'm not sure if it was coincidence or something stranger that had us at that art museum, but I'm certain my father wouldn't have hidden anything there. However, if he had hidden something of great importance in another Beard painting, it would explain his odd, almost desperate reaction to me reaching out to touch it.

I look at the painting now and wish that my curiosity alone could unlock all of its secrets, but it remains as solid and uninspired as it had always been. Though I have no idea how any of this is meant to work, if this is meant to work at all and my imagination is not just simply getting away from me, I reach out my hand towards the canvas.

What I'm doing may be crazy, but it feels so right. I surge forward, pressing my fingers to the pliable canvas and feeling each hill and valley of the soft paint.

Nothing happens. I blink at the image, all of the animals depicted there seeming to stare back at me with their beady eyes. I try again, gripping the wooden frame this time, but it's impermeable. Panic starts to rise, and I force myself to breathe through it, to calm down, to try again.

This time, I close my eyes. Instead of just thinking that this train of thought is sound, I choose to believe it. It's not an easy thing, even after everything I've learned the last several weeks and everything I've seen, to truly believe in something so impossible. But I am nothing but the product of something impossible.

Eyes glued shut, I shift forward again, bringing my hand towards the painting. I move slowly, preparing myself to feel the texture of the paint and not puncture the canvas in my eagerness, but it doesn't come. It doesn't come the next moment either. And with the next, the only thing I feel is a bitter, punishing cold.

I try to curb my excitement, fearing that if I recognize the truth of what is happening, it will break the spell—and maybe my hand will be caught on the other side of the portal. I'm certainly not an expert in transdimensional amputation, but I'm not eager to become one.

Pushing forward another inch, my hand finally comes in contact with something that isn't the painting or the wall. It's cool and smooth, like the glossy cover of a book, but then my fingers bump an odd corner and I realize that there are actually two things there, a book and a notebook, by the feel of it. I wrap my hand around both and pull it back through.

I open my eyes just in time to see the materialization of the items from the artwork's surface. The painting itself seems to warp and distort around the books, as if reality is stitching itself up at the seams, preventing me from getting even a glimpse of the aether beyond.

"Woah," I murmur under my breath. But my examination is halted by the sound of Hugh's footsteps coming back through the quiet library. I take a step away from the painting and towards the nearest table as he comes into view.

"Here ya go, hun," he says, setting the coffee mug down on the table.

"Thanks, Hugh," I say with a smile.

"Of course. Do you need help with anything?"

I wave the items in my hand before I can think better of it. "All set."

He returns to his desk, though I don't dare look at what's in my hands until I hear his rolling chair come to a halt under his weight. Finally, I look down, my heart in my throat, and I am immediately disappointed. The book is nothing like what I expected. Maybe it's because of Dee's story but I pictured some dramatic hand-scrawled tome. Instead, it's a small paperback with a waxy cover, the kind you see neglected in the clearance bin of an indie bookstore. The name on the cover reads *Chief Raven Heart's Guide to Skinwalking* and the cover shows only the image of a large white wolf.

I grab for the book and flip through, convinced I'm missing something crucial, because this is not at all what I envisioned my father going through such lengths to hide. There are ten chapters, each one a step in the practice of "skinwalking." From what I can tell from my brief perusal of the introductory chapter, it is the Native American ideology of embodying the spirit of an animal. Annoyed, I toss the book back onto the table and pick up the notebook.

It's spiral-bound, yellow, and college-ruled. It actually looks exactly like the ones my mom would pick up for me from a stack at the dollar store before school would start each year. The design is more dated, since it's from twenty years ago, and it's well-worn from use.

I flip through page after page of notes from classes, many of which might actually be helpful moving forward. My dad's messy scrawl is so familiar that it makes my chest contract. His brain always seemed to work so quickly that it was a struggle for his hands to keep up. Halfway through the notebook, following several blank pages, I finally find something relevant.

Skinwalking, it says at the top of the page, like a heading. It's followed by a short list of other books.

Nameless Monsters and Unrelated Legends – Dr. Tyrone Heatherstone

Native American Nagual Legends and Lies – Dr. Gianna Gabris-Joust

Abominations: Monsters So Scary Even Nagual Quake – Arthur Fowl

I'm on my feet in an instant, rushing to the bookcases. Unsurprisingly, they don't make me search very hard. The shelves quake as they do their usual shuffle, but three shelves, which display each of the three books front and center on each, present themselves.

I start with the last one, of course, since an *abomination* is a concept that I've come to be interested in after having the insult directed at me several times now. It's labeled as preternatural fiction: horror, which is strange in itself, so I don't even wait until I'm seated back at the table before I crack it open. Its table of contents lists each type of creature in alphabetical order, so I easily identify the page on Skinwalkers.

Skinwalkers

Imagine you came across a Nagual in the woods who looked like you, shifted like you, and smelled of flesh and blood, as you do. You would accept them as a Nagual, right?

Now, what if I told you that he wore a pelt that looked very much like your animal form's skin, and still dripped with blood. What if I told you he slaughtered an animal, or even a Nagual—for the legend is unclear—and enchanted it to give him the same abilities as you. That he robbed the Universe of a life to give himself an extraordinary one.

And what if he looked at you like you would make a much better pelt.

I shudder as I set it down again. I understand why it was classified as horror now. It reads very much like a scary story meant to be told around a campfire. I'm still not sure how any of this adds up to anything notable, but I'm far from deterred.

Native American Nagual Legends and Lies turns out to be a much less aggressive accounting than the title suggests. It's labeled as educational material, but it seems more like a fact or fiction glossary. The author addresses elements of Native American religion, usually regarding shapeshifting, and determines if the legends refer to Nagual. The passage on skinwalking is short.

With the skinwalking legend, one is said to wear the charmed pelt of an animal and shift into its form. While this practice is documented quite frequently in Navajo myths and religion, there has been no formal documentation of this practice in effect. Many Nagual scholars believe that the invention of the enchanted pelt is a misrepresentation of a natural Nagual ability. One purveying theory is that if shifters gave the impression that their gift was limited by a physical talisman, neighboring tribes would be less afraid of the power they possessed. If the Nagual legend had been misunderstood, it is likely that the story was shaped into that of the Skinwalkers. We have determined this legend to be a LIE.

Nameless Monsters and Unrelated Legends is like an encyclopedia of preternatural beings. Unfortunately, this glossary isn't alphabetical, so I have to flip through the book in search of the right write-up. The book is a collection of creature names and a few lines of basic information about them. None of the "monsters" he mentions are actually nameless, just not categorized as a Nagual, magi, or a familiar hybrid breed. There's a section on the El Chupacabra that nearly distracts me, but I force myself to keep searching. Towards the end of the book, I finally find the section on Skinwalkers.

Stemming from Native American religions, the legend of skinwalking presents an opportunity to shapeshift outside of the natural blessing provided by the Universe. In theory, this would give anyone the ability to shapeshift, much in the way a Nagual can. There is little documentation to support the truth of this practice and the likelihood of such an act seems incredible. To become a Skinwalker, in the way the legend suggests, one would be required to take an animal's life—not for food or sustenance, or out of protection of one's safety and that of their family (all acts of violence the Universe allows for in modera-

tion.) One would be required to kill for the sport of gaining power. It is difficult to see how the Universe, which values the harmony of human and nature above all else, could allow such an act to transpire. It is more likely that this legend is untrue or misinterpreted from historical texts.

I lean back in my chair, staring at the books. My mind is racing as I try to connect the dots that the books refused to do for me. Then I shake my head. It's interesting from a theoretical perspective, but it doesn't add to anything tangible.

Except, these books weren't the ones my father hid. It had been Chief Ravenheart's step-by-step guide. And while the guide made the practice seem more spiritual than physical, all the other texts directly opposed that idea, even as they disproved the existence of skinwalkers entirely. Though I can't imagine any commercial nonfiction book, even one that seems very questionable in its validity, being allowed on shelves, it plainly declared *do this and you will become a shapeshifter!*

Individually none of these books, nor my father's notes mean much. However, when you cumulate all the sources, it suddenly seems a little bit less theoretical. Crazy, for sure, but not impossible.

I flip the page on his notebook, curious if he had any additional notes on the subject, but again I'm disappointed. The next page is blank and so is the one after. I let out one long, labored breath.

As taboo as the books made the practice out to be, it is a loophole that could make the possibility of my mom conceiving me a reality. My father turned himself into a being that looked, behaved, and essentially *became* a Nagual, at least for a short time. It's in no way science, and it even seems so far off from the rules of magic that I have come to understand since coming to Versi. The last text questioned the Universe's allowance of such manipulation of nature, but I suppose that I am proof that they did.

I have a hard time believing that my dad would slaughter an animal to complete the ritual—he was a gentle man who wouldn't even kill houseflies, though he did leave them to his Venus flytraps to be taken care of—but if that is the aspect of all this that is the hardest for me to believe, then I'm ready to accept this as truth.

My dad became a Skinwalker.

✺ 27 ✺
JET

Three weeks after Tempest's attack by the Full Moon Knights and we're no closer to finding them. Before Kiara went missing, I wouldn't think of three weeks being a considerable length of time. After, I counted every hour of every day hoping for an answer, one way or another. Then the days turned to weeks, which turned to months, and I stopped counting like everyone else. Now, I refuse to let time eat away at the significance of this case.

I'm reviewing the Full Moon Knight files again, specifically the petty crimes committed in the New England region in the last twenty years. Most were robberies or muggings, with all but one being non-violent. While basic necessities and camping supplies were the majority of what was taken in the robberies, there's a ritualistic element to the crimes. They always take place at midnight during a full moon and a calling card, of sorts, is left at the scene. Claw marks mar either the door, the checkout counter, or a wooden beam, but it's never been done by the same hand twice. In one of my dad's notes, he suggests that these robberies could be some sort of initiation.

The one time that the encounter became violent, an employee had been in the back office doing late-night inventory when the break-in occurred. He heard two people, a man and a woman, enter. He tried to confront them but was knocked out before he could so much as get a glimpse of the culprits. All he could tell the LOP was that the woman was called Helena. His jaw and nose were both broken from the blow, but he was otherwise unharmed, supporting my dad's theory, since we know the Knights have no qualms about committing senseless murder.

I shake my head as I set down the documents. More than twenty years of history and yet I don't feel like we're any closer to apprehending these monsters. And I'm no longer sure that the LOP has done everything it could.

There should be more files, more details, more urgency. My dad has only had a little involvement over the years, but Lieutenant Caro was almost always lead on the investigations, with several others assisting. With as competent as the LOP typically is, it's hard for me to accept that this is the one area where they have always gotten unlucky or outsmarted.

I think there's a bigger issue here, one I have to address with my father—and maybe even the director if I can manage it. Something about the Full Moon Knights case just doesn't add up.

As I pick up my phone to check the time, I hear the elevator shaft creak to life. I'm definitely pushing the boundaries of what my dad and I agreed on as far as my independent investigation, but I'm beyond caring now. With the state of the case files, there isn't going to be much more opportunity for an investigation anyway, just as my dad tried to warn me.

I'm not surprised when it's Tempest who steps off the elevator a minute later. She texted that she needed to talk to me, so I told her where I would be. Still, the sight of her takes the wind out of me. She has her messy curls pulled up into a high ponytail and her eyes are unnaturally wild, even more so than I've come to know. She's gorgeous and I let myself revel in the momentary distraction.

"What's wrong? " I ask.

"I've had just about the weirdest night of my life," Tempest says as she takes a seat at the edge of my desk. She does it as if she's done it a hundred times before. The familiarity of her gesture and the sudden presence of her long legs in my periphery further distract me. "Yes, weirder than being attacked by a werewolf cult, and if you don't believe me then let that be a testament to how freaking weird my night was."

Tempest recounts the events of her evening, starting with the story she heard from her new succubus friend. My chest tightens at the first mention of her insane theory and the sensation doesn't ease again until she confirms what she did, and what she found, at the library. Except it's not insane, because not only did it work and Tempest accessed a previously-thought-to-be-fictional abditory aether, she found the information she was looking for there.

"A Skinwalker," I say in awe, shaking my head.

"You know what it is?" she asks.

"Yeah, it's like the boogeyman: a scary story parents tell us to go to bed on time and eat our vegetables. To think that your dad became *that*... it's kind of—"

"Freaky?" Tempest asks, wrinkling her nose.

"I was going to say 'badass,' but yeah, it's definitely freaky too."

Tempest shivers and I notice she's only wearing a long-sleeve shirt. It was moderately warm today but now that night has set it, even the heated office has a chill. I take the sweatshirt from the back of my chair and offer it to her. Wordlessly, she accepts it and slips the too-large garment over her head. The hem falls to her thighs and the sleeves hang long past her hands.

"It got me thinking though, about the Full Moon Knights and Daria Payne. I think she knew that my mom was pregnant with me."

I frown. "That's impossible," I say, but at Tempest's schooling look, I concede that anything is possible where Tempest's conception is concerned. "Your mother couldn't have been pregnant yet. They left Versi in March, it would have been too early."

Tempest shakes her head. "A typical pregnancy has a forty-week gestation, which is ten months, not nine. There's some medical justification for why they say nine months that my aunt tried to explain to me once. Which means even if it was early—really early— Daria Payne *could* have known. If Daria was my mom's partner, she would have been closer to her than anyone even if they didn't like each other, right?"

She is right. Even if Daria and Melanie's relationship had been contentious, they still would have spent an exorbitant amount of time together. Enough to know a person as well as they know themselves.

"You think that's why Daria and her brother went after your mom? She didn't approve of the pregnancy?"

Tempest shakes her head. "I don't even think they were necessarily targeting my mom. I think they were targeting me."

The office is suddenly too warm. My neck feels flushed, and my head is spinning as I try to digest everything Tempest just unloaded on me. Tempest seems eerily calm. Content even.

"The Full Moon Knights called me an abomination that night, and they haven't been the only ones. I think Daria enlisted her brother to take the matter into their own hands, and once my mom killed them, the Full Moon Knights went after them in retaliation. If the rest of the Knights knew I existed, I don't believe they would have let me live."

"And the reason why they found out was because of me," I say hoarsely.

The touch Tempest places on my knee is light, barely more than a brush, but it makes my skin burn as if her fingertips are made of fire. Her gaze meets mine and the way her breath catches tells me that she's not unaffected either, which doesn't do anything to calm my nerves.

"This world would have swallowed me whole eventually, Jet. I don't love how exactly I got dragged into all of this, but I'm not sorry it was with you."

"I am sorry, though," I say, needing Tempest to understand. "There's so much going on in your life right now. I don't want to be a part of the problem. I want to be part of the solution."

She gives me a small smile that seems to have a secret in it.

"You are, Jet. Why do you think I came to you tonight?"

I was wondering that, actually. I know Andre and Tempest have been actively looking for answers the last couple of weeks. Sure, he could have just been busy, but the way Tempest is looking at me is different than it has been before. It's been different since last week on the rooftop. She's not as guarded. Not on edge. At least not around me.

"I trust you," she confesses, her voice soft.

Her words slam into my chest like the powerful blow of a freight train. My breath flatters. My heart momentarily stops before picking up at double-time. My head feels like it's whirring, but my step is steady as I get to my feet.

I'm suddenly towering over her, our chests so close together that a particularly deep breath from either of us would have us touching. But neither of us move a muscle for a long moment. Her wild eyes are bright with curiosity. Her lips are parted ever so slightly. I take it as an invitation.

I move my hand to cup the delicate curve of where her throat meets her jaw and finally do what I have been thinking about for weeks. I guide my lips to meet hers.

28

TEMPEST

Kissing Jet is a juxtaposition of opposing forces: shy but curious, uncertain but confident, frightened yet relieved. I wrap my arms around his neck, and he flexes the hand he has pressed into the desktop beside me, his thumb now brushing the outside of my thigh.

I've experienced a lot of oddities tonight, but this is not one of them. This feels as inevitable as falling asleep at the end of a long day. It's surreal enough for me to briefly question if I am already dreaming, but I know this is real.

The heat of his skin under my touch. The soft press of his lips as they explore mine. The throbbing of his heart where his chest is flush with my own.

The sound of an alarm cutting through the quiet office.

It's a low whooping noise that's not loud enough to startle, yet still jars me out of the kiss. I search Jet's face but he's frowning at the elevator bank. A moment later, it starts to hum with activity.

"What is it?" I ask.

"It's an alarm they ring throughout HQ to get the whole

office's attention," he says, though that doesn't really explain why it's ringing now. I'm still boxed in by his frame, and despite the prospect of getting caught in this compromising position, I'm not eager for him to let go.

"But there's no one here. I only saw the agent at the front desk when I came in."

"I know. I think it means they're calling all available agents. Something must be going on."

He finally breaks away from me and cold rushes in to fill the places where his heat had been. He doesn't reach for my hand again or even meet my eye as he hurriedly arranges the documents on his desk. I tell myself not to take it personally, that he was just caught off guard by the alarm and now he's in work mode, but his sudden withdrawal feels ominous.

There are voices as the elevator doors open, a lot more than I would have expected with the alarm only starting a few moments before. I hop off the desk and move my hands to check that my curls haven't escaped the ponytail I tamed them in. Within moments, I see several familiar agents and officers gathering at a cubicle by the front of the area, all speaking in urgent, hushed voices.

Jet closes the last file, obscuring the files from anyone's passing glance. When he finally looks at me, all the tenderness from our kiss is gone. His look is hard: a message.

This night is far from over.

❧ 29 ❧
JET

The alarm has only ever been used once when I was in the office, but that time it had just been a convenient way to get the entire building down into the training center on time. To my knowledge, it's never been used for its intended purpose.

"What's going on?" Tempest asks from my side, but I don't think she's actually expecting me to answer. I want to reach back and take her hand. I want to pull her close and pick back up where we left off. I want to tell her that she's the one person I want to see too, even when it doesn't make sense to. I want to say that I don't think we should be friends, that we should be more. But something is wrong and that has to take precedence.

I can see the urgency of the situation in the way my dad's cheek twitches as he presses his lips into a tight line. He's speaking with Lieutenant Caro and the director with a few other agents around them. I approach my father, who seems unsurprised to see me here despite the hour, though his brows pinch when he notices Tempest just behind me.

"The Full Moon Knights are thought to be behind a

bombing in the Lake George area," he says, not making me ask the question. I take a step back in my shock and I hear Tempest let out a small gasp. "There was a disturbance at one of the shops closed for the season. We suspect that it was one of their initiations, but they didn't realize there was a silent alarm. The owner of the shop lives down the street and went by to check it out. He's Nagual, so he called us before he even arrived. Once he did, he put up a fight against the Knights—knocked one of them unconscious. The other fled. This happened an hour ago, but the director just heard a report from the human police force that a bomb went off in that area, the same block as the shop. Our theory is that more Knights returned to harm the man in retaliation. A speed team has already been dispatched, but we need all available units to get to Lake George fast to handle this before anyone gets hurt."

"What can I do?" I ask, though I expect him to send me away. I think he'll tell me to take Tempest home and leave the rest to them, but this situation must have spooked him because he assigns us a job right away.

"Have Tempest help you in reviewing the Full Moon Knight files. See if you can find a ballpark number of how many Knights are in their organization. Between the report of their initial dissent and the suspected initiations since, we should be able to gather an approximate number."

"Yes, sir," I say, already moving towards my desk. Tempest follows, not being shy about grabbing for a stack of papers once she's there.

"There were three who attacked me in Crescentwood," she says. "Two were older but one was pretty young. Our age."

"There's been at least eight initiations," I say, sorting through the files. I trade a few papers with Tempest. "Here's the report from the queen's assassination attempt. A few

Knights are mentioned by name, but only one was appre-hended that night. He said he had a brother, so account for that." Tempest nods and her eyes immediately start scanning the paperwork. I count the initiation files. Not eight, like I suspected, but nine, not including the new member being tested tonight. There's no way to tell if the second person reported at each of these crimes is the same person, and I'm not really sure if it matters. Any number we decide on will be an estimation. What if the initiations aren't done for every new member of their pack? What if they aren't actual initiations at all? What if the details missing from these files are obscuring critical information?

There are more questions than I'm comfortable with, but we can only do what we can with the resources we have. Worrying about the rest won't help now.

As Tempest and I read, more protectors arrive at HQ. There is a flurry of activity as they get everything they need to move out: weapons, potions, charms, and other gear. The ground floor of the LOPHQ, beyond the lobby, is mainly a garage for all the vehicles registered to the LOP. There's an entire fleet of black cars and vans to transport our units to the Adirondack tourist town about an hour and a half from here.

"Six," Tempest says finally. "That's the count from the assassination attempt, minus Dannon Carter and his brother, whoever he is. That's also not including the Don. That's who the wolf woman said they wanted to bring me back to. I can't tell if he was part of the first attack."

"Probably best to assume that he wasn't, for the time being. Plus, my nine gives us seventeen suspected Knights in total."

Tempest shudders. "Way too many, in my opinion." I nod my agreement.

"Let's tell my dad," I say. We cross the busy office area to my dad's open office door, but the director is in there and the volume of their voices suggests now is not a good time to interrupt.

"It's all hands on deck," Director Sanchez says. "The other two speed teams are already en route. Caro and I are leaving now with the units on hand. I want you to call in the rest of the organization and meet us as soon as possible."

"Yes, ma'am," my dad says. Elena doesn't waste any time pushing past us, giving a tight nod in acknowledgment as she barrels out the door. I see Brody jogging from a huddle of cubicles on the other side of the office. In a few short strides, he joins us in the doorway. My dad sees us outside and waves us in.

"Another bomb has gone off. So far, no casualties, only substantial property damage. Human police are closing off the area, but they have no idea what we're dealing with. Our first speed team has already arrived and apprehended two of the Knights, but another four were seen in the area. Two more speed teams are leaving now to trace the other Knights. The director got the FBI's blessing to take over jurisdiction, so she's leaving to take care of this quickly and quietly."

"We have evidence to suggest there are fifteen Knights in operation," I say. "But there are potentially three additional members: the new initiate, Dannon Carter's brother, and someone called the Don, who seems to be their leader."

My dad curses. "And only six were seen. I can't deny that I was hoping we may have caught a break tonight and be able to put an end to the Knights for good."

"Let us help," Brody says, ready to jump into the fray despite his late arrival. "Jet and I know the Knights as well as any agent, if not more."

"We won't get in the way," I say, agreeing with his sentiment. "We'll just be extra sets of eyes and ears. The director said it's all hands on deck."

My father considers this with a frown, but eventually, he gives a curt nod. "See if you can catch up with Lieutenant Caro's squadron. But no matter what we may face, you are not to engage. Am I understood?"

"Yes, sir," Brody and I chorus.

"Tempest," my dad calls before we can leave. "I need you to make a comprehensive list of everything you learned about the Knights from the night of your attack. Detailed descriptions of the three involved and anything they may have said."

Tempest nods. "Of course."

I know we had several reports written up on Tempest's experience so I'm not sure if my dad is assigning her the task in earnest or if it's just to give her a job that requires her staying put and out of harm's way. Either way, I'm grateful.

Tempest, Brody, and I leave my dad's office and make the short walk back to my desk. Brody grabs a few things from the top of his and I take that moment to face Tempest.

"Don't do anything reckless," she tells me. While she makes an effort to look tough, crossing her arms and scowling up at me, I can see the worry in her eyes. A lock of her messy, dark hair falls in front of them and instinctively, I take a half step forward to tuck it behind her ear. She bites her lip, seemingly to stop herself from saying more.

"Let's go," Brody says, turning to face us, though I'm still watching Tempest too intently to look back at him.

"You've got work to do," I tell Tempest. She nods but she doesn't move away. "Go on, princess," I say, nodding towards the desk.

"Do not call me that," she snarls—actually snarls, with bared teeth and everything. I have to press my lips together to stop from laughing, though I can't hide the smirk that replaces it.

She shoulders past us towards my desk, not bothering to spare Brody or me a second glance as we make our way across the office. As we approach the elevators, I shake my head, but Brody reads me like an open book.

"You're so screwed," he says, smiling.

"Yeah," I agree, though even I can admit that I sound happy about it.

Marring the splendor of the Adirondacks' breathtaking beauty of green rolling hills and glistening blue water is the town of Lake George. The night is too dark to see it properly, but I've been a couple times in the past and can picture it perfectly even amongst the chaos. Strips of tourist-trap shops selling five-dollar sunglasses and ten-dollar t-shirts line the streets. Criminally overpriced water-front restaurants and bars overlook the lake, but they're all rundown due to their only reprieve from the near-constant foot traffic being the harsh winter months. Elisa loves the party-town atmosphere, but I've never been impressed.

Tonight, the tourist town looks very different from what I remember. It's smoldering.

Sirens ring out discordantly, the wail of human ambulances and police cars clashing with the high-pitch alarms of our vehicles. Thankfully, it doesn't look like anyone is receiving emergency care, which is a promising sign. We're ushered out of the van we arrived in, dressed in a matching dark gray LOP uniform. All the excited anticipation of being allowed to participate in the assignment dissipated on the drive over, which

Caro managed in under an hour, thanks to the empty road in the late night.

Police officers and protectors run down the smokey streets, a sight made eerie by the heavy smog that hangs over the dark town. I see the director talking to the chief of the human police force. He's frowning and rubbing at his neck in confusion, likely as Director Sanchez tries to convince him to leave the scene so we can do our job to the best of our ability. Surely someone much higher up the hierarchy than him approved the handover of jurisdiction and he's hesitant to abandon an active crime scene with suspected assailants still on the loose.

This is why the LOP takes such drastic measures to avoid getting involved with human affairs in the first place. Only a small faction of government officials are aware of the preternatural, some of whom are preternatural themselves. It's enough to allow us open access to resources we may need, but not enough to risk our exposure, of course. Often the FBI, CIA, or Department of Homeland Security invite the LOP onto their "unusual" cases as consulting agents, and we generally have enough authority to conduct our independent investigations without people asking too many questions. But whenever a situation arises that throws us and humans together, it requires crafty wording, a few calls made to D.C., and a confoundment charm or two to help smooth things over.

That's what I see happening now, the director offering her phone to the police chief. His eyes go impossibly wide as he speaks to whoever is on the other end of the line. When he hands the phone back to Director Sanchez, she offers him a small bundle of herbs and black salt, which the man takes with confusion, and then his eyes become preternaturally glassy as he stuffs the oddment into his pocket. A moment later, he's calling for his men to retreat.

"Listen up," Caro announces as we gather around him in the street. "Another two Knights have been apprehended by the speed teams, with several other traces having been identified and are now under pursuit. This is great news, of course, though it has little bearing on our role here tonight. We will be doing rescue and recovery. All residents have been evacuated from the area, but we are looking for anyone who may have been missed or anything of interest. Based on the small blast radius, we have deduced that the bombs used by the Knights are rudimentary, homemade devices, but they still managed to do considerable damage, as you can see. Be on alert, and if anything useful is identified, come to me first."

We're each assigned to a specific area to start going through the rubble and split off, not hesitating to dive into our work. I do so without complaint for several long minutes, but then curiosity has me opening myself up to my ability to trace. The terrain is unfamiliar, with so many people around who I can't identify: human law enforcement, emergency responders, and our league, and yet I can recognize the lingering traces of the Full Moon Knights amongst them. None are exactly the same as the ones I followed in Crescentwood to find Tempest under attack, but there is an earthy undertone to their sweet-and-sour scent that's familiar.

I'm not sure if I've ever been able to trace by breed of Nagual before, or if the wildness of the Knights is just so ingrained in their bones and their blood that it somehow has permeated their trace as well. I can tell that at least four Knights have been running through this area recently, and the concentration by a couple of armored cars up the road tells me that five are sequestered inside those vehicles, the number that Caro implied had been arrested.

I've always had an interest in the speed teams. Every protector-hopeful is. They are the most elite of the protector units, chosen for their speed, of course, but also their superior ability to trace. They are also the only unit where one's Nagual form plays a factor. Typically, the LOP is open to all types of preternatural with a wide range of abilities, but for the speed teams, where physical prowess is critical to their functionality, it has to be taken into account. Because being fast for a rabbit is still nothing compared to being fast for a wolf, or raptor, or bear. I imagine as a panther, and with my talent, I stand a real chance of making it onto a speed team one day. I file that ambition away and try to ignore the itch of my instincts asking me to abandon Caro's assignment and set off into the New York wilderness on my own hunt.

In my periphery, I see Brody shift into his golden retriever form now that all humans have been cleared from the scene and shove his snout under several overturned slabs of concrete. He nudges at it with his head and makes a few whining noises that have me sighing and jogging over to help him. I lift the concrete chunk and it reveals an isolated area of scorched flooring. I look around and notice that the damage to this particular area is acute. Black puddles are now cauterized into charred mounds of plastic, probably from those cheap sunglasses. There are piles of ash and smoking remains of wire racks and hangers.

"Great find," I tell Brody before calling out to Caro. He's pretty far across the road so it takes him a few moments to jog over. With all the Nagual protectors now shifting into their animal forms at will, I'm a little surprised that he doesn't too. I try to remember his animal form. I know he is Nagual, but was it therianthrope or lycanthrope? Not bakeneko, I don't think.

"What do you got, boys?" he asks as he approaches.

"I think this is where one of the bombs was placed," I say.

Brody shifts back beside me. "There's evidence of foreign materials and acute destruction."

Caro looks around, taking in the scene for himself. "Good find, I'll make a note of it. Carry on." He takes a step away and I step forward, though Brody beats me to voicing his dissent.

"Sir, shouldn't we get a forensic team in here now? This could be evidence."

"Yeah, something in the bomb's construction could tell us more about where it was built," I jump in. "Which could give the speed teams some more direction and help them track down the rest of the Knights."

Caro gives us a tight smile. "Your enthusiasm is appreciated, as always, boys, but save the protector work for the actual protectors. I can assure you that our forensic teams will look into this after we have done our job here tonight, but I'm certain their findings will only be interesting to note for our report. So, as I said, carry on."

Something clicks then, and I do something I have never done before. I disrespect a figure of authority. I take another step forward. "I'm not sure I trust you to actually include this in the report."

Caro's eyes turn steely as they fix on me. I've never noticed the color before, I assumed his eyes were a light blue, but right now, in the dark, they look more like ghostly gray.

"Pardon?" he says, his tone is as flat and hard as the concrete slab I moved a moment ago.

Still, I don't back down. I roll my shoulders back as I say, "For the last twenty-four years a substantial number of reports on the Full Moon Knights appear to have been purposefully lacking critical details, and I noticed a pattern, Lieutenant Caro. All of those reports had you assigned to them."

"What, exactly, are you accusing me of, cadet?" his voice is no louder than a whisper and yet he wields that one word like a whip, the sound cracking through the tension.

"Nothing," I say, because it was not meant to be an accusation, though with his reaction, I'm starting to reconsider. "But as a *cadet*, I just learned the proper protocol and procedures for how to handle an active investigation, and this is not it."

A growl escapes his throat. "You are dismissed, Cadet Delancey. If you cannot understand the nuances between learning in a classroom lecture and active fieldwork then I don't want you within tracing distance of my crime scene. Cadet Bates, get back to work," he barks.

He turns away from us but does not immediately move out of earshot, so Brody and I just exchange a long, knowing look. Brody might not have had enough time with the files to come to the same conclusion that I have, but he did see them. That, paired with Lieutenant Caro's reaction, is enough to make him suspicious too. To be fair, I'm sure any officer would be upset to be accused of incompetence by a cadet, but my instincts tell me that Caro is too defensive. So, I'm glad to see in the sharp edge of Brody's hazel eyes that he got the same impression.

With a sharp nod, I turn on my heels and make my way *out of tracing distance* of Lieutenant Caro. I turn the block out of eyesight and head right for the street where our vehicles are parked. Right to where I know I can find the director. I have every intention of marching up to Director Sanchez herself, even if that means risking everything that I've worked so hard for in my pursuit to join the LOP by making an accusation of this nature. To my relief, I see my dad has arrived just a moment before I do. He exchanges a few hushed words with the director before starting off in the opposite direction. I call after him and he pulls up short, frowning at me.

"Jet, I allowed you to come so you could be put to work," he starts.

I run up to meet him. "I know," I say. I'm out of breath but not from the short run. My heart is racing fast enough to suggest I'm on mile twenty-five of a marathon. "I know," I say again. "And I know how this is going to sound so I really need you to take me seriously for a moment, not just as a son, but as a protector. Okay?"

My dad is still frowning but I recognize the glint of curiosity in his eyes.

"What is it, cadet?" he says, and this time I don't think he means it to be impersonal. I think he wants me to know that he will do as I asked and take me seriously as a colleague. Or at least try to.

"I have a few things I need to tell you," I start, thinking of the neglected case files, my new suspicions of Caro, and the mysterious brother that Dannon Carter was so certain would free him of prison, suggesting that at least one of the Knights was in a position to do so. "But before I do, I need you to answer something for me. What kind of Nagual is Lieutenant Caro?"

My father's scowl deepens, the wrinkles between his brows creasing. "I don't see how that is pertinent. We, as an organization as well as people, need to be above profiling based solely on one's Nagual form."

Somehow my heart manages to race faster, so fast that I can feel it skipping beats as it tries to keep up with a race it suddenly knows it can win, even if the cost is great.

"I know. I would never want that, but Lieutenant Caro *is* a lycanthrope, isn't he?" I already know the answer, based on my father's reluctance to share it alone. It still takes the small incline of his head for me to become certain of what my body has been sure of for the last several minutes.

"Dad, I don't have anything but circumstantial evidence, but all of my instincts are telling me that Lieutenant Caro is working with the Full Moon Knights."

I expect horror. I expect rage at the audacity of my accusation, similar to Caro's own. I don't expect the slight narrowing of my father's eyes and a question.

"How sure are you?"

"More than I ever have been," I say with a relieved sigh.

He nods, but true to his word, it's not my dad who gives the next order, it's Lieutenant Delancey, one of the most competent and highly ranking officers of the LOP, my superior and role model. "Tell me everything."

30

TEMPEST

Andre's face is pale as I finish telling him about what I found in the abditory aether and my theory on Daria going after my mother.

"Do you think it's possible?" I ask him. We're on the fourth floor of the LOPHQ, sitting on two of the cubicles we claimed.

Even though it's the middle of the night now, all the cadets who hadn't been at HQ when the rest of the protectors moved out to Lake George, or who hadn't been otherwise too preoccupied celebrating the holiday, came into HQ to do some reconnaissance. Since they're all used to my lurking around at this point, between my training with Andre and the few lectures I've shadowed, no one questions why I hang around to help.

The trouble is that there really isn't much to do besides wait for some further direction, and everyone out in the field is clearly too preoccupied to actually assign anything to us. So now there are twelve protectors-in-training, and me, just hanging around.

"I think anything is possible," Andre says, like a confession. He rubs aggressively at his brow. "Wow, Tempest, I mean if that's really what your parents did, it's kind of amazing. And kind of scary. I'm not sure if you should be telling anyone about this."

"I'm not telling anyone," I say. "I'm telling you." I nudge his foot with mine.

The cubicles are arranged so that every squadron has its own huddle space amongst the chaos of the open-concept office floor. The high-ranking protectors have offices along the back and left-most walls, with the right side of the room reserved for conference rooms. The cadets all started in one pod, but as we realized that there wasn't much of anything to search for on the databases yet, we spread out to entertain ourselves.

"I'm so bored," Ale announces, standing up from her desk. She walks over to where Andre and I are sitting. "I'm so mad I missed the first alert. I want to be out in the field."

"Yeah, I was on a date. What's your excuse?" Andre teases.

"Same, actually," Ale says with a sigh.

"With who?" I demand.

A furious blush colors her cheeks. "Doesn't matter," she mutters. I narrow my eyes at her, but I let her keep the secret, for now. "I'm just saying that I am way too useful to be babysitting the rest of these idiots. Gary and Leonard went to the archive room to pull the files on the Full Moon Knights thirty minutes ago and aren't back yet."

"The Full Moon Knight files aren't even in the archive room," I say, moving to the desk where I know they had been left. "Jet has them." I bring the stack back over to the group and hand them to Ale. She thumbs through the files but it's much too quick for her to have actually read them. "Has anyone else questioned the logic of all the protectors being in one place?"

"Not all the protectors," Andre says with a wink. "We're here."

Ale rolls her eyes. "I'm serious."

"The Knights are crafty," Andre says. "If they are all in the Lake George area and the director thinks we can finally get the jump on them then I can see why they needed everyone there."

"While we're stuck back here," Ale complains. "This sucks."

Andre's phone starts to vibrate so he fishes it out of his pocket. He beams and shakes it in Ale's direction. "Our luck is about to change, chica." He dances away from us a few feet, answering the phone.

"Lieutenant," he says in greeting. The rest of the cadets and I look on curiously. "Really? That's great." There is a lot of nodding and then Andre is quiet for a long moment as he bounces from foot to foot. "Understood. I can get going right away. Are you sure? No, of course. I'm sure she'll be grateful for the opportunity. We'll get right on it. Thank you, sir."

He hangs up and returns to us. "There's good news, bad news, and worse news—for you all. It's great news for me, I'm going to have a blast." He flinches. "That may have been the wrong choice of words."

"Just spit it out," Ale insists.

"The Knights are officially responsible for bombing a tourist strip in Lake George, which is the bad bit, obviously. Thankfully there are no casualties since that area is mostly closed up for the season. They've apprehended several members of the Full Moon Knights, and our speed teams are in pursuit of the others, with another several traces locked in."

There is a collective sigh of relief, though my heart feels

unexpectedly heavy from the news. I'm thrilled, of course, that the Full Moon Knights are being arrested. It means that soon I may even be able to put all of this behind me and return to some semblance of a normal life. Though I'm not sure if I know what normal would be for me anymore. That's not what worries me, though, which is worrisome in itself.

Jet is no doubt one of the fastest Nagual at the LOP, and I know he's particularly skilled at tracing as well. He may only be a cadet, but if it means catching the Full Moon Knights, I have no doubt he'd be the first to volunteer his services. The idea of him going after them on his own is more terrifying than it has any right to be.

"What's the rest of it?" I ask Andre. "The part you're all hyped up about."

"Well, there's been a domestic disturbance in Killington, about an hour north of here. And since there aren't any agents around to handle it, Caro asked me to go check it out."

"By yourself?" I ask at the same time Ale whines, "Really? That's not fair."

"It's just a welfare check, nothing fun," he says, patting Ale's head. She huffs and shoos him off. "But no, Caro wants me to take Tempest. He said it would be good exposure for her."

"She's not even an actual cadet," Ale complains. Then with a quick look at me, "No offense."

I shrug. "None taken." I look back to Andre. "But I'm not supposed to leave campus."

"Sure, but if all the Full Moon Knights are hours away in Lake George, this is probably the best time for you to sneak out. Besides, the order came from Caro, and he said the director approved it, so you're good to go. If you don't want to, I can probably bring someone else."

Alejandra looks all too eager to volunteer, so I quickly say, "No, I want to."

Andre beams. "Awesome. Let's get you some gear then, girl."

Andre takes me to the prep rooms on the third floor. There are several of them, each with a certain specialty. One is essentially an armory with all the weapons I never got around to playing with in the training room. Andre walks right by that one explaining, "We'll only take a couple of tasers on the off chance something gets out of hand, but we won't need anything more than that since it's a welfare call."

The next contains spare uniforms and Andre has me find one in my size. He directs me to wear one of the special shifting belts too. I give him a disapproving look, since we both know there is just about zero chance I shift during this assignment, but he just shrugs. "You never know." Sighing, I accept it and head into a changing room while Andre explains what we'll be doing from the other side of the door.

"There's a Ms. Vasselboro who's called the LOP on her husband a few times now. She's not listed as a shifter, but he's known to be a therianthrope: a Mastiff, I think Caro said, so he's a big guy. He threatened her and she got scared enough to call it in. Caro said she doesn't want to press charges, but he wants us to go up there and make sure."

"And he really doesn't think there's a problem with me going?" I ask as I wiggle into the cargo pants that come standard with the uniform. It's my size but since the uniforms are unisex it fits a little large in strange places.

"I mean, if you think about it, it couldn't be safer, if all the Knights are being actively apprehended in New York. And students in the Protector Program are invited on assignments all the time."

But it doesn't always end well, I think, remembering Jet's story about Kiara.

Now fully dressed, I look at myself in the changing room's mirror. The style is more athletic than a human police uniform but much dressier than army fatigues, though they clearly took some inspiration there. Everything is a shade of gray from heather to charcoal. Despite the cool styling, I just feel silly. I'm dwarfed by the length of the polo shirt and tucking it in somehow makes it look worse. Thankfully there is a nylon jacket made of thick wool that I can use to hide the rest of the outfit.

I throw open the door to find Andre fiddling with two tasers.

"Badass," he says, appraising the uniform. I shake my head, not believing him for a second but appreciating his unwavering support anyway.

He holds up the stun guns in his hand. "As you probably could have guessed, these aren't quite like the human equivalent."

"I would hope not," I say, accepting mine. "That would be boring."

He laughs. "There's no wires, for one thing. When you shoot it sends out what we call a button dart. Upon impact, it prevents the ability to shift and renders the affected's speed to that more similar to a human's, which will make them easier to apprehend. These are a new design which comes with two rounds instead of one."

I take the device, bright blue with a yellow stripe on the handle, and let the weight of it settle in my hands.

"How's it feel?" Andre asks.

"Badass," I admit.

31

JET

My dad listens intently, nodding in some places as I give my explanation, frowning at others, and asking more than a few follow-up questions. I don't detect any doubt in his voice, and I am never made to feel silly, even as I tell him some of the leaps in logic I've had to make for this to add up to the opinion I've come to.

"I'm going to entrust you with something you are not to repeat to anyone, not even Brody. Is that understood?" he asks. I nod, my heart lodging itself in my throat as I wait for him to continue. "The director has been conducting an internal investigation into the lack of care taken with the Full Moon Knight files. It came to our attention earlier this month when we reviewed them in light of Tempest's attack. Part of Lieutenant Caro's participation in this case has been a test, of sorts. He knows when to share information and when to hold back, but he's held back enough to warrant our concern. I must admit that allowing you access to the case files was, in part, a test of my own. Suspecting Caro has made me biased, I'm afraid, so

I'm reassured to see that you have come to a similar conclusion."

Relief is too mild of an emotion to describe the weight I feel falling off my shoulders.

"What do we do now?"

"We have to handle this delicately. We can't have anyone else learning of this and causing undue alarm, and we can't have Caro knowing we suspect him."

"But we can't have let him interfere with our investigation either."

"No," my father agrees with a nod. "I'll retrieve Brody. I doubt that Elena will need much convincing beyond what her internal investigation has been suggesting, but his perspective will help make the case. She'll likely reassign him for tonight, until she can enact a plan to get the truth from him once and for all."

I nod. "What can I do?"

"Go to the director and wait for me there. You may be a cadet, son, but your commitment to this organization has been more invaluable than you can know."

I nod. "Thank you, dad. For trusting me in this."

"You've earned it. I believe you'll be the best of us someday. Now, go. We don't have any time to waste."

I find the director the next block over. She's talking to Sergeant Koss but dismisses her to answer a phone call. I hang back a few feet, not wanting to intrude, and not willing to start the sensitive conversation without my dad. Her call is brief and spoken almost entirely in short-hand, though when her eyes land on me, she seems grateful for an audience to share what she learned.

"Another two Knights have been picked up by their trace. Speed teams are tracking them down now."

"That makes seven, right?" She nods. I don't count Lieutenant Caro out loud, but I say, "That's nearly half their organization. That's great."

The director wrinkles her nose. "I don't trust it."

"Ma'am?" I ask.

"Their initiations have gotten out of hand before but never with this level of retaliation. Either the Full Moon Knights have become very sloppy, or we're missing something."

I frown. With all the excitement tonight, I hadn't considered that. With the director's assessment, I play back the events of the night in my head with a fresh perspective, and she's right. It does seem too easy. But with five in custody, and the LOP in active pursuit of another three, it's hard to suss out why.

"Never mind that," she says, waving her hand. "What can I do for you, Cadet Delancey?"

"I was just wondering that myself," a smooth voice says. I turn to face Lieutenant Caro, seeming eerily relaxed given all I now know.

"My father got pulled away by another agent," I lie as I face the director. "But he asked me to let you know he has an urgent matter to discuss with you."

She nods with nonchalance. "Thank you, cadet. I'll find him as soon as I'm able." She turns to Caro. "Lieutenant?"

It's clear I've been dismissed so I take a couple of steps back, but I don't go far. In all honesty, I don't trust him to be alone with the director. So, until I'm ordered away, I'm staying put.

"I just wanted to update you that I received a call from a woman named Helena Vasselboro for a domestic disturbance just north of campus. You'll remember that I've been monitoring her situation for the last several months, so I took the liberty of assigning one of our cadets to make a house call."

The director's eyes narrow, and if I didn't know the extent of her suspicion of Caro from what my father said, it would be obvious to me now. And yet Caro is the picture of insouciance under her scrutiny.

"I would request that all matters of LOP business be directed through me," she says cooly. "As is standard."

"Of course, ma'am. But given how stretched thin we are tonight, I didn't want to interrupt you with such trivial matters. It's a simple house call, nothing a cadet has not shadowed before."

"Except they will not be shadowing tonight since all our agents are here," she continues with a frown. "They will be running point."

"It's a big ask, but the cadet is more than capable. He was instructed to bring one of his classmates with him, so I'm sure the pair will handle the matter with competence."

"Who did you send?" the director asks. And somehow I know who he'll say before he says it.

"Cadet Gonzales."

For the second, or perhaps fifth, time tonight, I act without thinking, taking large strides into the fray of a situation I have no business involving myself.

"Who did he bring with him?" I ask. My instincts are screaming again. No, not a scream. A roar.

"I'm not sure. I did not specify, so that matter was left to the cadet's discretion."

"You're lying," I say, just in time for my dad, Brody, and Sergeant Koss to join us. I don't know Lieutenant Caro well enough to know his tells, but his eyes seem to change, they somehow became unnaturally bright gray as he spoke, the same way they had been when he scolded me earlier tonight. They look almost like two full moons.

Several things occur to me at once, and they all pour out of my mouth as a stream of consciousness.

"You're lying," I say again. But even if by some chance he isn't, and Andre truly did have full autonomy to choose whoever he wanted to go with him on the assignment, the result would have been the same. "You sent Tempest with him. This is a setup."

I look up towards the sky just to confirm what I already know. "There was never an initiation tonight. The previous nine initiations have all taken place under a full moon at midnight. There's no moon tonight, and the suspected initiation started around nine p.m., much too early. There was a woman named Helena identified at one of the scenes, a suspected Knight, and I'm willing to bet that's the same Helena who you're claiming made the domestic disturbance call. I can't trace the three Knights who attacked Tempest in this area at all. All of this has been a distraction."

Lieutenant Caro snarls and shifts, turning into a wolf with blue-black fur. My father and Sergeant Koss had inched closer to him during my speech, not quite preventing him from running, but blocking him from making a quick escape. My dad shifts, his Great Dane form nearly the same size and shape as wolf-Caro, though one-on-one I'm certain Caro would still come out on top. Fortunately, Sergeant Koss' form is bigger. Much bigger. She's a bear shifter, and originally hailing from Alaska, her form takes the shape of a Kodiak bear, meaning she stands more than nine feet tall.

Caro cowers away and backs up towards me and the panther form I've now shifted into. I let out a roar, making him retreat until he's firmly between all three of us, looking cornered and panicked. We're drawing a scene, so Sergeant Koss' bear form bats her massive paw at the wolf, effectively knocking him unconscious with minimal effort. Quickly, we all shift back but Caro.

"Put him in a separate transport van," Director Sanchez says. "He'll be the first we interrogate. She points at my father, "Call headquarters and find out where Caro sent Gonzales and Maverick." She looks at Koss. "Have the speed teams redirect their efforts. We need our fastest units heading northeast immediately. We have no idea what to expect, but we cannot allow Cadet Gonzales and Tempest to face it on their own."

My father and Koss are already pulling out their phones to make their calls, so I don't hesitate to say, "Send me."

All heads snap in my direction, though I only meet the director's eyes. "The speed teams have been tracing southwest, right? They're farther than I am, and I'm fast. I can trace. I swear I won't take on the Knights myself, but like you said, Andre and Tempest have no idea what to expect. Even if I get there a moment before the speed teams, that could make all the difference."

I hear my dad start to object but the director doesn't wait to hear him out. "Go."

I don't hesitate another moment. My shift takes me, my body changing before my mind has even decided to do it. I'm moving faster than I ever have before, into the darkest hour of the night. The one that makes you question the certainty of dawn.

❧ 32 ❧

TEMPEST

With violet and white flashing lights, Andre pulls into the driveway of a dumpy modular home on a dark hillside. The roof is unkempt, nearly caved in, and it sits on several acres of unmaintained land. I would think that the place is abandoned except for a light shining from a back room in the house. Despite this, there is only the chirp of cicadas to greet us as we exit the car.

It's strange to be off the Versi campus after these last few weeks, though not as strange as it should be. I expected to feel some residual fear or anxiety, despite knowing that the Full Moon Knights are otherwise preoccupied nearly two hours away, but I honestly didn't feel much of anything on the drive over to Killington. Now I'm nervous, though I think that's just from the eerie feel of this place, the unnatural quiet, and the prospect of what Andre and I may have to do to protect this woman from her husband if things take a turn.

I fumble with the taser on my belt, making sure it's secure.

"You ready, chica?" Andre asks. I give a curt nod, but Andre must see through it because he offers me a smile. "It's going to be okay. I'll run point." I nod again, this time with a bit more confidence.

As we walk towards the stairs that lead to the door of the home, I experience a brief flash of deja vu. I try to recall the memory it feels like I'm experiencing, but it's elusive and I can't spare the time to consider it now. We have a job to do.

Andre clicks on a flashlight and lets the light beam draw paths in the yard. With nothing looking amiss, he ascends the stairs and knocks on the front door. There's no reply, though the chorus of crickets is so loud that they start to drown out the drumming of my heart. Andre gives me a questioning look and I shrug. I may have observed a few Protector Program classes now but I'm certainly not the best person to be asking what to do next. In fact, I may be the worst person to ask. The worst person to be here.

This time Andre knocks with the butt of the flashlight, the noise loud enough to echo against the hillside. "League of Protectors," he says with a tone more authoritative than anything I've heard from him before. "Open up." After another silent beat. "We have cause to enter the residence. Speak now or we'll enter by force."

It's not enough to persuade whoever is on the other side of the door. If there's someone on the other side, which I now doubt.

"She made the call from this property, didn't she?" I ask, suddenly nervous about what we might actually find inside, or what it means if we don't find anything.

The wind whistles, nearly drowning out my voice. I tug my LOP-issued jacket tighter around me. Earlier tonight had been deceptively moderate for this late in the year, but all at once it feels like winter is setting in. Thankfully there's no chance of snow tonight, but I wouldn't be surprised if we got some before the weekend is through.

"No, it was a cell," Andre explains. "It was traced to the tower nearest here but that doesn't necessarily mean she called from the house."

I let out a relieved breath. At this point, I'm not sure if it's better if we find her or if we don't. I hope she's safe, wherever she is, but I'm getting the uncanny feeling that Andre and I are out of our depth.

Andre unholsters his taser, so I do the same.

"We are entering. Place any weapons on the ground in front of you and put your hands up." He nods at me, so I remove the vile of petrifact powder from the pouch on the belt that Andre equipped me with before we left HQ. Andre takes it and dumps it over the door handle. Instantly, the residue eats away at the lock, corroding the metal, and leaving only a rusty finish. Andre kicks at it, once, twice, and then the lock hinge pings as his violent blows throw open the door.

I stand at the ready while Andre pushes the door open. I'm braced for a fight that never comes.

It's a one-bedroom home, if we can call it that. There is only a dirty sleeping bag in a corner and the frame of a couch with exposed springs instead of cushions and moth-eaten upholstery on the arms. I get a full tour of the kitchen in the small space, three counter units, and a pale square of wood where a stove must have once resided. Andre does a quick sweep of the bedroom and bathroom, but he's back with me in the main living space after only a few seconds.

"All clear," he says.

I holster my taser again. "This doesn't make sense."

"She could have gone for help," Andre offers. "And he could have fled."

I shake my head and gesture to the house. "No, I mean this." My parents always made sure I felt comfortable growing up, but I remember times we lived in motel rooms and one-bedroom apartments in neglected neighborhoods. Still, that was nothing compared to this. This place is inhabitable. I don't think it's the Vasselboro's residence at all.

We don't hang around any longer. We retreat to the car where Andre tries to call Lieutenant Caro. He doesn't have much service, so he walks around the edge of the property trying to get a signal. I lean against the front of the car, trying to place the feeling I had earlier. Something about this isn't adding up, and I'm too jaded from my experiences since being introduced to the preternatural world to chalk it up to a weird circumstance.

It's dark tonight, darker than I've seen in weeks thanks to the new moon. I've always understood why we call it a new moon when it appears like there isn't a moon at all, because despite the perception, the moon is only ever just out of our view. But tonight, it's so impossibly dark, with only the constellations to mar the midnight sky, I could easily believe that the moon is gone forever.

Andre had flicked off the lone bulb in the main room since it was making a humming noise that made us worry about faulty wiring, but even if there had been a sliver of moonlight, I would have noticed the sudden flooding of light in the distance.

"Andre," I call out, drawing his attention to the barn on the far side of the property. I watch him blink at it uncertainly, as if he's trying to convince himself the light had always been on.

"I can't call for backup," Andre says, gesturing to his phone. I take a peak at mine again, hoping for a single bar, but it's just as useless as his. Really, we have a magic campus full of shapeshifters and alchemists, and yet we don't have a solution to shitty cell service?

I watch as Andre thinks through our options. Finally, with a thick swallow that tells me he isn't happy with the decision he's come to, he says, "Let's head back towards town and get some direction from Caro on how to proceed. If Helena Vasselboro is still on the premise—"

His words are cut off by a blood-curdling scream. It's feminine and full of terror. Our heads snap towards each other, and I see my own panic mirrored in Andre's eyes.

"Stay here," he tells me, but then he's shifted, his hyena form taking off across the huge yard and towards the barnhouse.

"Yeah, right," I say, though I know he's too far to hear me. I sprint to catch up with him, though my human legs are as inadequate as my human lungs. Once this night is over, I really have to make more of an effort to learn to shift.

About halfway across the yard, I pull up short. It finally hits me, the reason why so much about this night feels familiar. It reminds me of Jet's story, of him and Kiara shadowing an assignment and everything going wrong so quickly. There's a lot about tonight that is different from what he went through, but too much is similar for my comfort.

"Andre!" I call out as he gets to the barn's door, but the winter wind is drowning me out again, and he's just too far away to hear. I curse and take up my jog again. I make myself another promise, this time to add running to my training regimen. I'm still yelling Andre's name. He's shifted back into his human form now, clothes and LOP gear intact thanks to the mechanism on his uniform's belt. I see him take out his taser, push open the door, and barrel through.

After another minute of pushing myself beyond any physical capacity that I've needed to before, I make it to the cracked barn door. I don't think before I throw myself through, knowing that something about this situation is very wrong, and yet knowing that with Andre inside there is nothing I can do but follow.

Still, nothing, not even my anxiety, could have prepared me for what I find. The barn itself is empty save for livestock stalls with a dusting of forgotten hay. Andre is standing at the center of stained cement flooring, his body between a woman's and not one, but two men. There is only one light above us, but it's so bright compared to the vast darkness outside that my skull throbs. I blame that for how long it takes me to recognize the truth of our situation.

The woman that Andre is so valiantly trying to protect has blood dripping from her hands, but I soon notice that the wounds are self-inflicted. She's dug crescent-shaped punctures into her own palms with the ragged nails of her claws. And they are claws, though she is still in her human form. My eyes trail up the rest of her: bony frame, dirty, knotted hair, and gray eyes almost lifeless with how translucent they are. I know exactly who "Ms. Vasselboro" is. She's the same Full Moon Knight who nearly took my life as she took my parents.

I unholster my taser and train it directly at her. Andre whirls on me, confusion clouding his bright eyes, but then he sees the cruel twist of Helena's smile and looks back at me again.

"Why, little Miss Maverick, what a pleasure it is to see you again."

Without any further preamble, she lunges. But she doesn't move towards me, something I only realize too late, after I've already dodged to my right. She goes for Andre, springing so fast that he never even has the chance to move before she's on him, her claws at his throat.

I lift my taser, aiming it at Helena again but she smiles victoriously.

"You don't want to do that, girlie. Your boyfriend's throat will be on the floor before your little toy gets within a foot of me."

Andre's wide eyes meet mine and I see the same shock and hopelessness in them that I know must be in mine. I'm shuddering from the cold even as my skin heats with the sudden spike in my blood pressure. I lower the taser and relax an infinitesimal degree as Helena's hand releases from Andre's throat, though she doesn't move it away.

I risk a glance at the men behind me. I don't recognize either of them, which has me wondering how big the Full Moon Knight network truly is if the LOP thinks they have the whole organization under their supervision in New York. The prospect is terrifying, more so than even this moment.

"I'm the one you want," I tell Helena. "You don't want to kill him, you want to kill me. Let him go."

"Oh, we aren't going to kill you," she says. "The Don has a better use for you."

I'm just about to tell Helena exactly what she and the Don can do when the barn's back door squeals open. There's no mistaking the wolf who enters as anyone but the Don. It's the largest wolf I've ever seen, for one thing, but its fur is snowy white.

In two, slow strides, he arrives beside his men, shifting into his human form. The bulkier of the two hands him a robe and the man wraps it around himself. It's the style of a smoking jacket, but instead of looking regal and classy, it comes across as a cheap mockery. There's nothing meek about the man, though. He's alarmingly tall, pushing closer to seven feet than six, but thin, like he too has gone much too long without a proper meal. He has more pride in his appearance than his subordinates, straighter teeth and recently washed hair, but his skin is just as marked, and his eyes are equally gray and wild in the way all the Knights seem to share. His smooth face has undereye bags so dark that I'm not actually sure that they aren't bruises.

"Tempest Maverick. Or should I say Tempest Darnell," he muses. He speaks with all the twisted charisma of a cult leader. "It truly is a pleasure to meet your acquaintance. I was devastated to discover that I knew so little about you for the first seventeen years of your life, so I've taken great measures to remedy that of late."

"You don't know anything about me," I say cooly, my voice not betraying the panic I feel rising in my chest.

"That's simply not true," he says, stalking closer to circle me. I don't want to turn my back on the Don, but it seems like a worse idea to show my back to the other Knights, so I maintain my stance. The Don is playing with me, but I know his Knights aren't as patient. "You'd be surprised by the resources I have available to me."

I feel stupid, so unbelievably stupid, for trusting Versi to be safe, for coming to blindly trust the people in it just because they weren't scar-marked or snarling. Isn't this exactly what my aunt warned me about? Why did I refuse to listen?

"What do you want?" I demand. He clicks his tongue.

"A great many things. But firstly, for you to understand that we are not the villains in this story. The Universe gifted our people with our powers in order to protect the balance of nature, but it is only the Full Moon Knights who have been relentless in our pursuits. Our Nagual brethren are weak-willed, and easily distracted by the frivolities of humanity. They blasphemously befriend the magi for selfish gains and allow hybrids to taint the places which are meant to be sacred to our kind."

"Let me get this straight. You protect the balance of the Universe but only so long as you are seen as superior to everyone else on this planet. Can you see where I'm getting a little mixed up?" I ask with deceptive calm. I can't let my unease show. Not with Andre's life on the line.

I don't know why I'm goading him on, other than I'm hoping to buy us some time. If this Universe truly has any sense of harmony at all, it will allow someone to come to our aid.

"Nature has a food chain, little devil. That *is* balance. Our kind was always meant to be at the top of it, and we will be again once we get your grandmother to step down from her false throne. She is the villain in all of this. You will come to understand that."

I snort. "And you think I'll somehow play a role in her stepping down? I am not the bartering chip you think I am. That woman and I may share some blood, but she is not my family."

"Oh, that is simply not true, devil. You see, you should not exist."

"I keep being told that, and yet, here I am." I gesture to myself, sweeping a hand over my pathetically ill-fitting uniform. I look about as ferocious as a kindergartener dressed up as a scarecrow for Halloween.

"Here you are," he muses pleasantly, somehow a scarier reaction than if he snarled with his sharp teeth. "You are an abomination, my dear. One who presents as a Nagual, I am told, and I may have allowed that had I not also been informed of *what* you are. Have you shifted since your first time, little devil? Or shall I be the one to enlighten you?"

"Go right ahead."

I remember the Knights being thoroughly unimpressed by my animal form, so I'm surprised by the Don's interest. I don't think I care what I am at this point, but if it keeps the Don talking rather than attacking, I'm all aboard his crazy theory train.

I sneak a glance at Andre, and I am relieved to see that Helena is only lazily holding him back now. He's been disarmed and his arms are wrapped behind his back by Helena's, but the imminent threat is gone. He meets my eyes and gives a small nod, I think encouraging me to pander.

"A *fox.*" He says it like the secret meaning should be obvious. I send another glance at Andre who looks equally as confused by the weight of the Don's sentiment. "There are many legends of foxes being more than they seem. They are very clever creatures, you know. Sometimes even called trickster spirits."

I laugh, incredulous. "You think I'm a trickster *spirit?* I hate to break it to you, but I am a Nagual, and not even a very good one considering I can't really shift."

"I don't believe that. In fact, I think you can be much more. One does not rob a bank just to take the till. You stole your life from the Universe, so I suspect you took something more with you. I believe you to be the weapon I need to dismantle the Maverick monarch."

"Why have you Knights tried to kill me then?" I ask.

"My brood are an eager sort, and they often act without thought. I do not wish for your death, child, just as I did not wish for your mother's. It was her betrayal that sealed her fate. But you are precious to me. I cannot have your death. You will agree to shift for me, and should you disappoint, your friend will have his life ended here. Should you succeed, I will grant leniency and allow your friend to live this night. I hear you have grown fond of this one."

My stomach twists at the horror of his words. The Knights are monsters, and I don't trust the Don's leniency for a single second. A glance back at Andre tells me he doesn't believe it either. I know his stance too, it's not his carefree bounce, it's the powerful posture that suggests he's preparing to fight.

This time he doesn't nod so much as dip his eyes, but I understand his meaning all the same. I turn to face the Don. I roll my shoulders back and start to stretch out my hands at my sides as if I do possess some great power that I am ready to release.

"Fine," I say. "But just remember that you asked for it."

33

TEMPEST

Nothing happens, of course, and yet the Full Moon Knights are taken by surprise as Andre shifts into his hyena form and bounds away from Helena. At the same time, I reach for my taser and whip it out of its holster. I aim at Helena, but between my lack of target practice and her quick reflexes as she lunges after Andre, I miss.

Not wanting to waste a moment, I swing around to face another one of the Full Moon Knights lackeys. I'm just in time. Who I guess to be the larger of the Knights is bounding towards me, his massive wolf form covered in thick, red-brown fur.

Thankfully, this makes him a larger target, so my second shot hits home, clipping him in the side. He lets out a howl, his last before his involuntary shift back into human form. He must not know that the dart was designed for that very purpose because he struggles against the cage that is his human body, snarling and gasping as if the lack of access to his wolf form is putting him in physical pain.

I only get a fraction of a second to revel in my success

before another wolf knocks into me, taking me to the ground. It's Helena, her slim but powerful body pinning me beneath her. I dodge the snap of her maw, an echo of my first attack by the Full Moon Knights so profound that I'm momentarily disoriented, unsure if I'm in pain or just remembering it, but feeling, very acutely, that I am about to die. Because despite the Don's insistence that he needs me, I know Helena, I've faced her before, and I don't doubt for a second that now that I've refused to cooperate, she'll eagerly go for the kill.

I'm quickly reminded of the last time I was in this position. It wasn't under the threat of the Full Moon Knights, it was with Jet's panther form on top of me, coaching me through fighting techniques and warning me of this very moment. He's right, against the Knights with their wolf forms and bloodlust, I'll never win with what I learned about self-defense these last few weeks. But I know more than I did in Crescentwood, which means I can put up a good fight.

I still have the taser in my hand, useless as it is now, but it packs a punch as I swing it against Helena's temple. She howls, the volume making my eardrums throb, and blowing hot, mustard breath in my face that has me gagging and rolling over. The hit must have disoriented Helena a bit because she rolls too, momentarily giving me the upper hand. She shifts beneath me, trying to throw me off with her human claws rather than her wolf ones, but I learned how to root my hips from practicing this exact scenario with Andre.

I use this single second of success to do a quick scan of my surroundings, trying to decide where to go should I make my escape from Helena's grasp. Andre is on the other side of the barn, throwing himself at the other wolf, a blur of fur and growls as they clash together. The Don stands back, watching the chaos dispassionately, as if this is nothing more than a brief

interlude in his master plan. The wolf I humanized is still struggling to understand what I did to him. It's like being separated
from his Nagual ability has rendered him useless. He's
forgotten that he is a large man with plenty of power in his
human form.

It gives me an idea.

Andre's taser is still laying on the ground where Helena
discarded it, not five feet from me. At that moment, I decide
what I need to do and bring my elbow down on Helena's
human nose. There is a satisfying crunch that leaves her
howling again, but then she's shifting, her growing form
launching me out of my posture. I use the momentum to my
advantage, jumping off of her before her paws can wrap around
me, and lunge for the taser.

The force sends me into the ground hard. I hear a pop and
feel my left kneecap shatter as it takes the full weight of my fall.
Pain explodes from that point, making brilliant, golden fire-
works burst behind my eyes. The taser is wrapped in my hands
now, and that's enough for me to force myself to blink the
sparkling stardust from my vision and focus on Helena's
growling wolf form. Drool drips from her bared maw as she
corners me against the steel gate of the abandoned horse stall.

She prowls forward, taking deliberate, sure steps, and
though I can't be sure with her in this form, it looks like her
mouth is tilting up into a satisfied smile. She thinks she's won.
And considering that I'm in more pain than I can ever remember, certain that standing will be impossible, I can understand
why. But she doesn't know that I have the taser curled in my
palm. So, when she lunges, I raise my hand, sending a dart
squarely into her chest.

Just like the first Knight, she shifts back in a rage, confused
and unaccepting as she wrestles with her suddenly human

body. She buckles over, then falls to her knees, her human teeth gnashing as she tries to make sense of her current state.

"Tempest!" I hear Andre cry out. He's human again, his hands open wide, signaling me to toss the taser. He has the other wolf pinned beneath his foot but it's clear he's about to lose his hold. I toss it, but it's a terrible throw from this angle, sending the taser wide. Andre dives for it, but the wolf does too. They clash together again, at first as humans, and then in their animal forms.

As they struggle for the taser, the Don stops in front of me, a furious scowl making him as ugly as his followers.

"What a disgusting display of all that my people are fighting against," he says. "Stealing the power of a Nagual is despicable—and how eager you are to engage in these vile acts. Just like your father. Just like your traitorous mother."

I try to pull myself up into a seat, but my entire leg is shrieking with the pain of my shattered patella. I can almost feel the cracks in the bone. At least three, but maybe more if I move it from this angle.

"She knew the truth, you know. Yet when it mattered the most, she failed to put an end to the Maverick rule. Your mother was selfish and short-sighted. She colluded with that magic-wielding filth to give herself a devil child, and I find great pleasure in knowing that I will use her child to complete the Universe's will after all." The Don smiles. "Bring him forth."

If it wasn't for the steady throb of my knee, I would think my heart had stopped. Both of the male Knights, in their human forms, step up beside where the Don stands with Andre between them. He's struggling against their hold, but the men have seemed to remember that they are imposing forces even regulated to their human selves. I wait for Andre to shift, to break free, but he doesn't. Finally, his gaze meets mine and his fight winks out.

My eyes widen, furiously trying to tell him that the door is right behind him. He can shift, he can run. He can find help and be free of this trap that was only ever intended to hurt me. I may even survive it. If the Don thinks he needs me for some back-assed higher purpose he's convinced himself of, then I could make it through this night.

Andre's eyes bore into mine and eventually, he nods. Relief has my chest concaving. He'll go. I just need to buy him some time, a minute, maybe two. Then this nightmare can be over for him.

"This is your last chance to prove yourself to me, little devil," the Don coos. "Do it now or the boy dies."

Panic bubbles up again, but I push it down to do my part in saving Andre.

"I don't know how to do what you're asking," I say. "But I want to. I can't shift yet, but if you can teach me, I'll do it."

"She's lying," Helena snarls, coming around the Don. She looks more unhinged than I've ever seen her, though maybe that's because her nose is bent at a painful angle with drying blood smeared across her upper lip.

"I'm not," I say quickly. "I'll do anything if that means you'll let Andre go." And I mean it too, I cast my eyes back to his and he gives me a small, sad smile. Why isn't he running? The men are paying more attention to their Don and Helena than him, and only the Don is capable of shifting now. He can make it, he can escape. So why isn't he going?

I tear my gaze away, not wanting to garner any more suspicion and risk his ability to get free. Just another minute and everything will be fine. One more minute.

"Please," I plead, and I'm no longer posturing. "Please," I

beg again. "I'll go with you. I'll learn to shift; I'll figure it out if I can—whatever it is you think I can do. I don't have any love for the queen, you're right. I can find a way to do what you've asked, but only if you let him go free. If you hurt him at all, I will *never* help you."

"Ah, the swan song of a falling hero," the Don muses. He takes another step forward and I try to stand on instinct. My left leg throbs with fresh spikes of pain shooting out in every direction. "We'll find a way to make you my weapon." He crouches down, his face now close enough to mine that I can feel the heat of his breath in the space between us. This close, he seems older than I originally thought. Maybe in his mid-sixties. There is something about him that's familiar. Not in a way that tells me I've seen him before, but in a way that tells me I know him. It's in his eyes, still gray like all the Full Moon Knights, but a darker shade, just like my mother's.

"I do believe you mean what you say. You'll help us, Tempest, dear. I'm sure of it."

"I'm not." Helena's melodic voice cuts through the uncanny quiet. "She's a liar. An abomination. A plague to be purged. Do not be deceived, my Don. End her now and be done with it."

I watch over the Don's shoulder as she moves like a flash of light, fast enough to suggest that the potion in the dart I shot her with is wearing off. She lunges for me, her dagger nails curled into claws, but I don't so much as flinch.

It's the Don's turn to surge with speed so fast that should I have blinked, I'd have missed it. But I don't blink. I don't move as he stands, catches Helena mid-stride, cups each side of her jaw with the gentleness of a lover, and snaps her neck. A noise between a gasp and a sob escapes me. Helena's body crumples to the floor.

"Let's move out," the Don says, turning to face his men. "Bring Helena's body. She may have betrayed me in the end, but she served our cause faithfully for years. She'll receive a proper burial."

"The boy, sir?" one of the Knights calls out.

"Leave him," he replies. "He's already dead."

The Knights release Andre and he falls to his knees as they move towards Helena. I'm frozen for a moment, trying to process what they said.

Andre is clearly not dead. The Don said that if I went with him, he wouldn't harm Andre. If he hasn't gone back on his promise yet, I don't see why he would now.

No one stops me from surging towards him, my injury forgotten either from the adrenaline of the moment or the strange heat that is starting to course through me. I awkwardly drag my leg as I shuffle to him. His face is now pinched with pain, but he doesn't make a single noise. It's only as I put my hands on his shoulders that I notice the blood.

Now that I'm close I can tell that the gray of his uniform has turned a shade darker. A few drops of blood fall onto the floor, but too quickly it grows into a small puddle.

"Andre, I don't know what is happening, but you have to shift," I say breathlessly. He shakes his head. "You have to," I argue. "You weren't injured in your boudas form. You can wait it out until you get help."

It might not help still, Andre warned me before that a fatal wound will be fatal no matter our form, but there's no way for me to tell if that's what Andre is facing now. He did also say that a shift in a weakened state can do more harm than good, but Andre is so strong. I know he can survive it.

He shakes his head again. "I can't, Tempest."

Andre lifts the edge of his shirt to reveal a patch of skin

above his right hip that is marred by a red welt. I frown, not recognizing what it is at first, but then it hits me. I heard Andre's taser go off and assumed he shot the Knight with it, but *he* was the one with his ability to shift temporarily neutralized. That's why he didn't run away. He couldn't.

It's then I see the real issue. The flesh of his left abdomen has been split open by the scratch of three claws. The wounds are deep, and even with all the blood, I can see the unnatural puckering of his muscle beneath.

For one horrible moment, I think I'm dissociating. I can't feel anything, not my pain, not the cold, not the blood roaring in my ears, or the fear coursing through my veins. I am empty. Then there is a single throb of my heart and awareness comes crashing back into me, along with heat, like I'm being roasted alive, from the inside out.

"No," I say, panic gripping me again. The fever is building, making my skin feel oddly tight and itchy. "We'll get you fate's root. It helped me. It'll help you."

"I didn't pack any," Andre says.

I want to scream. Why didn't we pack any? But of course, it wasn't negligence. We were purposely misled, I'm certain of it now. Someone wanted us in this exact position, at the Full Moon Knights' mercy.

"Bring the girl. We must go," I hear the Don say from the other side of the barn.

I turn my fury on him and the approaching men. They pull up short. While his Knights are wide-eyed, the Don's eyes are hooded, a pleased expression crossing his too-familiar features.

"Careful," he says. "She is revealing her true nature."

I don't know what nature they think that is besides pissed, though I am *hot*. So uncomfortably hot that it feels like someone dragged the sun inside the barn. Andre reaches out and squeezes my arm and I am momentarily worried that his hand will be burned.

"Give them hell," he says with a sad smile.

In a trance, I get to my feet. I'm sure somewhere in the back of my brain I am registering the great amount of pain I am putting myself in, but I can't feel it. I can't feel anything but fire.

"Reveal yourself to me, oh deceptor!" the Don cries out in rapture. He falls onto his knees, and though I once again feel like I'm in the thrall of dissociation, I feel like a flip is being switched inside of me.

And then I feel nothing at all.

The overhead light bursts, but there is only a moment of plunging darkness before a gold ghost light fills the air around me. On my skin, the air is starting to warp and shimmer, like pavement sizzling in the summer sun. A new, unfamiliar pain rips through me, making my heart feel like it's burning to ash. A tortured cry passes through my lips as the anguish becomes unbearable.

The barn is now filled with brilliant yellow and violet-orange. The air is acrid with the smell of smoke, like something besides my organs is on fire. I can't see the source of the light, it's too blinding, and even that is causing me pain.

My body is on fire and yet I feel like a god. I'm a being made of nothing but rage and power. The light becomes brighter and brighter until I truly am blinded by it. Then, all at once, the night becomes dark and cold again, and I fall.

With my sizzling body now curled on the cool concrete floor, the pain finally dissipates. I smile.

. . .

The night is nothing but unrelenting blackness. There's no light. No stars. No moon. Nothing but an engulfing, endless dark.

Then I remember to open my eyes.

When my vision adjusts to the soft, flickering amber light, all I see is carnage. The source of light is not the one that had been overhead. There is no longer an overhead. The barn's roof has caved in, beams of charred wood littering the concrete. Even that has been scorched, black soot in a circle just a couple of feet from where I lay. The wall closest to us is on fire, though it's smoldering rather than roaring. Still, it's enough to make me worried. The barn is made entirely of wood. If pieces of it are on fire, it could be mere moments before the entire thing goes up in flames, right?

I have no idea how fire works, if I'm honest. Though between the thick curtain of smoke I'm huffing into my lungs and my general confusion over what has happened here, I have no idea how most things work at the moment.

I glance around and see four bodies lying on the floor. All but one of them is charred beyond recognition.

Andre.

Sore and disoriented, I move to get to my feet. That's when pain flares in my left leg, so sudden and acute that I nearly topple over and lose my lunch. Lunch, the last meal I ate. I had coffee with Dee just that afternoon. How had so much happened in a single night?

But it's not night now. I'm not sure how I can tell since the world is still oppressively dark, but I can feel it in the change of the atmosphere. I don't doubt that soon the blue-black horizon will give way to a violet twilight.

I fight my way to my feet and limp the short distance to where Andre lays. There's not so much as a flake of ash on his uniform, though the wetness of his shirt is just as concerning. His eyes flutter open and his lips curl into the smile I've come to know and love so much. My heart squeezes painfully. I'm so, so grateful to see him, somehow equally unharmed by whatever exploded to cause the fire.

"You're alive," I say with a sigh.

"Thanks to you making bacon out of those guys," he says breathily. At least that's what I think he's saying. His words make no sense, so either he is feeling the effects of the smoke inhalation more than I am, or I'm more delirious than I thought.

Wood cracks as fire eats away at it and my eyes widen in alarm.

"We have to get out of here." Andre tries to shake his head, but I don't let him fight me on this. "This place could go up any second. I know it's going to hurt," I say. There's no time to argue about this. Andre must realize this too because despite him opening his mouth to do just that, he nods and tries to sit up. He winces and I hook my hands under his armpits to pull him to his feet. It's hard to do without putting any extra weight on my left leg, the only way to keep the agony within functional limits.

We're so slow, but eventually, we're limping out the barn doors. It's just in time too. I hear several more cracks, a pop of heat, and soon the smoldering wall is burning steadily. By the time we're outside, the other walls are catching too. Another section of the roof concaves.

I look over at Andre, to wonder aloud if we should risk trying to move again, but I jolt as I realize just how pale he is. The warm firelight must have disguised it, or our short journey spent him, because it's clear now that he is ghostly pale. Deathly pale, even. I reach out to place my hand on his forehead—as if having a fever would explain his pallor rather than the amount of blood pooling out of his abdomen. His skin isn't hot to my touch, it's ice cold.

"Andre," my voice is brittle and panicked. "Let's get you to the car. There has to be something there; fate's root or another medicine bundle."

He gives a weak nod, and we start our shuffle again. The expanse between the burning barn and where the LOP-issued car is parked feels endless. It was a far trek when I had been running, but with the state of us both, we are barely inching across the property.

After a few laborious minutes, I offer to run ahead. Andre tries to shake his head but only manages a jerk. "No. Stay with me."

Something in my chest cracks in half, making my breath come out like ragged pants.

I almost argue, but I'm not sure if I could manage the run anyway. I'd hate to leave him only to fall myself.

It's not until I see droplets of water fall onto my arm that I realize I'm crying. No, not crying. Sobbing, that's why my chest is heaving like this.

"We did it," he says breathily. "We survived the Full Moon Knights, Tempest."

For some reason, him saying 'survived' has another sob tearing through my chest, leaving a prickling, achy feeling behind. I curl against him, though I'm careful not to put any pressure on his wound.

"Shh," he tries to soothe, which only makes me cry harder. He's trying to comfort me when he's the one dying. "Don't cry, Tempest. There's something I need to tell you."

We're forced to stop when he opens his mouth to speak, and a coughing fit overcomes him. I watch in horror as a fresh spurt of blood seeps through his shirt. Then I notice it's on his collar too, and true grief sets in. There isn't enough time. We're too far, and Andre is too far gone.

It's at that same moment that I hear the distant pitch of a siren meant only for preternatural hearing. Hope, agony, and defeat all swirl in the empty cavity where my heart had once been.

"It can wait, Andre. The protectors are coming. Don't you hear? Tell me later, okay? Save your energy. Promise me." I pull him forward again. For a moment he fights, but then he lurches forward, his pace glacial.

"I've been keeping it from you all this time. Please, Tempest."

I nod. Maybe if I can keep him talking, he can hold out long enough for the LOP to arrive. Only another couple of minutes. Three at most. They will have medicine bundles. Andre would be okay. He can survive this.

The ghost of a smile crosses his lips. "I let you win the rock-climbing competition."

My crying stops all at once. "I— You— What?" He does stop walking and I'm surprised enough to let him.

He chuckles and fresh blood, somehow redder than it had been, seeps through his uniform and onto mine. But his laugh is as infectious as it always has been and suddenly, I'm laughing too even as my heart is breaking. Because I now know that a few minutes is too much to ask for. Andre isn't going to make it. He's saying goodbye. And I want to hate him for it, but I'm just too damn sad. "You just seemed so down that day," he continues. "You looked like someone who could really use a win. So, I let you win."

I think I'm going to laugh again, but it's another round of

sobs that escapes instead. I'm shaking my head now. I don't want to let him go. I can't lose another person I love.

"That's harpy shit," I say. "I won fair and square."

"Come on, chica," he teases weakly. He eases himself down into a seat on the grass. We're nowhere near the car, maybe a third of the way to the street. "You know I'm the best."

I snivel in reply. He squeezes my hand, a burst of strength that is more disheartening than reassuring. Like he knows it may be his last. I fall onto the ground beside him.

"All I've ever wanted is to be a hero, Tempest. Thank you for letting me be yours." His voice falters, trailing off as his eyes flutter closed.

"Andre," I say, shaking his shoulder roughly. Far rougher than I have any right to, given the situation. "Andre, stay awake," I demand. "Open your eyes." He lays back, even as I'm shaking harder.

Still, Andre doesn't answer. His eyes don't open and after another moment his chest does not rise or fall.

"No," I moan. "No, Andre, please. You can't go. I need you."

"Tempest!" I hear a voice shout. For a gut-wrenching moment, I think it's Andre, but the voice came from too far away, and it's too deep. Familiar, but not the voice I need to hear. There is a curse and then shouting, "We need medical here *now!*"

I clutch Andre closer to my chest, sobbing into the dry shoulder of his uniform. A moment later, strong arms are wrapping around me.

"Tempest," the voice softly murmurs against my ear. "You have to let him go."

I argue. I fight. But then there are other protectors with medicine bundles moving towards us, moving for Andre, and I know they're going to try to help him. I do let him go, even though I know they won't succeed, I let them try.

The arms are gathering me to my feet, tucking me against a warm, familiar frame. I've never been so glad to see him, even as I refuse to meet his eye, instead burying myself in the soft fabric of his uniform. One arm is wrapped around my waist, while his opposite hand is holding my head against his chest, prohibiting me from looking over my shoulder at Andre and the inferno that now engulfs the barn.

My chest heaves against his. Gently he strokes my matted hair. Jet's lips move against my ear, whispering in soft tones that everything will be alright. That everything will be okay now.

Graciously, I accept his lies.

❧ 34 ❧
JET

"We have every reason to believe that the same devices used in the bombing at Lake George were utilized at the Killington barn. Ms. Maverick cannot recall how she and Cadet Gonzales managed to avoid the effects of the blast due to excessive smoke inhalation, but the iron stalls could have provided enough cover for them to escape the barn unharmed before it went up from the fire."

The director is briefing out to a crowded room of agents, officers, and members of the preternatural press. After two days of chaos, things are finally cooling down enough for us all to take stock of the events that occurred over the weekend, in one of the longest, most challenging, successful, and tragic nights in LOP history.

"But why would the Knights use the bomb on themselves?" one of the members of the press calls out.

Director Sanchez nods, having expected this question. It was one our officers deliberated upon for hours over the last few days.

"We can't be sure, of course, but Ms. Maverick identified another Knight who was present during their attack, but not included as one of the fatalities. It is our belief that he double-crossed the other Knights by setting the bomb to be detonated prematurely. Ms. Maverick's report states that the leader of the Full Moon Knights made it clear that she would join ranks with them or be killed. They likely brought the bomb as a tactic to pressure her into aligning with them. We believe that when it became evident that she would not, this rogue Knight put his own plan in action."

Director Sanchez looks out, scanning the crowd. Her expression is serious, even grim, and yet she seems completely in control.

"I understand that there may be frustration around the lack of clarity during the events in Killington that stole the life of a promising young cadet, Andre Gonzales. I assure you that we are doing all that we can to understand the full scope of what took place, especially in an effort to bring peace to the Gonzales family. In the meantime, let's focus on the fact that we have seven Full Moon Knights in custody with another three dead. This is only the beginning of the end of their reign of terror. Thank you."

With that succinct dismissal, the crowd starts to disperse. The journalists are the first to go, all eager to write up their interpretation of the briefing to have it printed in tomorrow's edition of the Versi Sun. The protectors start to file out too. I don't see Brody in the crowd, I haven't seen him since the early morning on Saturday when I assured him that Tempest was safe, though shaken.

I think he's taking the news about Andre hard. A lot of our classmates are. It's the first time that a lot of them are seeing the truth of how dangerous our chosen path can really be. I bet a few will declare new majors come next semester. It was the same last year after Kiara disappeared, and later declared dead. Both were freak events, totally unprecedented, and yet two students died in two years—no more than kids. I wouldn't be surprised if some of those journalists call for the cancellation of the Protector Program completely.

I'm about to head for the back staircase when a voice calls out to me.

"Cadet Delancey." I turn in surprise to face the director. "Do you have a minute?"

"Ma'am," I say in deference. She nods towards her office, so I file in after her. It's an open space with nice furniture, though every inch of her desk is covered with files and devices.

"Have a seat." She gestures to one of the two plush chairs across from her desk. I take the one closest to her. My hands are suddenly sweating so I try to wipe them on my jeans. She takes her own chair, settling in behind her desk with all the euphoria of someone who has been on their feet all day. Once she's seated, she steeples her hands and regards me.

"Several of my officers have spoken highly of you in the last few months," she says. "And I saw your deductive reasoning skills for myself when we were in Lake George. It was impressive for a cadet. Hell, it would have been impressive for a seasoned agent. You have a lot of potential, Jet, and I think many of us are curious to see how you continue to grow in the next few years."

"Thank you, ma'am," I say, trying to instill enough confidence into my voice so that I don't sound quite as breathless, but her praise took me by surprise. I'm ecstatic to know I'm being recognized for all my work, but given everything that happened in the last several days, I'm not feeling all that celebratory.

"However, I did not ask you here just to tell you to keep up the good work—though I hope you do. I want to discuss the matter of our former lieutenant, Brendon Caro with you."

I swallow thickly. It's common knowledge that one of the LOP's own is facing an internal review pending negligence that impacted the LOP's ability to pursue the Full Moon Knights more thoroughly, but very few people are privy to the full extent of what transpired. Even Brody, who had been present for the most-damning evidence against Caro, had been told only what was strictly need-to-know and sworn to secrecy. I think he understood enough of what was going on to piece things together for himself, but he hasn't mentioned it to me yet.

"My father mentioned that he's being held for further questioning by the queen."

"Yes," she says with a nod. "We don't have much in the way of evidence to prove his collusion with the Full Moon Knights, and we fear that any further investigation will incite panic at Versi. People may start to distrust the League of Protectors." Her gaze trails above my head and to the closed door, as if she's trying to see past it. "In fact, I believe it'll already be starting. We cannot allow Brendon Caro to go free. His connection to the Full Moon Knights is of primary concern, and with his knowledge of the LOP procedures, he poses a real threat to our organization."

I nod, though none of this sounds simple. In fact, it's making my head ache.

"We allowed Lieutenant Caro to work against us for years. He's been a part of this organization since before the inception of the Full Moon Knights, longer than myself and most of our highest-ranking officers. We also cannot be certain that Caro was working alone, and any official investigations to dissuade this fear may cause alarm, which presents a unique problem. That's where you come in."

"Ma'am?" I ask, not understanding how I can have anything to do with this.

She gives me a wry smile. "It is in our best interest to limit the knowledge of Caro's involvement to those already in the know, but my officers have responsibilities that they cannot neglect in doing any... extracurricular investigations. However, with your previous interest—and success—in your independent studies, we feel that if anyone will be able to sniff out evidence that allows us to put Caro away, or unearth any further betrayal within the LOP ranks, it would be you."

After I recover from my initial shock, I'm flattered.

"What does my involvement look like?"

"We hope that Caro has implicated himself sometime in his career here. We'd need you to comb through his cases, personal effects, and devices. The time you spend at HQ working on the 'independent study' will also allow you to better integrate yourself with members of the LOP. We don't have any reason to suspect another one of our own is trading information to the Knights, but given the situation with Caro, we cannot be too careful now. There is a lot more to discuss, but it's imperative that we put a plan in motion right away. Not just for the sake of the LOP, but for Tempest too. The Full Moon Knights have proven time and time again that they will not rest until she is dead, and they do not care about who they hurt in the process. Cadet Gonzales is proof of that."

I feel strangely numb as I leave the LOPHQ and turn right into the business district. The room Tempest has been put up in is on the hospital's ground floor, so it only takes a few minutes for me to arrive. For the first time since she's been admitted, her room is empty. Her aunt drove up the day before and is staying in our guest room, though I think this is the first time she's actually left Tempest's side. She was technically conscious the first night, though between what they gave her for the pain and her grief over Andre, she really wasn't in a position to do much more than answer the LOP's most pressing questions.

They sedated her yesterday to do the surgery on her knee, and my mom and sister have been taking turns staying with her ever since, despite the doctor's insistence that she won't wake until tomorrow with the dosage of potion they gave her.

I stalk into the room, taking care to make my footfalls quiet, as if she is simply sleeping and not in a medically induced coma. Even though it's clear she's healing, and quickly, she looks wrong. Too pale. Too restless, even in her sleep. Her cheeks are hollow, like she's missed a week of meals the several hours in which she's been unconscious. I want to be sick.

It's impossible not to remember the few times I came here to visit Brody's mom with him. It's impossible not to think of Andre and Kiara, and how close Tempest came to not being here at all. It makes me feel grateful that she survived, followed by gut-wrenching guilt that they didn't.

Grief is always devastating, but there's something particularly horrifying about it happening when it's not meant to. Death is something that should only come for the old and the sickly, and pain should only ever be felt by those who have inflicted it. Healthy people should not fall to illness and teenagers should not lose the possibilities of forever because of an accident.

People say that the Universe, life, God—whatever it is they want to call it—works in mysterious ways and always has a plan, but I'm not sure I can understand how this can serve anyone's plan, and I'm not sure I'm the kind of person who can put my faith in a higher power who would do such a thing. The only thing I can put my faith in is myself and my actions.

I've been told countless times, by my therapist and my family, that I need to get comfortable with not having control, and it's taken me a long time to even wrap my head around that. But, as well-meaning as they are, they don't understand the compulsion I feel to do all that I can. I now know I can't control everything all the time, but I can control aspects of what life has put in front of me—and I'd be stupid not to take those opportunities.

That's why I have to agree to the director's proposition. I think I knew from the moment she asked that I would say yes, but being here, seeing Tempest so hurt *again*, and knowing that I can be the person who takes her out of harm's way once and for all, it's clear to me that this was never really a choice. Having her safe will always win out over having her in my life.

I wish it didn't have to be mutually exclusive, but that's where I've grown. That's where I must give up control. That's where I would have once fought to have everything and lost myself in the process.

So, while I hate my options, and it hurts to consider, I'll have to let her go. I will let her go. Even if she hates me for it, she'll be alive to do so.

35

TEMPEST

I wake to the warm rays of the late morning sun. I'm in a hospital room, though I immediately recognize it as a different one from the last time. While many things are the same: the metal contraption that looks more fit for a torture chamber than as my bed, the sickly-sweet smell of antiseptic, the impersonal touches meant to liven up the ultimately depressing space, there are several things that are different. There's something purple and shimmering in my IV drip, for one thing, which tells me immediately that I'm at Versi.

Another similarity from the last time I did this, less than a month ago, is that my aunt is curled up on an uncomfortable-looking chair, somehow managing to get some sleep.

"Laura" I whisper at her, not entirely sure why I'm keeping my voice down at all. She stirs, and then she's awake, alert, and staring at me with wide eyes.

"Tempest," she says with a relieved breath. She looks like she wants to reach out to me but then pulls up short. She swallows thickly, nods as if accepting something, and says, "I hope it's okay that I'm here."

I want to burst into tears. "*Of course* it's okay," I impress, feeling terrible that she could ever consider the possibility that I wouldn't want her to be. "Thank you. I— I'm really happy you are, but I hate that I made you come all this way."

She shakes her head. "I drove up with Brian. Stacy and Tisha are covering our shifts."

"Brian's here?" I ask, not understanding. I don't think there's a rule that humans can't come to the Versi campus, magi *are* humans after all, so there's no biological blockers in the campus wards. I can see my aunt being granted admittance, given the circumstances, but Brian isn't family—not yet.

"He went to some place called the Grove to get us coffee and bagels," she explains, though once she meets my eye, it's clear she gets my meaning. "Oh. Yeah, well I couldn't exactly tell him that more wild dogs attacked you, so I kind of told him everything on the drive up here."

A small, sad smile crosses her lips and understanding passes between us so acutely that it almost feels tangible.

"Tempest, I can't say I regret everything I did when it managed to keep you safe for so long, but I've come to see after these last several weeks that the only person my lies protected was me. It let me avoid hard conversations, first with you, and then with Brian. I know I messed up a lot where you're concerned, but when it came to Brian, I decided the truth could either drive a wedge between us or bring us closer. So, I took a shot in the dark."

I'm so surprised by her confession that I take in a sharp breath. It proves to be too much excitement for my healing lungs to manage. I cough and a small army of nurses funnel into the room at the sound to make sure I'm not having spontaneous respiratory arrest. All four of them choose an area to poke and prod at: my knee, which feels tender, my kidney, which hurts only from the force of said prodding, my arm where the IV has been inserted, and the buttons on the monitor in which is proclaiming me to have a steady, though increasing, pulse. Apparently, having decided that I'm fine, the four nurses shift into two-inch versions of themselves, all with glittering pixie wings, and fly out of the room in the same flurry they arrived.

Aunt Laura's eyes are wide as saucers. "I'm not sure I'll ever get used to that."

"Me either," I admit. "How did Brian take it?"

"He thought I was kidding at first. Once I convinced him I wasn't, he nearly pulled over to check if I had a head injury. I eventually proved that I wasn't crazy, which backfired because then he was *very* mad. By which I mean, he silently fumed for a few minutes before he started asking follow-up questions—this is Brian we're talking about."

I chuckle, though the sound is hoarse, like my voice is being raked over sandpaper.

"So, he went through all five stages of grief over the six-hour drive and has been ceaselessly curious ever since. He's actually been at the Grove for close to an hour, so either he got lost, is frozen in shock after watching another Nagual shift, or he's bothering poor Brody Bates with all his questions again."

This time when I laugh the sound is clearer, even as my heart clenches.

Grief. The five stages. I can't be sure where on the spectrum I'm falling yet since all I can feel right now is numbness. That's denial, I think.

Laura must read the shift on my face because hers falls. "I'm sorry about your friend, honey. Everyone has been saying that you two were close."

I nod, but the movement shakes loose a tear that now trickles down my cheek.

"It's my fault," I say, because I have to. I have to confront this even though I'm not ready to hear my aunt's eager insistence that it's not.

I know he didn't die by my hand, but the truth is that he never would have been in that position if it wasn't for me. The Full Moon Knights came after me. They orchestrated the attack to get to me. They used Andre as leverage to convince me to help them. All of it, every part of it, comes down to me. So, while it wasn't my hand, my vendetta, or my master plan, it is still my fault and I can't handle anyone's insistence otherwise.

To my surprise and relief, my aunt doesn't argue the point. She pinches her lips together in a frown and takes a deep breath.

"He sounds like a very noble young man," she says instead. "And that he cared about you very much."

The dam in my chest breaks and tears spill over onto my cheeks. My aunt is moving in an instant, sitting herself on the side of my bed, careful not to jostle my injured leg. She's pulling me into her chest and smoothing my hair, the way she has held me so many times before.

"I'm so tired, Laura," I choke out after a few long moments. "I'm tired of loving people just to lose them."

"I know, honey," she coos gently. "I know. Losing them is the tough bit, but eventually, you remember how it felt to love them in the first place. That won't ever make the pain go away, but you'll remember that getting to love them was worth it."

The next two days pass in a blur of friendly faces, kind words, and boundless grief, but then I'm given a clean bill of health from the preternatural doctor, an alchemy set's worth of potions to drink and herbs to burn, and a pair of crutches to help me keep weight off my nearly healed knee for the next few days.

I'm due to come in for a follow-up in a week, but there's no doubt that my reconstructed patella, with the newly grown shards of bone that I am very happy to have been fully unconscious for, will be as good as new by then. Despite everything, I'm immensely grateful for the magic of this strange world.

The Delancey family hosts a send-off dinner for my aunt and Brian. It's a fairly intimate affair, only family—the Delancey family that is—and my aunt and Brian are on the road with plenty of time for them to manage a full night of sleep before their shifts in the morning.

On their way out, Laura pulls me aside.

"You're sure that you want to stay? I spoke to Dylan about it, they said they could spare some agents to monitor things in Maryland while they round up the last of the Knights. You could come home. We could make it work."

I smile. There is a part of me that wants that, for things to go back to normal. I could return with my aunt, reconnect with my friends, and try to figure out what my future would look like in the human world. But I was never meant for normal, and despite everything, Versi has come to feel like home, and that's as much as I can ever hope for. There's no going back now.

"We could," I agree with a small smile. "But I think I need to spend some time figuring out how I fit into this world, and I think this is the best place to do it."

Brian comes up beside me, placing his hand on my shoulder. "You can't exactly put the genie back in the bottle now," he agrees. He's wearing a wide smile, evidence that he's still taking all this preternatural weirdness well. Maybe too well. I make a mental note to never let him hear about skinwalking.

My dad hid what he learned for a reason. Well-intended or not, some secrets are meant to stay secrets. It was my dad's burden to carry, and now it's mine, but I'm oddly okay with that. Though one world-changing secret is more than enough for me.

Brian grabs his and Laura's suitcases from the front porch and starts to load them into their car. Laura waits until he's gone to continue.

"I watched your dad go through this, and I guess I experienced it too, in a way. Choosing between two worlds—it's not easy. You have to choose whichever life can give you the future you want. Or whatever is closest to it. Either way, I'll support you as best as I can."

"Thank you, Laura," I say, giving her a hug. "I love you."

"I love you too, honey." Her voice is tight with emotion. "So much."

Brian returns to give me my goodbye hug and secure yet another promise that I'll fly home for Thanksgiving, somehow only a few weeks away. Then they're pulling out of the Delancey's driveway and towards Versi's Main Street in a picture-perfect tableau that I never thought I would see; my worlds meshing together seamlessly despite the strangeness of it all.

When night sets in and the Delancey family heads off to bed, I'm left in their quiet house much too wired to try to sleep. I'm taking over the guest room for the next few days with Diane's insistence that the second-story bedroom is much more manageable than my dorm. Since the idea of being completely alone is still enough to make me inconsolably sad, I'm essentially moved in for the rest of the week.

But my presence in the Delancey household only highlights the lack of Jet's. The first couple of days I assumed he was busy dealing with the fallout at the LOP and convinced myself not to have my feelings hurt. It was easier in the daylight when I was surrounded by friends and had my aunt at my side. It was harder at night when I had only the shimmering purple potion in the IV drip and my grief to keep me company.

I spent those first couple of nights laying awake, waiting for Jet to appear for one of our midnight chats. I waited for him to find a way to sneak me up to a rooftop, to confess all the things we aren't brave enough to say except for in the dark. Yet he never came. Not even once.

I'm not willing to wait anymore. So, when I hear the soft footsteps of someone crossing the Delancey's lawn late that night, I head for the back door. I throw it open before Jet can. He's still a few feet away, crouched in his panther form.

It takes me a moment to realize that he's waiting for me. I thought I was so clever, surprising him, but of course, his keen animal instincts are still several times better than my own. I must be a pathetic sight too. He's all long, dark limbs, meanwhile, I'm a shapeshifter who still can't shift, heartbroken and hobbling around on crutches. Despite this, I swing myself down the four doorsteps and manage to cross my arms without knocking the crutches over.

"Cowardice doesn't suit you," I say. He growls in response, but I'm not threatened.

Apparently, the chastisement is enough to have him actually face me though. He shifts into his human form and scowls. He's no less dangerous like this but I'm uniquely unaffected. Anger will do that to a girl.

Though a part of me wishes he would whisk me up to the rooftop now, I know that even if I could physically manage the climb, my doctors would have some choice words to say about it. So, I plant myself on the bottom stair instead, letting the crutches fall onto the grass, and pat the seat beside me for Jet to join. He only hesitates for a moment, but then we're seated beside each other in the dark, in a way that feels painfully familiar.

"The director thinks there's another mole in the LOP," he says, surprising a gasp out of me. "She didn't say it in that many words, but they're spooked after the truth came out about Caro. They need someone to find hard evidence and figure out if he was working with someone else at HQ, and she asked me to be the one to do it."

"You're a student, Jet. She can't make you—"

"She's not," he says, cutting me off. "I want this, Tempest. More than anything."

More than me, I realize. And while I can't fault him for that, it still hurts as badly as a physical blow.

"There are still Knights out there and Caro can't be held without cause forever. If there are people at the LOPHQ working with them then I need to be able to earn their trust, and I can't do that if I'm with you. I really like you, Tempest. I want things to work out with us, but I just need some time. I can go undercover, help put this all to rest, and then we can pick things right back up where we left it."

I shake my head. There is a stinging pain behind my eyes that I'm trying to blink away.

"You can't ask me to just wait around for you to want to be with me," I say. I see Jet open his mouth to argue so I continue quickly, "Just like I can't ask you not to do this."

Despite my level tone, anger is burning again, making my

skin feel prickly and hot. I'm reminded of feeling heat more acutely sometime recently, but I can't recall what would have caused the sensation, so I banish the errant thought.

I don't like that Jet is deciding to do this, and I hate that in the process he is once again deciding me too. But if I have to beg a guy to want to be with me then I definitely shouldn't be with him. I always thought that dating someone was supposed to be about liking the other person enough to want to work through the hard parts, but maybe that's why I've never done much dating at all.

"I'm sor—" he starts to apologize, but I don't let him. I don't want to hear him say that he likes me, just not enough. I'm already too heartbroken to allow any more fissures.

"I'm going to be sticking around," I say instead, plowing through any chance of a subtle change in subject. "I know the Full Moon Knights aren't the threat they once were, but I think Versi is right for me."

Jet finally glances at me, a small smile curving the corner of his lips. "I'm really glad, Tempest. I think you're going to do really great here."

I nod, but there's really not much more to say. I know Jet can feel it too. Thankfully he doesn't make me suffer more than a moment before he's getting to his feet and clearing his throat.

"I hope you get some sleep," he says with all the cordial aloofness of the night shift fae nurses at the hospital.

I give a pitiful, "You too," in reply.

It's only when a gust of cool air clashes against my cheeks that I realize I must be crying again. Jet's already gone, the light to his room above me flicking on before I can even wipe the tears from my face. I feel silly getting upset over this when there are so many more important things to be upset about right now, and I don't think my body can handle the loss of any more electrolytes with all the crying I've done for Andre this week.

I fight up to my feet, cursing in frustration at my clumsy human body that isn't quite healing fast enough. It's a constant reminder of my weakness. That I'm not as strong as he was, as good as he was, and yet I get to be here, pathetically shiftless, when he is not.

I fumble for my crutches and give up once it's clear I can't bend down to get them. These stairs don't have a railing either, so I genuinely don't know how I'm going to get up them again. The thought of calling for Jet to help me actually makes me want to melt into a puddle of mortification, so I hobble away from both, limping awkwardly as I go. It doesn't hurt, it's just made nearly impossible by the brace I'm wearing. I nearly rip it off as I approach the tree line, but now that I'm moving, I can't seem to stop.

I don't have a destination and know I'll have to turn around in a moment, but I'm just so angry and sad and frustrated and *hot* that if I don't expel some of this pent-up energy now, I'm sure I'll explode.

With the quiet night and the endless throngs of trees that flank me as I move through the perimeter of the Versi campus at the most speed I can manage, my mind starts to slip away from me. For the first time since I've suffered from my dissociations, I welcome the feeling like a friend. I don't want to be in control of my mind anymore. I want to take the back seat for a while, just let life happen to me, rather than constantly feeling the impact of it happening.

Maybe this time, just this one night, it's okay if I just slip into my insanity. So, with a contented sigh, I do.

But insanity is a lot bigger than I expected.

The forest is taller now, like someone stretched the treetops to six times their usual height. Everything I pass is somehow larger than it had once been. The rock that had been up ahead is now a boulder at my side. The grass is no longer just beneath my feet, but my hands too. No, not hands. Paws.

I laugh, so surprised by my accidental shift, and it comes out in a high-pitched yip. The sound of it makes me laugh harder, and the cycle continues. I'm running now, at full speed, though I feel a little shaky on my four tiny, furry legs. More brown than red, though it's hard to tell in the dark.

I'm a fox. I forgot the Don had said that after everything else that happened that night. But I do feel like a fox now. It's like now that I know it, it seems impossible that I ever could have not known it before. It's a part of me, half of me, in fact. And I want to rejoice in the knowledge that I'm not actually crazy. I'm just Nagual. It's bizarre and elating and so freaking weird, but it also feels *right*. More right than anything ever has before.

For the first time in my life, even in a small, strange body, I feel truly powerful. It doesn't even scare me. In fact, I welcome the feeling. If I'm going to be an abomination, I might as well embrace it.

~

Printed in the USA
CPSIA information can be obtained
at www.ICGtesting.com
JSHW022153150824
68219JS00004B/219

9 781963 558029

MATERIAL
WITNESS